MURDER IN THE KITCHEN

Savannah smiled and picked up her fork, intending to pilfer the last bite of raspberry tart off Tammy's plate when she wasn't looking. But no sooner had she reached across the table to do so than a nerve-shattering scream came from the kitchen area.

Savannah dropped the fork and leapt to her feet.

During her time as a police officer, Savannah had heard more than a thousand screams. Screams of rage, pain, fear, and drunkenness. People screaming for all sorts of reasons, and sometimes for no reason at all other than to attract attention or express a minor annoyance.

But there as only one reason for that sort of scream—a cry that went straight into the heart and the marrow of the bones, causing those who heard it to steel themselves for the worst life had to offer.

Nobody screamed like that unless somebody was dead . . .

Books by G.A. McKevett

Published by Kensington Publishing Corporation

G.A. McKEVETT

Killer
GOURMET

A SAVANNAH REID MYSTERY

KENSINGTON BOOKS
www.kensingtonbooks.com

KENSINGTON BOOKS are published by

Kensington Publishing Corp.
119 West 40th Street
New York, NY 10018

All Kensington titles, imprints and distributed lines are available at special quantity discounts for bulk purchases for sales promotion, premiums, fund-raising, educational or institutional use. Special book excerpts or customized printings can also be created to fit specific needs. For details, write or phone the office of the Kensington Special Sales Manager: Kensington Publishing Corp., 119 West 40th Street, New York, NY, 10018. Attn. Special Sales Department. Phone: 1-800-221-2647.

Kensington and the K logo Reg. U.S. Pat. & TM Off.

ISBN-13: 978-0-7582-7658-2
ISBN-10: 0-7582-7658-3
First Kensington Hardcover Edition: April 2015
First Kensington Mass Market Edition: February 2016

eISBN-13: 978-1-4967-0239-5
eISBN-10: 1-4967-0239-5
First Kensington Electronic Edition: February 2016

10 9 8 7 6 5 4 3 2 1

Printed in the United States of America

For Gwen and Jim

Amazing as individuals,
together you are synergy extraordinaire!

May you always be able to look
into each other's eyes and say,

Tá isteach Mo Chroi istigh ionat.
(My heart is in you.)

I want to thank Leslie Connell for her support and assistance, which she lovingly supplies, year after year. What would I do without you, dear Leslie?

I also wish to thank all the fans who write to me, sharing their thoughts and offering endless encouragement. Your stories touch my heart, and I enjoy your letters more than you know. I can be reached at:

sonja@sonjamassie.com
and
facebook.com/gwendolynnarden.mckevett

Chapter 1

"I want you to know, boy . . . it's about all I can do to gag down this fine supper you bought me."

Savannah Reid stared at the chili cheese dog in her hand, thought of the divine meal she was missing elsewhere, and momentarily wondered why she had married the guy sitting next to her on the bus bench.

The seat was liberally frosted with seagull poop, which added its own special charm to the dining ambiance. As did the X-rated language of the graffiti on the mud-streaked stucco wall next to them and the piles of rusty, mangled vehicles in the junkyard across the street.

He took her to all the best places.

She certainly hadn't married him for his "table" manners either, she decided as she gave him a sideways glance—just in time to see a blob of chili ooze from the end of his frankfurter and slide down the front of his orange-and-purple plaid thrift store shirt.

Nor for his fashion sense.

His mother had sent him the shirt as a Christmas present.

Not for his relatives either.

"Sorry, babe," replied her beloved. Detective Sergeant Dirk Coulter stuffed the other half of the hot dog into his face and talked around it. "I was looking forward to piggin' out on all that free gourmet crap, too. But a man's gotta do what a man's gotta do."

"Yeah, but a woman shouldn't have to do what a man's gotta do just because she's married to him."

He wadded the soggy hot dog wrapper into a tight ball and, with his best NBA-wannabe shot, launched it toward a nearby open-topped trash can.

Michael Jordan himself couldn't have done better, Savannah thought as she feigned keen, wifely interest. After all, she understood that this mini-display of manly prowess was for her benefit.

Dirk had always been a bit of a show-off. But she had noticed an uptick in these demonstrations since they'd said, "I do." Apparently, Dirk thought it necessary to continually remind his bride that she had snagged herself a true hunk—a dude positively chockablock with testosterone.

The wrapper clipped the edge of the trash can, ricocheted, and landed on the sidewalk a few inches away.

Oh well. She stifled a giggle. *Michael probably would've done a tad better.*

As Dirk got up, walked the three steps to the can, picked up his trash, and deposited it inside, she placed a couple of chalk marks on the positive side of her mental Husband Tally Board. The guy might be a slob at home, but when it came to public areas, he was no litterbug.

And he loved cats, dogs, children, and her. Unconditionally. So she cut him some slack in the table manners and fashion sense departments.

"I wonder what they're having," she said, her mood sliding back down into the Culinary Valley of Despair.

He settled next to her on the bench and eyed the remains of her hot dog with poorly disguised greed spawned of unadulterated gluttony.

"Beef Wellington?" she wondered aloud. "Lobster thermidor? I'm pretty sure I heard John say something about raspberry tart drizzled with a sauce made of Chambord and Chantilly cream."

"What the hell's that?"

"Glorified berry pie and whipped cream." She sighed, chin dropping, shoulders sagging. "But it still sounds amazing."

"Yeah, it does. Sorry, darlin'." He slipped his arm around her and pulled her close to his side. He leaned his head down to hers, nuzzled her ear, and whispered, "How's about I make it up to you when we hit the hay tonight? Berry pie might be sorta messy in bed, but we can think of something to do with a can of whipped cream. We'll pretend it's Chantilly."

She wriggled closer, enjoying his body warmth. The sun was setting, and even in sunny Southern California, that meant the chill of evening was upon them.

"Now I remember why I married you," she said, laying her hand on his thigh, which even through his tattered jeans felt deliciously hard against her palm—in a manly man's thigh sort of way.

He grinned down at her and waggled one eyebrow. "Oh, I know why you married me. Free, uncomplicated, hot sex on demand."

"And even more important . . . lawn maintenance."

He laughed and tweaked a lock of the ratted, scraggly silver hair hanging down into her eyes. "You look pretty cute as an elderly broad. Makes me glad we're gonna grow old and decrepit together."

"Aw. You sweet talker, you."

"No, seriously. That gray wig looks kinda sexy on you. The extra padding, too."

"I'm not wearing any extra padding tonight. Didn't have time to put it on."

He gulped. "Oh."

"And you were doing so well."

"It's in all the right places."

"A smart husband knows when to stop while he's ahead."

"Gotcha."

They sat silently for a while as she finished her hot dog and ignored his longing looks as the last bite went down the hatch.

Since the moment they had met—back when dinosaurs had frolicked in the La Brea Tar Pits—he had harbored the false notion that she might offer him the occasional, unwanted last bites of her meals and snacks. Apparently, some finicky-eating female in his past had left him with the mistaken notion this was standard, respectable lady behavior.

And maybe it was. But Savannah and her appetite could hardly be considered "standard."

She was surprised he still held out hope.

Leaning her head on his shoulder, she closed her eyes, taking a break from her constant surveillance of the area. They'd been at it for three hours, and her eyes were nearly as tired as her buttocks were sore from sitting on the hard, wooden bench.

Playing the part of "sitting duck" to lure in a couple of cruel, idiotic criminals wasn't half as much fun as one might imagine, she had decided two hours and forty-five minutes ago. Especially when she and Dirk hadn't seen hide nor hair nor ugly mug of either one of the miscreants in all that time.

If that hot dog truck hadn't come along, the evening would have been a total bust—a nonevent on her social calendar.

Except for her husband's warm arm around her.

Eyes closed, Savannah savored the night air—the deliciously cool refreshment of it, its faint pungency—as it carried the sea-scented fog from the beach areas of the tiny town into the less picturesque areas. Like the neighborhood where they were playing "vulnerable, come-and-get-me decoys."

Of Southern California's beach communities, San Carmelita was, without a doubt, one of the most beautiful. Known for its quaint Spanish-style architecture, ancient founding mission, perfect sands, and surfer-friendly beaches, as well as its Main Street lined with antique shops, boutiques, and fine restaurants, San Carmelita thrived on tourism.

Every weekend, tourists from the Los Angeles area flocked to the town to escape the city smog, heat, and most important the congestion—both vehicular and human. Local merchants—from the little souvenir kiosks near the beach to the luxury hotels and restaurants on the hillsides—depended upon that reliable influx of cash.

But lately, charming little San Carmelita had been making the evening news on the major Los Angeles stations almost every evening. And it was for yet another dark, sinister reason.

Mom and Pop Whops.

That was the cutesy name the media had coined to

describe these random, cruel blitz attacks on unsuspecting senior citizens. In the past fifteen days, there had been six attacks on elderly couples. Although none of the victims had died, four of the six had been badly hurt, and one poor woman was still in a coma. Her prognosis: Grim.

For the past three nights, Savannah and Dirk had posed as an older twosome, positioning themselves in the areas where the majority of the attacks had occurred. Tonight they had staked out a city bus bench on the same block as a senior citizens center and a church known to be attended mostly by the over-sixty-five set.

The perpetrators had been described as a pair of wannabe gangbangers in their late teens—one tall and thin, the other short and squat. The tall one wore a distinctive black stocking cap with a red-and-white stripe across the top from front to back. He had delivered the sucker punches to their victims, while the other one—bald, short, and pudgy—filmed the assaults with his cell phone.

As a devoted and protective granddaughter of a southern octogenarian grandma, Savannah wanted nothing in the world more than to get her hands on these punks and show them the downside of attacking someone who could actually fight back.

Granny Reid had raised Savannah and her eight siblings to have respect for their elders and to protect those who couldn't defend themselves. Even if it meant missing a gourmet dinner, Savannah was determined to catch these guys and do Gran proud.

Savannah grinned just thinking of the can of "whoop ass" she'd like to open on those overgrown delinquents. When she was finished with them, every man, woman, and child in the greater Los Angeles area would have

seen their nasty pusses on the six o'clock news and
would know that they'd had their clock cleaned by an
over-forty, abundantly curvaceous female.

Sweet.

Dirk nudged her. "Hey, look over there."

She opened her eyes, expecting to maybe see a suspect. But when she spotted the couple he was referring
to, she smiled. It was an elderly woman and man, walking down the steps of the nearby church, hand in hand,
whispering sweet nothings to each other and giggling
like a couple of teenagers in the throes of "cherry pink
and apple blossom white" love.

The couple walked in their direction but didn't even
seem to notice the younger twosome as they passed, fo-
cusing solely on each other. The woman wore a lavender floral print dress with white patent leather flats and
carried a matching purse. Her long silver hair had been
twisted into a bun at the nape of her neck, and she had
fastened a sprig of fresh-cut lilac at the top of the twist.

Her gentleman escort was equally festive in a comple-
mentary purple shirt, an orchid paisley tie, and white
slacks with creases ironed military sharp.

Once the couple had passed them, Savannah gave
Dirk's thigh a squeeze and said, "I want to be just like
them when we get that age."

"Well dressed?"

"All lovey-dovey."

"We will be."

"Well dressed?"

"Naw, I'll still be in jeans and a Harley T-shirt, but
we'll still be all goo-goo for each other like that."

"You figure?"

"Yeah." He chuckled, breathing hot dog and onions
on her. "We got a late start, you and me, not gettin'

married till we were in our forties. We have a bunch of lost time to make up for."

She smiled up at him. "I like the way you think."

He grinned and winked at her, causing her to forget about his onion breath and the smear of chili on his chin. Nobody was perfect, and he didn't seem to mind, or even notice, when her mascara was smeared, giving her raccoon eyes, or when the hot, dry Santa Ana winds blew, causing her thick, dark curls to stand on end.

Years ago, for some reason that she couldn't imagine, he seemed to have decided that she was pretty much perfect in every way. And she had decided that was his most endearing virtue.

You could overlook a lot of nonsense in a guy who overlooked your faults or considered them "cute."

In Savannah's estimation, unconditional love was, without a doubt, the sexiest personality trait any man could possess. Having a husband who was crazy about you and tried to impress you with slam-dunked hot dog wrappers made things like onion breath not such a big deal.

Though she did jot a mental note to herself: *The next time he orders onions on his hot dog or hamburger, make sure you do, too.*

It was a simple matter of self-preservation.

In companionable silence, they watched as the older couple made their way down the block and turned at the corner to cross the street. The man stepped off the curb gingerly, and the woman cupped his elbow, offering a bit of gentle support.

"See there?" Dirk nodded in their direction. "When we get that age, if you need help gettin' around, I'll give you a hand like that."

Savannah's mind replayed a succession of quick flashbacks from not so long ago. Scenes of Dirk offering her all forms of assistance. Some far more intimate than simply helping someone cross the street.

When she had been recuperating from grave injuries caused by multiple gunshot wounds, he had helped her with such pathetically simple things as rolling over in bed and making her way to the bathroom.

"You already did, darlin'," she said.

He turned his head and looked down at her as tears moistened their eyes.

"And I'll do it again if, God forbid, I ever need to," he said, his voice husky. "You know that."

"I do. I most surely do."

She gulped and cleared her throat, then readjusted the wig that was feeling more scratchy and uncomfortable by the moment.

Glancing down at her watch, she said, "It's after eight. Reckon if we left now and hightailed it over to the restaurant, there'd be some of that good grub left?"

Dirk readjusted his position on the bench and reached back to rub a sore spot in the region of his tailbone. "Tempting, ain't it? Nothin' going on around here. I told you we should've staked out that bingo parlor."

Looking up and down the dark street—deserted except for the couple that was now a block and a half away—Savannah had to admit that, perhaps, he was right.

Of course, she admitted it silently to herself.

Years ago, in a moment of foolish, ill-conceived generosity, she had uttered the ridiculous words, "You're right."

Her humble confession should have garnered her a

nomination for sainthood. But instead, she had been re-warded with years of pompous, incessant, and highly annoying reminders of *The Day He Had Been Right!*

Day and night, she had been bombarded with such gems as "You aren't always right, you know, Miss Smarty-Pants Savannah! Remember that day when . . ." and "You think you're so smart, but I can remember that time when you were just wrong, wrong, wrong!"

Yes, that had been her reward for her charitable admission.

Never again.

Granny Reid hadn't raised any dummies.

Well, actually, she had, but Savannah wasn't one of them. Now that she had learned her lesson the hard way, Satan would be wearing ice skates the next time she'd utter those fateful words aloud.

"Do you really wanna split?" he asked, nudging her in the ribs. "I don't know about lobster therma . . . whatchamacallit . . . but if Ryan and John have got anything else left over, something that recently mooed, I'd be happy to take it off their hands."

Savannah weighed her options carefully, and it wasn't easy.

She had two passions in life: eating amazing food and nabbing bad guys and making them pay for their evil ways. Both she found to be deeply soul-satisfying. And there was hardly ever a conflict of interest between the two obsessions. As a former cop, Dirk's previous partner, and now a private detective, she had no qualms at all about chewing a Godiva truffle while chasing, tackling, and cuffing a perpetrator. Or pulling her 9 mm Beretta with her right hand while holding a KFC original-recipe drumstick in her left.

Multitasking? No-o-o problem.

But having to weigh the chance of savoring a once-in-a-lifetime meal against catching a numbskull, elder abuser . . . a hefty decision like that nearly blew her mental fuses.

Only for a few seconds.

"We'll stick around a while longer," she told him with a resolute tone of voice that contained only the tiniest note of disappointment.

"For Gran," he said softly.

"Exactly."

A second later, like an instant reward from heaven for her virtuous sacrifice, Savannah caught sight of two shadowy figures creeping out of an alleyway about 150 feet from the bus bench.

One tall and thin. The other short and squat.

She nudged Dirk's thigh just as he elbowed her ribs. She could feel him tense beside her and hear his breath quicken.

Even in the semidarkness, she could clearly see the black cap with a red-and-white stripe across the top, as described by the victims who had actually gotten a look at their attacker.

When he and his cohort passed beneath a streetlamp and Savannah saw that his companion was, indeed, short, squat, and bald, her heart rate doubled.

Their actions and body language told her they were up to no good. No doubt about it. They snuck along, going out of their way to stay in the shadows, and when they couldn't, they scurried through the lighted areas, their shoulders hunched, the collars of their jackets pulled up around their faces.

They were heading away from the bus bench and Savannah and Dirk.

And toward the elderly churchgoers.

Outrage and fury rose in Savannah's spirit, as bitter and strong as Granny Reid's leftover coffee. How dare they even consider hurting such an elegant, loving old couple!

"It's not gonna happen," Savannah whispered, more to herself than anyone else. "Not tonight."

"You're damned right it's not," Dirk muttered as they left the bench and hurried toward the suspicious two-some.

Savannah had already drawn her 9 mm Beretta from her shoulder holster and switched off the safety. She didn't intend to use it unless absolutely necessary. But she would do whatever it took to keep those precious people from becoming these cruel idiots' next victims.

If she could get there in time to stop it.

As the ugly predators drew closer to their prey, she and Dirk rushed toward them, moving quickly, trying to be quiet and not attract attention to themselves.

Savannah eyed the distances between the various couples. She didn't like what she saw.

She and Dirk weren't going to get there in time.

"Shit," she heard Dirk mumble under his breath.

"Yeah," she replied a bit breathlessly.

She and Dirk started running as fast as they could—caution and stealth no longer a concern.

Her mind raced through half a dozen scenarios, possible ways to handle the situation.

Dirk could simply yell, "Freeze! San Carmelita Police Department!"

Of course, if he did, they would most certainly *not* freeze.

They would run like hell, duck down some alley, and get clean away. With them having over a half a block's head start, Savannah and Dirk would have a heckuva time catching them.

Savannah knew that this might be the only chance they'd have to nab this pair. If she and Dirk blew it, there was no telling how many more people would be hurt, even killed, before these maniacs found another way to entertain themselves.

But as Savannah watched the elderly gentleman lean over and place a kiss on his wife's cheek, then another on the top of her head, Savannah knew she couldn't let it happen. She couldn't even let it "almost" happen.

She couldn't allow harm to come to that nice couple, even if it meant losing the perps.

Apparently, Dirk had come to the same conclusion. "I gotta announce," he told her. She could hear his frustration in those three breathless words.

"I know," she answered.

The attackers had nearly reached their intended victims. They were less than ten feet from the couple and would be on them in seconds.

The tall guy nudged his partner. The short one pulled something from his pocket and held it up in front of his face.

"A phone!" Savannah told Dirk. "He's getting ready to film it!"

The tall one took two more running steps and was even with the couple. He raised his right fist—

"Stop!" Dirk roared. "Police! Freeze!"

For half a second, Savannah started to raise her weapon and aim it at the attacker, but he was too close to the couple, and she was too far away to take the shot, even if she needed to.

The miscreant pair whirled around to face Dirk and Savannah.

A slight smirk crossed the taller one's face when he saw their gray hair and baggy clothes. That was enough for Savannah to raise her Beretta. Her finger was off the trigger, but judging from the way the guy's smirk vanished, he didn't notice her precaution.

From the corner of her eye, Savannah could see that Dirk was doing the same.

"Down on the ground!" Dirk shouted. "Now!"

"You too," Savannah yelled to the shorter guy. "Down on your knees! Do it!"

Savannah and Dirk were nearly close enough to grab them when it happened—a flurry of activity so fast, furious, and confusing that, for several seconds, her mind couldn't process what she was seeing.

Much like the battles between cartoon cats and dogs that Savannah had watched as a child on television, the brouhaha taking place before her looked like a whirlwind with the occasional arm, leg, fist, foot, and white patent leather purse protruding from the cyclone's center.

She and Dirk froze, watching in disbelief as the two would-be attackers took a terrible beating from their intended victims.

"You scumbag degenerate! Oughta be ashamed of yourself!" Savannah heard the old woman shout has she walloped the short one on the side of the head with her purse. The blow knocked him to his knees.

A well-aimed kick to the groin from a matching white patent leather shoe sent him the rest of the way down. He curled into a fetal position on the sidewalk, screaming as he indelicately clutched what remained of his grievously injured male pride.

Half a second later, Savannah saw the older man's fist fly and heard the distinct sound of a bone cracking—in this case, a jawbone. The tall guy catapulted backward and fell across his disabled and demoralized companion, who was still receiving blow after enthusiastic blow from the deadly, Sunday-Go-To-Meetin' white purse.

Savannah shot a quick glance at Dirk. The look on his face registered the shock she felt at this unexpected turn of events. His mouth was hanging open. His eyes were bugged.

He holstered his Smith & Wesson and cleared his throat. "Ma'am. Uh, lady."

The pocketbook-wielding granny took no notice, but continued to clobber her victim with gleeful abandon.

"Ma'am," Dirk said, approaching her. "You should probably stop now. He's down."

"Yeah," Savannah said, feeling just a bit sorry—but only a wee bit—for the guy who was squirming around like an earthworm on a hot sidewalk. "He ain't going anywhere, I assure you."

Meanwhile, the husband had rolled the tall kid onto his belly, expertly jerked his arms behind him, and was holding his wrists tight. "Here you go, officer," he told Dirk with a satisfied smirk. "All ready for cuffing."

The man seemed to notice that his wife was still dispensing her own brand of vigilante justice, because he reached over and tapped her lightly on the kneecap. "That'll do, Martha honey," he said softly. "These nice policemen can take it from here."

She paused, purse held high above her head, and administered one last whack. "I'm just making sure he doesn't do this again!"

"Oh, I think you've fixed his wagon, right and proper," Savannah told her. "Believe me. He won't be doing several things for quite a while. If ever."

Gingerly, Savannah reached for the purse while getting ready to block, if it should happen to swing her way.

Dirk squatted beside the tall perp and snapped handcuffs onto him. Then he did the same to the short guy with the green face.

Savannah helped Dirk pull the first one to his feet. But when they attempted to get the other one to rise, he howled so loudly that they decided to just leave him where he lay.

From his shirt pocket, Dirk took his cell phone. He punched in some numbers and said, "We've got 'em. Send a radio car for one . . ."

He looked down at the squirmer. ". . . and roll an ambulance for number two."

He listened a moment, then chuckled. "Nope. Wasn't us. In fact, wait'll you read my report on this one."

He hung up and turned to the couple. The gentleman was readjusting his orchid paisley tie as his lady smoothed her flower-spangled skirt back into place.

"Who the hell are you two?" Dirk asked them.

The old man grinned broadly. "Retired CO. Folsom."

Savannah chuckled to herself. Corrections officer at a maximum security prison. That made sense. "And your lady here?" she asked.

The woman turned to Savannah, her eyes agleam with a mixture of dark and light humor. "Retired CO. Pelican Bay State Prison," she said. "Psychiatric unit."

Laughing, Savannah patted her on the shoulder. "If you don't mind me saying so, ma'am . . . when you and your fella strolled by us earlier, looking all sweet and lovey-dovey, I was thinking I wanted to be just like you when I grow up."

The woman laughed. "But after seeing this, you've changed your mind. Sorry about that."

"Oh, please don't apologize. After seeing what you two just accomplished, I'm determined to be exactly like you!"

Martha slid her arm around her husband's waist and gazed up at him adoringly. "Well, what do you think of that, Herman?" she said. "At this late date, I've become a celebrity, somebody's idol."

Herman kissed his wife on the forehead. "Baby, you've always been my star."

Savannah smiled. Yes, if she and Dirk were very lucky, they might grow up to be just like Martha and Herman.

Something to look forward to.

Chapter 2

"What a difference three years can make, huh? This is a whole new neighborhood," Savannah said to Dirk as she pulled her classic Mustang into a parking spot directly in front of Ryan and John's new restaurant and cut the key.

"Yeah, no kidding," he replied with a sniff. "Four or five years ago, I wouldn't have walked down this street unless I had my gun, a Taser, and a billy club and was wearing a bulletproof vest."

Though he might have been exaggerating a tad, Savannah wasn't about to argue the point with him. Not that long ago Mission Street had been a dark, dreary thoroughfare, where only the very brave or incredibly foolish San Carmelitans had dared to tread after sundown. On even the shortest of strolls, hapless visitors would have garnered all sorts of colorful invitations. They would have received offers galore to purchase illicit pharmaceuticals of all varieties.

They would have been given the opportunity to drop coins, or preferably bills, into dirty disposable cups.

Individuals wearing skimpy and garish clothing would have provided equally dirty and disposable relationships.

Best of all, the area had provided the chance to rid oneself of that heavy, pesky wallet that was weighing down one's pants pocket.

But a few years back, when the mayor and several city council members had been up for reelection, actions had been taken to gentrify the 200-year-old Mission District's neighborhood. The city elders decided that the heart of their town deserved better.

The pothole-pocked street had been repaved. Empty, abandoned lots had been cleared of weeds and garbage and transformed into well-maintained, brightly lit, metered parking lots. Palm trees had been planted in even, majestic rows on either side of the street. Broken cement sidewalks had been jackhammered, then torn out and replaced with elegant herringbone brickwork. Owners of shabby storefronts had been cited and told to "shape up or ship out."

The tattoo parlors and pawn shops had "shipped out." Charming boutiques, coffee shops, beauty spas, and antique stores had taken their place. And the Mission District was now the area of choice for tourists, young lovers, senior citizens, and well-behaved children to while away a pleasant afternoon or enjoy a romantic evening.

Now, with the opening of their friends' new restaurant, Savannah and Dirk would have reasons of their own to frequent the area.

"I'm glad Ryan and John decided to stick this joint here instead of on the beach, like they were thinking about," Dirk said as they got out of the Mustang and walked up to the front door of the restaurant. "First big storm, we'd have been down there with them all night long, piling up sandbags so that they wouldn't get flooded. And I would've pulled that muscle in my back that always gives me trouble, and I'd have been out of work for months. Dodged a bullet on that one, that's for sure."

Savannah smiled and wondered if every man on earth complained bitterly about natural catastrophes and their negative effects on his life . . . before they even occurred. Probably not. Just her luck, there was only one guy like that on the planet. And of course, she'd married him.

As they reached the restaurant's entrance, she noted the latest addition to the storefront—an elegant, crimson awning. At the sight of the scrolled REJUVENE emblazoned in white script on the front of the awning, Savannah felt a surge of pride.

Probably better than anyone else, Savannah knew what this new enterprise meant to her dear, longtime friends. This was, indeed, a venture born of love and creativity.

"I'm so happy for them," she told Dirk. "They've been wanting to open a restaurant for as long as we've known them. This is their dream come true."

"I think it's a stupid idea. Even *I* know that most restaurants fail."

"So nobody should even try?"

"Not unless they want to lose their shirts."

"Thank goodness everybody doesn't think like you do. There's something to be said for entrepreneurial spirit, you know. Nothing ventured, nothing gained."

He sniffed and shrugged. "Nothing ventured, no cold, hard cash flushed down the crapper."

Savannah shook her head. "Make sure you don't share those great words of wisdom with them. Okay?"

He gave her a grin and reached down for her hand. "Of course not. I'm a married man now with the wife to teach me the proper way to talk to people."

She gave his fingers an affectionate squeeze. Her heart filled with wifely pleasure and satisfaction. Perhaps her efforts had not been in vain, after all. "Really? Have I helped you? Socially, I mean."

"Sure you have. You've taught me well. I've learned that if I say the wrong thing, you'll kick me under the table. When you've got those pointy-toed shoes on, it hurts like a sonofabitch."

Her bubble of self-satisfaction deflated a bit, but she told herself, *Oh well, whatever works. The proof's in the puddin'.*

Adequately self-consoled, she leaned on the restaurant's front door and peered through its ornate, beveled-glass window.

When she saw the dark, empty interior, her heart sank into her sensible, old-lady, thrift store shoes.

"Oh, shoot," she said. "I knew it. They're gone. We missed all of that amazing food."

She turned to Dirk. The stricken look on his face told her that he was as heartbroken as she. But faced with such a loss, she couldn't summon an ounce of compassion or goodwill toward him.

This was his fault.

It was all his fault.

Normally, under such circumstances, she would insist that he make it up to her. But there was no way. Some opportunities, once missed, were gone forever.

"I'll just betcha that raspberry tart was amazing. Did

I mention Ryan said it was topped with Chambord sauce?"

"—And Chantilly cream, whatever the hell that is. Yeah, yeah. I'm never gonna live it down. I told you that you didn't have to go to the station house with me. I told you I'd book them and do the fives by myself. But no. . . . You wanted to see it through to the end. That's what you said. Those were your exact words. 'I want to see it through to the end.' I remember it well. You—"

"Oh, for heaven's sake, hush. I remember what I said. I just thought we'd get here in time to at least sample that tart. Hey! Wait a minute. What if they're back there in the kitchen? They might've even done the whole tasting routine back there instead of the dining room."

She already had him by the sleeve and was dragging him around the corner of the building and back toward the alley.

"Aw, come on, Van. Give it up, babe. It's over. Grieve the loss and move on."

But the visions of Chambord sauce dancing in her head wouldn't allow her to give up so easily.

Granny Reid had taught the young Savannah and her siblings that the good Lord up above had a book in which He kept track of the virtuous and evil goings-on taking place on the earth below. Sooner or later, bad deeds got punished and good deeds got rewarded. It all worked out in the long run. Some called it "karma." Others called it "reaping and sowing." But one way or the other, the scales of Justice got leveled in the end.

By helping Dirk catch those slimeballs, she had done society a great boon. And to her way of thinking, God was in his Heaven above, and she wasn't going to let Him forget that she had a great big piece of raspberry tart coming to her.

As they entered the alley that passed behind the restaurant and its adjoining businesses, Savannah was a bit surprised at the shabbiness of the area—in direct contrast to the newly renovated street. The stench of rotting food garbage, and a few other smells that she didn't care to identify, weren't nearly as disturbing as the sight and sounds that greeted them in this nether region.

Dark shadows moved in the dim light as the creatures of the night scurried, crept, slunk, and sought refuge behind garbage cans, dilapidated cardboard boxes, wooden pallets, discarded doors, window frames, tires, and rusting bicycle frames.

Savannah fought her natural, instinctive urge to lift her skirt and run, screaming like a squeamish girlie girl back to more civilized and sanitized surroundings.

If she did that, Dirk would never let her live it down, and she would never again be able to tease him by reenacting his less than graceful "Spider Dance."

To gain control over her phobias, she told herself that the furry critters she saw darting through piles of litter were cute, fuzzy kitties. Every single one of them. Even the ones with bald, scaly tails and beady little eyes.

Then to strain her already taut nerves, something moved in the shadows off to their right. A much larger, darker, and more menacing shape than the ones darting around their feet.

"Halt!" Dirk shouted as both he and Savannah once again reached for their weapons. "Police!"

Yelling "halt" was something else that Savannah frequently teased Dirk about. "Who do you think you are?" she would ask him. "A Marine drill sergeant? The Sheriff of Nottingham? Dude, nobody says 'halt' anymore."

But she wouldn't be teasing him about it tonight, because it worked. The large, dark figure to their right did exactly as he was told. He even put his hands in the air for good measure.

"Hey, man, no problem. I didn't know you guys were the police," the fellow said as he slowly moved into a patch of light.

Savannah had seen more than her share of shabbily attired street folk in her day. But this fellow made most of them look like Fifth Avenue haute couture. By the dim light she couldn't tell for sure if the clothes he wore had once been military camouflage or if they were simple civilian attire that was now mottled with a decade's worth of soil and stains.

His matted beard hung nearly to his waist, as did his filthy, tangled hair.

He lowered his hands slightly and held them out in a gesture of supplication. "Really, man, all I was gonna do," he said, "is tell you guys that there's no point in knocking on that back door there. I already tried it and got nothing."

Savannah put her Beretta back in its holster. "You mean, you asked them for a handout? For something to eat?"

The guy lowered his hands and nodded. "I asked them really nice, too, and just about got my head bit off. It ain't the Mexican joint anymore. Those guys were real nice and would give anybody that asked a little something at closing time. But now the place has changed hands. And the new owners don't give a damn about nobody but themselves."

Savannah thought of the countless kind and charitable acts she had seen Ryan and John perform during her long friendship with them, and her indignation rose. "Well, now, I wouldn't go so far as to say they don't care. Maybe you just asked at a bad time or—"

"Naw, they made it pretty clear any time would be a bad time. I won't be asking again, that's for sure. Who needs a door slammed in their face twice? And if I was you guys, I'd steer clear, too. I think they've all left and gone home, anyway."

Savannah glanced down at her ragtag clothing, then at Dirk's, and she stifled a giggle. No wonder this poor fellow thought that they, like himself, had come begging for their supper.

"That's okay," she said. "We'll take our chances, but thank you for the advice."

Dirk reached into his pocket and pulled out a couple of crumpled bills. Holding them out to the man, he said, "Here you go, buddy. There used to be a hot dog stand down there across from the mission. If it's still there you can get yourself a pretty good double chili cheese dog."

Even through the matted beard, Savannah could see him smile as he accepted the money. "Thank you, sir," he said. "I sure appreciate it. I think they tore down that hot dog stand when they put in all the palm trees. But they left the pizza place alone, and at closing time they'll sell you a slice for half price."

"Good luck, then," Dirk told him as the man shuffled away, limping. "You have a good evening and stay out of trouble."

"Will do, sir. You and your good lady, too."

Happy and relieved that the situation had ended

well, Savannah hurried up to the back door of the restaurant and gave it a hearty knock.

"What're you doing?" Dirk asked her. "The guy just told you, they're gone."

"And with a gourmet dinner at stake, do you really think I'm going to just take his word for it?" she asked, banging on the door even harder.

Dirk chuckled. "I've always been the one with the reputation for going out of his way to get free food. And now look at you, leaving no stone unturned."

Savannah tried one more time, knocking with all her might. Tomorrow her knuckles would probably be bruised—but all for a good cause. "Yeah, but you'll make a fool out of yourself for a stale donut and a cup of cold coffee. Me, I will debase myself only for the very best."

Reluctantly, she turned away from the door, surrendering the battle. The war was lost. She had to admit it was over and abandon all hope as gracefully and with as much dignity as she could muster.

"Dadgum-it!" She kicked a metal trash can beside the door. And because the simple act of violence felt so satisfying, she kicked it twice more just for good measure.

"Jeez, Van," Dirk said. "It was one meal. I hate to say it, babe, but you might be overreacting just a little bit."

She turned on him with a vengeance. "One meal? Ryan and John invited us to join them for a chef's audition! And not just any chef. A world-class chef! Even they can't believe their good luck in maybe getting Chef Baldwin Norwood to run their restaurant. He was here tonight, cooking just for them—and Tammy and Waycross and us, if we'd been here. It was a private dinner where one of the best chefs in the world was trying to impress them and us! Can you even imagine how good that would've been?"

Dirk thought it over for a long time. Then his face fell, his entire mood deflating to match hers. "You're right," he said. "It would've been amazing. Damn."

Yes, Savannah thought, *he's got it. He understands now.*

She turned on her heel and marched back around the building toward the street. Dirk trudged along behind her, muttering to himself. It was something about "life opportunities wasted" and "never to return again."

Finally, she thought, *he feels just as rotten and disappointed as I do. Mission accomplished.*

"You don't really think this is *all* my fault, do you?" Dirk asked Savannah as they walked up the sidewalk to the quaint little Spanish-style house that had been Savannah's home for years and Dirk's a matter of months.

Deciding he had suffered long enough, she laced her arm through his and gave it a companionable squeeze. "No, of course not. It was those scuzzballs' fault. And if you'd busted them all by yourself, and I hadn't gotten a piece of it, I'd be a lot more bitter about that than I am over a lost tart."

"Then why did you say it was all my fault earlier?"

She giggled. "A gal's gotta blame some stuff on her husband. There's only so much crap that you can blame on the government."

He laughed with her, leaned over, and kissed the top of her gray wig. "That's true," he said. "But that should apply to husbands, too, and not just wives. The next thing that goes wrong around here, it's going to be either your fault or the governor's."

As Savannah passed beneath the lush arbor of crimson bougainvillea that arched over her front door, she glanced at the front window, instinctively knowing what she would see there.

Two black, matching silhouettes that were always visible when she returned home. Waiting, watching, eager for "Mom" to arrive.

Her pair of ebony fur-babies, her favorite felines in the world, Diamante and Cleopatra.

Before her marriage to Dirk these two had been her nearest and dearest family members. Together, they now held second place, but they didn't appear to mind their demotion. It meant having Dirk around all the time instead of once in a while. And that translated into extra treats and almost endless petting.

Dirk was one of those men who actually loved cats. So the girls hadn't found it all that difficult to train "Dad" in the finer points of kitty spoiling.

"Aw, look. How cute." He pointed to the window. "The kids are waiting for us."

"Of course they are," Savannah replied. "It's past their dinnertime. We'll be lucky if the beasts don't gnaw our feet off the moment we get inside."

Just as Savannah was sliding her key into the front door lock, she heard her next-door neighbor's door open and slam shut.

Then there was a scurrying of feet along the sidewalk, and a shout. "Hey! Savannah, Dirk. Wait a minute. I've got something for you."

Savannah sighed and steeled herself. It was Mrs. Normandy, her nosy, intrusive neighbor with the lousy sense of timing. The dear lady had an uncanny ability to schedule her impromptu and unannounced visits at the most inconvenient times.

It wasn't that Savannah didn't like her neighbor. She truly believed that Mrs. Normandy had a good heart and meant well. But she always seemed to time her visits when Savannah was the most exhausted and wanted nothing more than a hot bubble bath, some sort of soothing beverage, and a bite of chocolate.

Pasting her best fake smile on her face, Savannah turned to greet the woman. "Aw, Mrs. Normandy, how lovely to see you, bless your heart. And at such a late hour. I'd have thought you'd be snug as a bug in a rug, snoozing away in your bed by now."

"I should be asleep at this hour," Mrs. Normandy said with a huff and a puff as she made her way up the few steps to the porch. "It's long past my bedtime for sure. But I made a promise that as soon as you two got home I'd bring this over and put it right in your hands."

She held out a lovely wicker basket that was covered with a fine linen napkin. One corner of the cloth was embroidered with an elegant, scrolled *S*.

Recognizing both the basket and the cloth, Savannah felt her heart leap with joy. "Oh, you dear, precious lady," she said as she took the basket from her neighbor and clutched it to her chest. "You have no idea how grateful I am at this moment."

With eyes that were pretty sharp for a woman older than ninety, Mrs. Normandy looked Savannah over from head to toe, then scrutinized Dirk in the same manner. She lifted her right eyebrow, and one side of her lip curled a bit as she took in the gray wig and ratty clothes.

When Mrs. Normandy had first moved in years ago she had frequently questioned the fact that, from time to time, Savannah left home and returned wearing unconventional clothing. Tattered homeless-lady outfits.

Garish hooker garb. Once in a while she even covered her hair with a baseball cap and dressed like a man.

On numerous occasions Savannah had attempted to explain the concept of undercover attire to her curious neighbor. Mrs. Normandy had failed to grasp the idea, and Savannah had given up trying to enlighten her. She suspected that the elderly lady somewhat enjoyed having eccentrics for neighbors. It added a bit of color to her otherwise mundane life.

"Thank you, Mrs. Normandy," Dirk said. "We really appreciate your staying up late just to give that to us."

Offering him a coquettish grin, the lady tossed her head and said, "Oh, I don't mind. I'd do about anything for one of San Carmelita's finest. I always did like a man in uniform."

Savannah stifled a chuckle. Cop groupies, they were everywhere. They came in all shapes, sizes . . . and apparently, all ages.

Dirk cleared his throat and gave her one of his most flirtatious smiles and a quick wink. "Serve and protect, ma'am," he said as he opened the door and ushered Savannah and the basket inside. "Serve and protect. If you need anything, you just give us a ring, and I'll be right over."

Mrs. Normandy giggled as she minced off the porch and back down the stairs. "Oh, I will," she said. "I most certainly will."

Savannah shook her head as she entered the foyer and tossed her purse onto Granny's heirloom piecrust table. "You shouldn't have said that," she told Dirk as he took off his shoulder holster and placed it and his Smith & Wesson on the top shelf of the coat closet.

"Now you'll never get rid of her. She's going to be like a sticker burr on the back of your trousers."

"Ah, I don't mind," he replied. "She's still way nicer than any of my neighbors in the trailer park. They never would've stayed up late to bring me a basket with goodies in it. I'd have been lucky to find a Tupperware container on the ground next to my door with a few crumbs left inside."

Savannah headed through the living room toward the kitchen, eager to turn on some lights and see the basket's contents. But suddenly, she found it difficult to walk. Two black cats, tracing figure eights between her ankles in a dark room, turned a simple task into a treacherous obstacle course.

"Di, Cleo, I swear one of these days I'm going to step on you and squash you flatter than a flitter. And when I do, don't you come running to me, howling about it, 'cause it'll be your own fault."

Dirk hurried ahead of her and flipped on the kitchen light.

"Come on, girls," he told the cats as he opened an overhead cupboard, took out some cat food, and began to fill their empty dishes. "Don't pay any attention to your cranky momma. She missed her gourmet dinner. She's never going to get over it, and we'll be hearing about it for the rest of our lives."

Their mistress utterly forgotten and abandoned, they ran to him, purring like a couple of cheap, twenty-five-cent motel bed vibrators, and buried their faces in the bowls.

But Savannah took no offense, because she was likewise distracted. Placing the basket on the counter, she slowly peeled back the linen napkin as she savored the anticipation.

More than once in the course of their relationship, Ryan and John had left a basket such as this on her front porch. And it had always contained something delectable—something that, at least temporarily, made life delicious and well worth living.

Unfortunately, the last time they had left a batch of butter rum muffins beside her door, a family of raccoons had discovered them first. Upon arriving home Savannah had wept to see the carnage of what would have been a purely orgasmic weekend breakfast.

No doubt that was the reason they had chosen to leave this offering with her neighbor.

"Well, what is it?" Dirk asked as he made his way to the refrigerator to get his cold, I'm-finally-off-duty beer.

The napkin removed, Savannah looked inside. And what she saw, nestled there against yet another snowy white napkin, was enough to buttress her belief in a benevolent higher power.

There was a God. And, at least for tonight, she appeared to be on His good side.

Granny was right—one good turn deserves another. And as far as Savannah was concerned, she had just been celestially rewarded in a mighty way.

"It's a big ol' raspberry tart," she told Dirk as he peered over her shoulder, trying to see the bounty. "And a jar of Chambord sauce and another one of Chantilly cream."

He leaned down and began to nuzzle her neck, his warm breath giving her delightful little shivers.

"Does this mean I'm out of the doghouse?" he asked,

nibbling her earlobe. "Off the hook, back in your good graces, and all that stuff?"

She turned, wrapped her arms around his waist, and pulled his body tight against hers. With her deepest, most sultry Southern drawl, she whispered, "Well now, that remains to be seen. It all depends. . . ."

He gave her a throaty chuckle. "Um-m-m. On what?"

"On how creative you can get with a jar of Chantilly cream."

Chapter 3

"I'm so excited, I'm just about to pee my pants!"

Savannah looked at the young woman sitting across the table from her and decided that her friend Tammy Hart was telling the truth. Tammy might be the quintessential blond, svelte, golden-tanned California beauty, but she had a problem holding her water, and she was almost always excited about something. So this sort of declaration was nothing out of the ordinary, and Savannah wasn't worried.

But sitting beside the squirming, effervescent Tammy was Waycross Reid, Savannah's younger brother. And it was pretty obvious by the red flush on his freckled cheeks that he wasn't accustomed to such earthy candor—at least, not on the part of females. Recently, he had immigrated to San Carmelita from a small, conservative, rural town in Georgia, and he still got embarrassed easily. One mention of any basic bodily function in mixed company and his face would turn the same color as his ginger mop of curls.

Savannah found it one of his most endearing qualities. As far as she was concerned, the ability to blush was a virtue all too rare in modern society.

"How about you?" Savannah asked him.

"Naw. I took care of business before we left the house."

Savannah laughed. "I was asking if you're excited."

"Oh. Well, sure. Who wouldn't be?" he replied, rearranging the napkin on his lap for the tenth time.

Waycross was always a bit uneasy at gatherings of any kind. Thus far, his life hadn't included very many formal, or even informal, social events—except high school football games and their hometown's annual barbecue cook-off.

While Savannah had enjoyed those activities herself in days gone by and missed them from time to time, she was glad to see her little brother branching out a bit. It was good for him.

She took a quick glance around the packed restaurant. Every seat was filled and waiters scurried from table to table, taking orders. Meanwhile, Ryan and John moved calmly and with great poise among their guests—ever the charming hosts.

As Savannah soaked in the ambiance, she took a moment to enjoy the room itself. She could see both of her friends' tastes reflected in its décor.

John's love of the old British gentlemen's clubs showed in the reclaimed, antique brick walls; the enormous gilt-framed mirrors; and the leather club chairs with their nail-head trim that had been placed invitingly in front of the lit fireplace in the waiting area. Like Ryan's and John's home, there were bookshelves everywhere, lined with beautiful old books and interesting artifacts they had collected from their world travels.

She could see Ryan's contemporary touches here and there, as well. She was sure he had chosen the amazing water feature behind the bar. It was a large, continuous slab of exquisite green slate, lit from above, with water cascading over its surface downward into a line of flickering flame.

To Savannah, just being here, inside the physical manifestation of their combined dreams, felt like being hugged by both of those glorious men at once. And she reveled in the warm and loving sensation that evoked.

Then, to think that she was actually going to get to eat the famous Chef Baldwin Norwood's scrumptious food in this magnificent setting . . . it was almost more than she could stand.

But she wasn't the only one thinking about food.

Waycross leaned closer to her and said, "If this supper's even half as good as that tasting thingamajig the other night, we're about to be treated to a humdinger of a spread."

Sitting beside Savannah, Dirk grumbled something under his breath.

"What was that?"

Savannah was almost afraid to ask. Dirk wasn't shy about making inappropriate comments, and the ones he mumbled to himself were often the worst.

"I just said we wouldn't know about that tasting thingamajig, 'cause we were protecting and serving and all that good stuff."

Tammy gave him and Savannah her most sympathetic smile. "And we're so proud of you for it, too," she gushed. "You got those horrible people off the streets, and I'm sure you saved lives. The way they were going, sooner or later, they would have killed somebody."

"Thank you, sugar," Savannah replied. "But tonight,

it's Ryan and John we're proud of. Just look at this place. Look at this crowd! Everybody who's anybody is here for this opening."

It was quite true that the beautiful and the famous had come to celebrate Ryan's and John's dream come true.

Everywhere Savannah looked, she saw celebrities: well-known actors, directors, and producers from the television and film industries; media moguls; titans of industry; sports figures; stars of the music world; respected journalists; and powerful politicians galore.

Then there was their little table. Peopled with nobodies.

The Moonlight Magnolia Detective Agency in all its lackluster "glory."

Frequently, Savannah felt outclassed when attending a function hosted by Ryan and John, although her longtime friends did everything they could to make her feel comfortable. Years ago, after a stint in the FBI, the twosome had become high-priced bodyguards for those who could afford only the best personal protection. She could hardly hold it against them that they traveled in A-list circles.

Due to the amiability of the pair, many of their clients had become close friends. Tonight that impressive, if eclectic, group had assembled here in this one exquisite setting to enjoy the fruits of their friends' labors.

The promise of eating food prepared by a world-class chef didn't exactly hurt either. Judging from the smiling faces and the sound of laughter and excited chatter, the crowd was looking forward to an awe-inspiring culinary experience.

As Ryan made a circuit around the room, meeting and greeting, he spotted Savannah and her gang and headed straight for their table. Bending from the waist like a Renaissance courtier, he kissed Savannah's hand and set her heart atwitter. Many times she had thought Ryan Stone would look tall, dark, and devastatingly handsome in a barrel—or in her more exotic fantasies, a loincloth. But tonight, wearing an Armani tux, he was positively delicious.

Now that she was a married woman, she tried not to think about how delectable Ryan Stone was with his bright green eyes, black hair, perfect bronze tan, and the musculature that would make a bodybuilder proud.

She was pretty sure that Dirk had included "Lusting After Stone" as a "Don't" in the fine print list of "Do's and Don'ts" on the back of their wedding certificate.

Not that Dirk was jealous or anything. Heavens, no. So what if a man's wife was dear friends with a walking, talking, just-fell-from-the-heavens Adonis? What guy would get his boxers in a bunch over a little thing like that?

"I'm so happy you were able to join us tonight, Savannah," Ryan said, his voice soft and rich as fine, claret velvet. He turned to Dirk, and with a tad less velvet in his tone he added, "And you, too, buddy. So glad you could make it."

Ryan leaned over and planted a kiss on the top of Tammy's glossy, golden head. She wriggled with delight—or maybe because she still needed to pee; Savannah wasn't sure which. Tammy's wriggles were frequent and pretty much all the same.

As Ryan shook hands with Waycross, she heard the subtle tinkling sound of a cell phone. Ryan reached into his jacket pocket, and as he took out his phone, he said to them at the table, "Forgive me. Apparently, we have another issue of some sort brewing in the kitchen."

His eyes scanned the text message, and he frowned. "Oh, man. This new chef and his team. . . ." He shook his head wearily. "I'm starting to wonder if we made the right choice. His food is amazing, but his personality sure leaves something to be desired."

"He's a horse's patootie?" Savannah offered.

"Precisely." Ryan stuck the phone back in his pocket and sighed. "I'll have to get back to you. Enjoy yourselves. This table's meals are on the house tonight, and I want you to sample as many dishes as you possibly can so that we can get a full report later."

They watched Ryan rush to a set of double swinging doors at the back of the dining room and disappear into the kitchen.

Dirk said, "Let's see now . . . sample as many dishes as we possibly can. Hmmm. That's an offer I certainly won't refuse." Picking up the menu, he gave it a quick scan and added, "Not that I can tell what any of this stuff is. What the hell is Crayfish Vol-Au-Vent?"

"Fancy puff pastry with crawdaddies inside. You'll like it," Savannah told him.

Dirk looked doubtful. "Crawdads. I don't think so. Aren't those like a poor man's lobster, and they look like big, nasty bugs?"

Tammy laughed. "So do shrimp, but you devour them any time you get your hands on—"

A loud racket suddenly erupted from the kitchen. Metal clanging. Breaking glass. Shouts of anger and alarm.

The entire room hushed as the diners turned toward the double doors in the rear of the room, their eyes wide, mouths open.

Savannah glanced toward the bar area, where John stood, a champagne bucket in his hands. The usually calm, collected, and debonair Brit raised one eyebrow, cleared his throat, and set the bucket on the bar.

As he hurried toward the back of the room, Savannah saw him run his fingers through his thick silver hair and lightly tweak the right corner of his lush mustache. Savannah knew him all too well. And for her, those simple gestures said it all: John Gibson was alarmed. In fact, he was nothing more or less than horrified.

"Whoa," Waycross said under his breath. "Sounds like a major fracas goin' down in there. Reckon we oughta go lend a hand?"

Savannah was already half out of her chair. "Yep, I reckon so. But just Dirk and me. Less of a stampede that way. You kids cool your heels and wait here at the table."

Savannah and Dirk were about halfway across the dining room when another enormous crash resounded throughout the building. Several of the guests rose to their feet, and a couple of ladies cried out in alarm.

Savannah held up her hands, fingers spread as though directing traffic. And in her best authoritative cop voice she said, "Now, now, don't y'all trouble your heads about a thing. Just relax and talk amongst yourselves. Drink some wine, swig some beer, down your cocktail, and relax. Your dinner's on its way."

Her admonition seemed to have a calming effect on the crowd, at least for the moment. They retook their seats, buried their noses in their beverage glasses, and resumed their conversations, though the tone of the place was certainly more animated than before.

Savannah wished she could heed her own advice and calm down. But as she neared the doors, the shouts from inside the kitchen only seemed to be escalating. Fast.

Dirk was the first one to burst through the doors. Immediately, he had to duck to avoid being hit in the head by a flying saucepan.

"Get out! Get out! Get out!" roared a deep, male voice. "I will not work this way! I told you, 'No one is allowed in my kitchen except my team. No one! Ever! No exceptions!'"

Savannah hurried into the room after Dirk, fully prepared to avoid any cooking utensils hurled in her direction. Her eyes scanned the chaotic scene, trying to make sense of the situation.

A woman wearing a white uniform jacket with red cuffs was squatting behind the counter—obviously taking cover.

A couple of male workers with stained aprons and terrified looks on their faces crouched beside some vegetable crates next to the rear door that opened onto the alleyway.

On the opposite side of the kitchen, near the stove, stood Ryan and John. They appeared to be in a face-off with an enormous hulk of a fellow, dressed in what even Savannah recognized as a chef's uniform—a white double-breasted jacket with black buttons and black piping. His long, curly silver hair was pulled back into a ponytail and his head was covered with a toque, the traditional hat worn by chefs the world over for hundreds of years.

Although Ryan Stone was exceptionally tall, this man was even taller. Savannah guessed Chef Baldwin Norwood must be six foot six or seven, weighing in at a tidy 350 plus pounds. His round face was flushed an alarming shade of crimson.

The last time Savannah had seen someone whose face was so red, that person had fallen at her feet a moment later, dead from a heart attack. She wouldn't have been surprised if the chef had suffered the same fate there on the spot in front of them all.

Granny Reid would have described his condition as "pitching a conniption fit."

In spite of the fact that the chef had an enormous knife in his hand, Ryan stepped closer to him, until the two men were nearly nose to nose.

"Chef Norwood, we must ask you to gain control of yourself immediately," Ryan said in a calm, but stern, voice. "We won't have you endangering the staff and upsetting our guests."

"Then get out of my kitchen and stay out!" Norwood shouted.

In an instant John had slipped beside Norwood and wrenched the knife from his hand. The chef howled from pain as his wrist was twisted.

He raised his fist and shook it in Ryan's face. "And now you attack me? You injure me? I'm just about to leave this establishment and take my team with me. Let's see how you do then! I will not tolerate any form of disrespect in my own kitchen!"

"May I remind you, sir," John said in his thick, aristocratic British accent, "this kitchen belongs to my partner and me. We are the employers and you, for all your expertise and grand reputation, are the employee. You will not resort to violence in this place, or you will be arrested. Do you understand, sir?"

Norwood gave a derisive snort and lifted his chin. "You're going to tell me how to run a kitchen? You two have been in the restaurant business, what, thirty minutes? And *you're* going to lay down the law to *me?*"

Dirk stepped forward and flipped open his badge, showing it to Norwood. "How about if I lay down some laws for you? When I stepped through that door just now, you nearly took off my head with a metal pan. You assaulted a police officer, dude. And if my friends here didn't need you to cook dinner for all those people out there, you'd already be facedown on the floor wearing handcuffs, lickin' tomato sauce off the tiles."

Ryan reached over and laid a hand on Dirk's shoulder. "Thank you, Detective Sergeant Coulter. But I think Chef Norwood has a much clearer understanding of the situation now than he had a few minutes ago when he threw that pan at you."

John nodded. "And I believe we all understand that the important thing is, we get this dinner service under way. We have a room full of hungry guests out there who are not going to be speaking well of this establishment"—he gave Norwood the infamous, full-on Gibson glare—"or its celebrated chef come tomorrow morning. We must turn things around straightaway unless we want to wake up to hideous reviews."

As the men continued to talk sense to the chef, Savannah watched the petite young woman in the red-trimmed coat as she stood and readjusted the red bandanna that held her mass of dark curls away from her face. Pretty in a girl-next-door, no-nonsense sort of way, she walked over to the two men kneeling behind the vegetable crates and gave them each a nudge on their shoulders. "Come on," she told them. "The excitement's over, and those stations aren't going to man themselves."

She hurried over to a computer screen and glanced over the orders listed there. "Five Chateaubriands, four lobster thermidors, seven beef Wellingtons. Let's get crackin', people."

Savannah turned and saw a small cluster of waiters and waitresses staring through the windows of the double doors. She hurried over to them, swung the doors open, and said, "Everything's fine. Just ducky, in fact. Go back to your tables and tell everybody there was a small accident. A few pans dropped, that's all. Their suppers will be up before they know it."

As the waitstaff scurried away to do her bidding, Savannah glanced over her shoulder once more at the chef and his team. She crossed her fingers, mentally knocked on an imaginary piece of wood, and hoped to high heaven that—for Ryan and John's sakes—they wouldn't make a big honkin' liar of her.

Because at the rate the kitchen staff was going, the guests of ReJuvene could consider themselves lucky if their delicacies were served blood-spatter-free.

"Gee, that was fun."

Savannah looked across the table and saw a version of her debonair friend that she had never seen before. Ryan's appearance belied his cheerful words that had been uttered with an unmistakable note of sarcasm.

His dark mane, usually without a hair astray, had escaped the confines of its liberally applied gel and was now hanging down over his eyes. A tuft in the back stood on end like a child's rebellious cowlick.

His face glistened with a sheen of sweat that Savannah had seen only once before—at the end of a particularly grueling tennis match.

Ryan looked positively worn to a frazzle.

So did John.

He was slouching in a chair beside Ryan's. His face

had the same haggard, dejected expression, and his arms hung down at his sides as though he were too weary to lift them.

"Yes, bloody good fun," John replied with even less enthusiasm. "Let's do it again tomorrow."

Ryan picked up a napkin from the table and wiped his brow. "And the next day and the next and the next."

John gave him a derisive half-grin and a poke in the ribs. "Whose idea was this—you and I becoming restaurateurs? I seem to recall you first broaching the topic one summer evening over a cup of granita in Salinas."

"Ugh, don't remind me." Ryan reached across the table, grabbed Dirk's by-now-warm beer, and drank nearly half the glass in one long draft.

"At least the party's about over," Dirk said as he shoveled the last bite of raspberry tart into his face, snatched the glass back from Ryan, and washed the mouthful down with what remained of his beer.

"And everybody seemed to have had a great time," Savannah added in her best cheerleader voice.

Tammy nodded enthusiastically. "That table where the press was sitting for sure! I saw them taking pictures of all the dishes. They were superimpressed. I could tell."

"How could they not be?" Waycross said as he carefully folded his napkin and laid it next to his empty plate. "That was a meal fit for a king . . . or a guy on his way to the electric chair."

He looked around the table and saw everyone giving him a strange look. Shrugging, he added, "Just sayin'. If I was on my way out of this world, that'd be my choice for a last meal. Okay?"

Ryan smiled, reached over, and patted the kid's broad shoulder. "Thank you, Waycross. That's about the nicest compliment we've received tonight."

Turning back to John, Ryan sighed and said, "Seriously, though, what are we going to do about Norwood?"

"The food was fantastic," John replied. "The service impeccable. Top drawer, all the way."

"But the attitude. That level of drama every night?" John shook his head wearily. "It can't be borne."

"Tomorrow we start looking for a new chef."

"Done. Life is too short to tolerate the likes of such an arrogant, violent cad as that—five-star chef or not. Surely we can find a sane individual who doesn't terrorize the staff."

Noticing that the last remaining guests were standing and gathering their things to leave, Ryan rose and hurried over to say good-bye and see them to the door.

"I'm sorry things didn't turn out as well as you'd hoped in all ways," Savannah told John, "but overall, the night was a rousing success."

Tammy nodded eagerly. "I heard that at the end of Disneyland's first day, Walt actually cried because of all the things that went wrong. And look how well that worked out in the end."

John reached over, took Tammy's hand, and kissed it. "Thank you, love. Rave reviews from one's nearest and dearest—that's what matters most. And you're right; all's well that ends well."

Savannah smiled and picked up her fork, intending to pilfer the last bite of raspberry tart off Tammy's plate when she wasn't looking. But no sooner had she reached across the table to do so than a nerve-shattering scream came from the kitchen area.

Savannah dropped the fork and leapt to her feet.

So did everyone else. En masse they rushed, once again, to the double swinging doors at the back of the room.

As they ran, they heard several more cries—each worse than the one before.

During her time as a police officer, Savannah had heard more than a thousand screams. Screams of rage, pain, fear, and drunkenness. People screaming for all sorts of reasons, and sometimes for no reason at all other than to attract attention or express a minor annoyance.

But there was only one reason for that sort of scream— a cry that went straight into the heart and the marrow of the bones, causing those who heard it to steel themselves for the worst life had to offer.

Nobody screamed like that unless somebody was dead.

Chapter 4

Once through the double doors, Savannah needed only a couple of seconds to spot the body. It lay on its back in a dark red puddle of gore on the floor in front of the stove.

She required a bit longer to identify the corpse.

The white of the chef's jacket was mostly stained crimson, but she could still discern the black buttons and piping. And the sheer bulk of the man alone told her it was Norwood.

Even though she was the first one into the room, the first to kneel beside him, and the first to press her fingers against his still warm, blood-slick neck, Savannah needed no one to tell her there would be no pulse.

The amount of damage that had been done to the body—multiple wounds that she could see on his chest and abdomen and several gaping slashes to his head—were some of the worst homicide injuries she had ever seen.

No one could have survived such an attack.

So absorbed was she by the gruesome sight that she was only vaguely aware of Dirk asking her, "Well? Is there a pulse?"

"No," she replied. "None."

She rose and turned to the young woman nearby, who was still screaming hysterically. She seemed to be stuck in some sort of horrible, nightmarish mind-warp, repeating the same gut-twisting shriek over and over and over again.

Savannah rushed to her and grabbed her by the shoulders. She shook her gently, trying to get her attention. But the woman was staring down at the gory figure on the floor, transfixed, her eyes wide with horror, as she continued to wail that terrible, shrill cry.

Savannah whirled her around, forcing her to stand with her back to the body as Dirk, Ryan, and John examined it.

Placing her hands on either side of the woman's face, Savannah held her head tightly, compelling her to look straight into her eyes.

"It's over now. Stop your screaming, sugar," Savannah told her in a voice both kind and stern. "Try to get ahold of yourself, darlin'. What's done is done. It's over."

For the first time, the woman appeared to see her, and she stopped crying. But she was breathing so deeply, so hard and fast, that Savannah knew she was hyperventilating.

"Come over here," Savannah told her. She led her toward the back door and sat her down on one of the vegetable crates where the same two fellows, who had been hiding there earlier, were cowering once again.

"Don't you two go anywhere," Savannah told the men. "That policeman over there is going to want to talk to you both, for sure."

The workers exchanged quick looks of apprehension.

"Don't worry," Savannah told them, anticipating the reason for their concern. "He's not the immigration police."

She glanced back at the scene behind her—at Dirk, who had moved away from the body and was now scouring the area around it for anything out of the ordinary that might be evidential.

Ryan and John were doing the same. Though it had been years since they had carried FBI badges, the skills and mind-sets of professional investigators never changed.

Just outside the now-open double doors, Tammy and Waycross watched silently, their sweet faces registering the full horror of the situation. Behind them stood several of the waitstaff, looking equally traumatized.

Savannah heard the woman sitting on the crates gagging, and a moment later the pungent stench of vomit joined the coppery scent of blood in the air.

That particular nauseating combination was a common odor that Savannah had smelled many times.

More than once, she had wondered if the millions of people who found the topic of murder so fascinating—even "romantic" in a perverse, macabre way—would have found the sordid reality so intriguing had they experienced it firsthand.

She suspected that five minutes at a real homicide scene would have put much of the public off their true crime shows forever.

One of the men left his hiding place behind the crates and stepped closer to her. "Your friend is not the immigration police?" He cleared his throat and shifted nervously from one foot to another, not meeting her eyes.

"No," she replied.

"What kind of police is he?"

Savannah looked at Dirk, who was speaking on his cell phone. She could hear just enough of his conversation to know that he was requesting Dr. Liu's presence. Dr. Jennifer Liu—the county coroner.

"Unfortunately," she said, "right now he's the murder police."

No matter how many years Savannah had known Dr. Liu, she would never get over the momentary surprise she felt when she saw the Asian beauty enter a crime scene. Tall, statuesque, and usually dressed in an outfit that would be more appropriate on a high-priced hooker, Dr. Jen hardly fit most people's idea of a medical examiner.

Tonight was no exception.

She entered the kitchen by way of the back door. And as was her habit, she left the accompanying CSI team momentarily outside so that she could have a solitary "first impression" look.

She was sporting a pair of over-the-knee, black leather boots with a matching miniskirt. Her blouse was sheer enough to be illegal, except for the two strategically placed and slightly less transparent front pockets.

Her waist-long, silky black hair was pulled back and fastened with a large clip embellished with peacock feathers and rhinestones.

Her exotic black eyes lit up when she spotted Savannah.

"When I heard that he was the one who called this in"—she gave a curt nod in Dirk's direction—"I was hoping you'd be here," she told Savannah.

Taking in the boots, the miniskirt, and the peekaboo blouse, Savannah said, "Sorry you got called away from your party. I'll bet it was a fun one."

Dr. Liu gave her a slightly confused look. "Party? What party?"

Savannah shrugged. "Oh, nothing. I just thought that . . . Never mind. Glad you're here." Savannah glanced down at the still-distraught young woman, whom she had now identified as Francia Fortun, the sous-chef.

Lowering her voice, Savannah whispered to the M.E., "It's a messy one. Very high on the Yuck Factor Scale."

The doctor gave a flippant nod of her head, which caused her peacock feathers to quiver a bit. Her beautiful face registered no trace of concern as she glanced around the room, looking for the victim.

Dr. Liu had seen it all. Her Yuck Factor Scale was set much higher than her fellow human beings, making her difficult to impress.

But Savannah did notice a momentary look of surprise that registered in those dark eyes when Dr. Liu spotted the corpse near the stove. Was that even a trace of revulsion that she saw cross the doctor's face?

Wonders never ceased.

But then, even hardened professionals like the county medical examiner seldom saw such a brutal homicide. Most killers were content with a bullet or two, or a few stabs to their victim's most vital areas.

This was definitely overkill in one of its most gruesome forms.

The doctor gave Dirk, Ryan, and John only a cursory nod before she walked over to the body and squatted beside it.

Savannah couldn't help grinning . . . just a little. Dr. Liu was an excellent coroner, but she was all female. And Savannah knew that any woman who owned a pair of boots as expensive as those would never kneel in a pool of blood while wearing them.

"Somebody did a thorough slice-and-dice on him," Liu said, accepting a pair of surgical gloves from Dirk.

"No kidding," Dirk replied. "Looks like his head went through one of these giant food processors."

Savannah heard Francia give a little groan and start to gag again.

For the sake of the young woman and the crates of vegetables that had already been fouled, Savannah reached down and pulled her to her feet.

"I think you've been in here about long enough," Savannah told her. "Let's get you to a more peaceful surrounding, and we can have a little talk just between us girls."

Savannah turned to the two workers and crooked her finger. "You fellas come along, too. Y'all are looking a bit peaked around the gills. Reckon you could use a change of scenery, too."

Savannah led the three into the dining room, where she suggested that the men take a seat in one corner.

As she led Francia to the opposite side of the room, she motioned for Tammy and Waycross.

They hurried over, eager to participate in any way. She knew they were dying of curiosity about the whole horrible affair, but they were well-trained enough to keep a low profile unless invited in.

"Tammy," Savannah said, "would you mind getting Francia here a glass of ice water? And Waycross, I think those two gentlemen over there in the corner could use a couple of cold beers to quiet their nerves."

She nodded toward where the waiters, the bartender, and a couple of busboys were huddled around the fire-place, whispering among themselves. "Get them some-thing, too, if they need it. And tell them not to leave until Dirk questions them. Okay?"

"Sure," Tammy said. "And how about you, Savannah? Can I get you something?"

Savannah sighed, feeling a few years older than her octogenarian grandmother. What a day this had turned out to be. So much for a relaxing, culinary treat.

"Oh, I'm sure my nerves could use a cold beer, too. But I'll pass and settle for ice water like Francia here."

"Actually," Francia interjected, "if they can have a beer, I want a glass of wine . . . if it's all the same to you. A full-bodied, dry Cab. After what I've seen tonight, I think I deserve it."

Tammy gave Savannah a questioning look. Savannah nodded.

"No problem," Tammy said with a tremulous, pseudo-bright smile. "One full-bodied, dry Cabernet Sauvignon coming up."

Tammy scurried away to get the wine and Waycross followed her to the bar for the beer. Savannah turned to Francia.

The sous-chef had removed her jacket and was wear-ing only a thin tank top underneath. Savannah tried not to stare at the fascinating array of tattoos that were now visible. But they were impressive.

She had everything from kitchen knives dripping with blood, to a collection of beautifully portrayed vegetables, to the words "I Cook to Live, I Live to Cook" inside an ornate banner. On her shoulder were salt and pepper shakers.

Obviously, Francia Fortun was a "foodie" of the first order, fully dedicated to her craft.

"Speaking of the traumatizing things you've seen tonight," Savannah began, "let's hear it all."

"All? You want me to relive everything I've just been through right now? I don't even know who you are—except some friend of Mr. Stone and Mr. Gibson. Why should I talk to you?"

"Because you have to talk to somebody. As a witness, you're going to have to give your statement, and if it isn't to me, it's going to be to that detective in the kitchen, Sergeant Dirk Coulter. Frankly, between the two of us, I'm the nice one. He wouldn't be letting you have a Cabernet Sauvignon, dry, full-bodied, or otherwise. So you ought to spill it all to me and consider yourself lucky."

"Are you a cop?" Francia's dark eyes reached deep into Savannah's. And it occurred to Savannah that this young woman—for all of her hysterical screaming earlier—was no shrinking violet.

"I used to be. As a matter of fact, for years I was Sergeant Coulter's partner. Now I'm a private investigator. So don't worry. I've been around this block once or twice before. You're safe with me."

Tammy arrived with the wine and water and placed the glasses in front of them. "If you need anything else," she said, "I'll be right over there in the bar area. You know, like some saltine crackers, or pretzels, or something to settle your stomach. I noticed you were having a problem earlier with a bit of nausea and—"

"I'm fine now. Okay?" Francia snapped back. "It

was just a bit of a shock, you know. But I'm all right. Or at least I would be if everybody would just leave me alone and let me drink this wine."

Tammy hurried away and found a seat out of earshot next to the bar.

Once Waycross had delivered the beers to the grateful men in the corner, he joined her. They sat, heads together, whispering to each other and pretending not to watch the interview on the other side of the room.

Savannah took a sip of her ice water and said in her gentlest "good cop" tone, "Feel free to guzzle every drop of that wine. I'll even get you another, if that's what you want. But you're going to have to tell me what happened in the kitchen earlier. Absolutely everything. Or you and I are going to be sitting at this table all night."

Francia did exactly that. She guzzled the wine so quickly that Savannah couldn't help bemoaning the waste of a good, dry cabernet. It went down the hatch so fast that it could've been nail polish remover and Francia wouldn't have tasted it.

"Okay." The sous-chef took a deep breath and slouched in her chair. "Ask anything you want. But you saw what I saw. Him lying there all cut up and bloody. That's it, that's all."

Savannah's heart sank. So much for an eyewitness to murder.

She should've known; it was never that easy.

But, of course, Francia Fortun could be lying.

Savannah looked her over, as she had several times already in the kitchen, searching for anything in her personal appearance that might give clues to her character.

She wasn't sure what the tattoos meant, other than that she was fiercely passionate about being a chef.

It was a bit tough reading the clothing of a person who was dressed in a uniform. The generic garb of the sous-chef—a white jacket with a red collar and cuffs and black pants—told her nothing.

Francia's skin had an olive tone, and her eyes were deep brown, nearly black. Now that she had calmed down, they were virtually expressionless. Her hair was a dark brunette, and she had dyed several bright blue streaks in the strands near her nape.

Okay, Savannah thought, *so she isn't afraid of needles or a little unconventional hair color. Hardly indicators of whether she's capable of hacking a guy to death.*

"Then you weren't in the kitchen when he was killed?"

"No."

"Where were you?"

"Out back in the alley with Manuel and Carlos."

Savannah nodded toward the two men in the opposite corner, who were draining their beer glasses with gusto. "Those guys over there?"

"Yeah."

"What are their jobs?"

"The tall, skinny guy is Manuel. He's a kitchen steward. The shorter, heavier guy is Carlos, the prep cook."

"And all three of you were out in the alley? Together?"

Francia nodded, toying with her glass.

Savannah's spirits sank a bit further. She had started with three possible murder witnesses, and after asking only a few questions, she was down to zero. Not only were all three absent from the murder scene, but they appeared to have alibis. One another.

"What were you three doing out there in the alley?" Savannah asked.

"Having a smoke. It was a tough service. We needed a break before we started the cleanup."

Savannah thought for a moment, took a drink of water, and said, "Before you went outside to have your smoke . . . where was the chef?"

"In the kitchen."

"Who else was in there with him?"

"Nobody. Just the three of us. The waiters and bus-boys were out here, cleaning up."

"Yes, I know. I saw them. When you last saw Chef Norwood, what was he doing?"

"Pigging out on the leftover desserts. He always does . . . I mean . . . *did* that. How do you think he got so big?"

Savannah couldn't help noticing a twinge of sarcasm in Francia's voice. Maybe a touch of bitterness, too.

"He did that all the time," Francia continued. "At the end of a service, if it wasn't nailed down, it went into his mouth. The guy definitely had some food issues."

Yes, there it was. Definitely more than a touch.

Francia Fortun had not liked her boss. No doubt about it.

But then, Savannah had spent only a couple of minutes in Norwood's presence and something told her that there weren't too many people on earth who had enjoyed his company.

She also suspected that, although there might be a lot of people at Norwood's funeral—him being a celebrity and all—there wouldn't be many genuine mourners.

Cynical and cold as the thought might be, Savannah had decided that, although most people improved the world while they lived in it, there were a few who actually improved the sad ol' earth by leaving it.

Chef Norwood struck her as maybe being one of those. So if there was no love lost between Francia and her boss, no big surprise there.

Savannah tried to remember all that Ryan and John had told her about Francia Fortune. They said she was a gifted chef in her own right, and originally, they had considered hiring her instead of her boss.

Savannah searched her memory, trying to recall why they had changed their minds and gone with Chef Norwood. She'd heard something about Norwood giving Francia a poor reference. Didn't he say she lacked the initiative necessary to run a kitchen? Maybe she was a good cook but not such a strong leader? Something like that.

Suddenly, it occurred to Savannah that Francia might have harbored a great deal of resentment toward her boss. More than just the common dislike that others might feel toward him. And who could blame her?

From what Savannah had observed, he wasn't exactly a sweetie pie who endeared himself to others. How many people had to have a deadly weapon snatched from their hand on their first night on a new job?

"How long had you known Chef Norwood?" Savannah asked.

"Seven years. It would have been eight years this next September twenty-fourth."

Savannah did a quick mental listing of those nearest and dearest to her heart. For the life of her, she wouldn't have been able to name the exact date when she had met them for the first time.

"There's something special about that day?" she asked. "Some reason why you would remember it so well?"

"Of course it was a special day. I'll remember it until I die. It was the day I won Capocuoca Extraordinaire."

When Savannah gave her a blank look, she added, "A chef's competition in Venice once a year. The grand prize is an apprenticeship with a master chef."

Tears flooded Francia's eyes. She quickly blinked them away, but more took their place. "That was the happiest day of my life. I felt like I'd won a huge lottery. No, better than a lottery jackpot. Finally, I could fulfill my destiny. I was on my way to accomplishing my dreams. I was so full of hope."

She took a used napkin from the table, held it to her face, and cried into it.

Savannah reached over and placed a hand on her shoulder. "There, there, darlin'," she said. "You just had an awful shock. A few tears are to be expected."

Finally, Francia composed herself, wiped her tears, and blew her nose on the napkin. She rumpled it and tossed it back onto the table. Suddenly, the pain and vulnerability disappeared from her face, to be replaced with anger and bitterness.

"But it is what it is," she said, her jaw tight, her eyes cold. "Nothing in life ever turns out the way you think it's going to. For every dream you have, there are ten assholes out there ready to stomp on it, to grind it into the dirt."

Savannah gulped, thinking that even on a bad day, even when half a box of chocolate truffles wouldn't lift her mood from the doldrums, she wouldn't have uttered a comment as caustic as that.

"Sometimes," Francia continued, "it doesn't even take ten of them. One can do it. One can ruin your life, destroy your hopes, turn you into somebody you don't even recognize anymore."

Shooting Savannah a quick, cautious look, the sous-chef reached for her wineglass and drained the last drop from it. Suddenly she looked uneasy, as if afraid she had said too much.

And she certainly had.

"He was that bad, was he?" Savannah said in her most sympathetic, big sister voice.

Francia shrugged, trying to look casual, but it was too late. "Yeah, he was that bad. Ask anybody here who worked with him. Ask any of his so-called friends who were here tonight. He thinks they came to support him, but they didn't. They were here because they were hoping to see him fall on his face, once and for all."

"Who were they, these people you're talking about?"

"I don't know for sure, because I was in the back the whole time, but I took a look at the reservation list when I first got here. And there were several of 'his' people."

"Like whom?"

"His ex-girlfriend, who hates his guts now. His former business partner, who's suing him, by the way. His current girlfriend, who must've figured out by now what a pig he is."

Savannah couldn't help brightening a bit. Maybe she wasn't at square one with zero possibilities. Perhaps she had some viable suspects after all.

She picked up her water glass, took a sip, and in as casual a manner as she could muster, she asked, "Of the folks you just mentioned, is there anybody in particular who stands out? Anybody you think could have done such a thing?"

"Who knows? All of them? None of them? He wasn't known for bringing out the best in people. But then, you know that. You saw him in action. You're the professional. What do you think?"

What do I think? Savannah asked herself. *I think ol' Chef Norwood had himself a passel of enemies inside this building tonight. And I think we're going to have a booger of a time trying to figure out which one got to him first.*

Chapter 5

As a general rule, Savannah was never happier than when those she loved most in the world were gathered around her kitchen table. Feeding friends and family was third on her list of great passions.

Number one was catching bad guys—and the occasional bad girl—and making them pay for their evil deeds.

Number two was taking a long, hot bubble bath while nibbling a piece of quality chocolate. And since she had married Dirk, the bubble bath/chocolate routine was solidly tied with hitting the sheets with her hubby. Whichever one she was doing at any given moment . . . that was number two.

But tonight, the guests who were gathered around her kitchen table were hardly in a festive mood.

Usually she was plying them with food and drink of the highest caliber. But since they had just consumed a large meal, no one was interested in the plate of home-baked chocolate chip and macadamia nut cookies she had set before them.

The gruesome sight they had all seen on the restaurant kitchen floor hadn't exactly whetted anyone's appetite either.

Ryan, John, and Tammy were all studying the screens of their tablets, peering at photos they had taken of the crime scene.

Still stuck in yesteryear, Savannah, Waycross, and Dirk had used their digital cameras and printed out the pictures from the printer stashed beneath Savannah's home office desk. Their photos were spread across the table, all the more lurid in the red light cast by the stained glass dragonfly lamp overhead.

"At least we've got the murder weapon," Ryan said, holding up his tablet for everyone to see and pointing to the close-up of a bloody knife that was lying on the floor between the stove and the body.

"You mean *weapons*," Dirk told him. He picked up one of the photos and shoved it under Ryan's nose. "Dr. Liu said it was probably that knife that did the damage on his belly area. She'll know for sure once she's got him on her table and can measure the depth of the stab wounds and all that. But she said it was a meat cleaver that opened up his head like that."

"Did you find it?" Waycross asked.

"Yeah. It was on the floor a few feet away, over near the garbage cans."

Ryan shuddered. "Grisly. I'm sure I saw worse when I was in the bureau, but it's been a while, for sure."

"Somebody had it out for him," Savannah said. "Big-time."

"I was wondering," Tammy said as she played with her bottle of mineral water and tried to avoid looking at the pictures, "if it had anything to do with the disturbance that went down earlier, when you guys had to go back there and settle things down."

"Those two guys, Carlos and Manuel, didn't seem to think so," Dirk replied. "When I squeezed them there at the restaurant, they said what happened earlier was no big deal. They've worked for Norwood a couple of years and said that's just par for the course with him. Apparently, he was even better at throwing fits than he was at cooking."

"And pots and pans," Savannah added. "Maybe he threw one at the wrong person and that led to him getting his hide perforated."

"Or maybe he just tossed one too many and sent somebody over the edge," Tammy suggested.

Waycross combed his fingers through his thick red curls and leaned back in his chair. "I'll tell you what. . . . I like to think of myself as a peace-loving sorta guy, and I've got all my front teeth to prove it. But I wouldn't abide somebody I worked for chuckin' skillets at me, right and left. That wouldn't happen more than once or twice before I'd be takin' some action of my own."

Savannah gave him a soft smile. Of all of her eight siblings, Waycross was her favorite. The eldest of her two brothers, he had been forced at a young age to assume the role of patriarch in their less than conventional family.

Their absentee father had done little to contribute to the raising of his younguns. As a long-distance truck driver, he spent most months of the year on the road and away from his family. Sadly, Savannah had figured out that this lifestyle suited him quite well. Far more than that of a caretaker father.

The caretaking of the nine-child Reid brood had

been left up to their mom, Shirley. But just as sadly, Shirley had been ill-suited for the role of motherhood. She much preferred to hold down a barstool at the local tavern than to assume less recreational duties like feeding hungry kids, washing dirty clothes, or applying bandages to skinned knees.

Eventually, the state of Georgia had intervened, and the children—all nine of them—had been placed in the custody of their grandparents, Granny and Grandpa Reid.

A short time later, Grandpa had gone to meet his Maker, and little Waycross had become the "man" of the family. Like Granny Reid and Savannah, he had done his best to fill the parental void for the rest of the children.

Although not all of them had become solid and upstanding members of society, most had managed to stay out of jail. And in the small backwoods town of McGill, Georgia, that pretty much constituted "turning out good."

"Now, Waycross," Savannah said, "you've got just enough of Granny in you that I wouldn't put it past you to give somebody a good skillet smack if you felt it was necessary. But that's a far cry from what we've got here."

"No kidding." Dirk pointed to the gruesome pictures spread across the table. "This attack wasn't just meant to slow Chef Norwood down or curtail his meanness."

"That's for sure." Savannah got up from her chair, walked over to the kitchen counter, and began to go through the motions of making another pot of coffee. Most of the night was gone already, but she knew they would be at it until the break of dawn.

Homicide investigation was many things, but it wasn't your usual nine-to-five job.

As she scooped up an extra portion of coffee, she added, "Whoever killed Chef Norwood, they weren't aiming to just take him down a notch or two. A bunch of stabs in the belly and, as if that wasn't enough, some nasty whacks across the head with a meat cleaver. Nope. Somebody intended to demolish that boy altogether."

"You're taking your bubble bath now? Let's see. . . . You're three hours behind me. So it's seven o'clock in the morning there in California."

Savannah settled back into the mountain of sparkling bubbles and felt her tense muscles begin to relax immediately. It wasn't just the deliciously hot water. It wasn't the flickering candlelight that gave the tiny bathroom its cozy ambience. It wasn't the fact that she had pulled the shades and locked the door, figuratively shutting out the world.

No, it was because Savannah was talking to her beloved grandmother. So far, nothing in her life had been so terrible that a talk with Granny Reid couldn't make it at least a bit better.

She pressed the cell phone a little tighter to her cheek and smiled. "Yes, Gran. It's only seven in the morning here."

"Then something's going on. You're a nighttime bath-taker, like me, unless there's something bad in the wind. A kidnapping? A robbery? Some man did his wife wrong and she took a baseball bat to him?"

"Murder."

There was a brief silence on the other end, then

Granny said, "Murder's bad, all right. As bad as it gets. Anybody we know?"

"The chef at Ryan and John's new restaurant. It happened last night at the end of dinner service. It was their grand opening. Somebody decided to cut him up into fish bait right there on the kitchen floor."

"Boy, howdy. That must've put a damper on the festivities."

Savannah chuckled in spite of the subject matter. How many people had a grandmother who would say a thing like that? She didn't know any. And if there was only one in the world, Savannah was glad she had her.

"It certainly did. And we were up all night trying to figure things out. I'm going to take this bath and go straight to bed. Dirk's already in there, snoring like a cartoon bulldog."

"Hmmm."

Savannah could practically hear Granny Reid's mental wheels whirring.

She scooped up a handful of bubbles and blew on them, sending their glistening iridescence into the air. "Okay, Gran. Whatcha up to? I can hear you thinking three thousand miles away. You're plotting mischief, I can tell."

Gran laughed. "That's the trouble with you, Miss Smarty-Pants. You think you know everything."

"Not everything," Savannah returned. "But I'm an expert on my grandma. And right about now, you're wishing with all your might that you were out here so you could help us with this case. Am I close?"

"Close? As usual, sweet pea, you're spot on. I've been saving up birthday and Christmas money, and it's about to burn a hole in my pocket. How would you and that new husband of yours feel about a visit from—?"

"Yes!" Savannah practically jumped out of her Victorian claw-foot bathtub.

"Are you sure? I don't want to impose on a couple of newly—"

"Dust off your suitcase and travelin' bonnet, Gran, and start makin' tracks in this direction. There's nothing we'd like better."

"Are you kidding?" Dirk said over his breakfast eggs and sausages later that morning after they had both taken a sleep that was little more than a glorified nap. "There's nothing I'd like better than a visit from Gran. As long as she understands we're working a case here and we're not gonna have time to take her to the beach and Disneyland and all that touristy stuff."

Savannah swallowed a bite of her eggs, mixed with a bit of grits and a dollop of cream gravy. "Of course she understands. Why do you think she's coming? As much as she adores the Mouse, you couldn't hog-tie her and drag her to Disneyland in the middle of a murder case. Knowing Granny, I reckon she'll want to be right here, smack-dab in the thick of things."

"You know, it's been proven that distracted driving is more dangerous than drunk driving," Savannah told her disgruntled passenger.

"Who's distracted?" Dirk shot back. "You're not talking on your cell phone. You're not texting. You're not even messing with the radio. What's distracting you?"

"Not *what*, *who*."

"Who?"

"You."

"I'm not distracting anybody. I'm just sitting here, minding my own business, not saying a word about the fact that you're the one driving and I'm just cooling my heels over here in the passenger seat."

"You'd better not put your heels on my seat. I just gave them a good cleaning with that special leather conditioner."

"You fuss more with this car than you do your hair."

"You're darned right I do. And that's why, until you get another car, I'm driving and you're riding shotgun."

His mood sank, if possible, even lower. His pouty lower lip protruded a bit farther. "They crunched my Buick. Flat as one of your grandma's pancakes."

"I know, sugar."

"They killed it."

"After that wreck, it was already dead. They were just putting it out of its misery."

"I miss that car. I had a lot of good times in that car."

"You ate a lot of junk food in that car. I think every taco wrapper and empty French fry bag was still on the back floorboard when we wrecked it."

"I'm never going to find a car as cool as that one was."

"You have to at least try. Sooner or later, you'll have to put a period to the end of your grief and move on. You'll have to risk your heart and learn to love again."

He turned to her and gave her a long, searching look. "You're messing with me, right?"

"Absolutely."

He snorted. "Well, that's nice. I'm heartbroken and my wife laughs at me. And worse yet, she won't even let me drive her car."

"That's right. She won't. She saw what you did to

yours. Let's face it, kiddo—one of these days you're going to actually have to break down and go car shopping. You know, spend money. Your least favorite activity."

"Oh, just hush and drive."

"I can't. Your poutiness is distracting me. Every time we go someplace—"

"—and you drive . . ."

"Yes, and I drive, you sit over there with a sour puss on, radiating your disapproval. Being the codependent, fix-everything-for-everybody sucker that I am, I can't concentrate on my driving. So cheer up before I wreck this car, too."

She was surprised to hear him chuckle under his breath.

"We'd have to break out the bicycles," he said.

"Yeah, right. Like that's gonna happen."

At least she had put a smile on his face for a moment. Her job was done. Her destiny fulfilled. All was right with the world.

And she had gotten off cheap. Usually, the arduous chore of lifting Dirk from the doldrums required food. And if he was in a particularly foul mood, the food had to be free. Now that they were married, and he contributed to her weekly grocery budget, it was much harder to use that as a ploy. *Her* food was now *his* food, and therefore no longer free.

But then, as a wife, she now possessed an even more potent weapon in her arsenal.

Sex.

And since he was quite good at it, she didn't exactly mind having to resort to such underhanded tactics. "Manipulation" had its advantages.

All in all, with this new marriage contract in place,

things had taken a definite turn for the better. While attempting to cheer him up, she frequently found herself feeling pretty chipper, when all was said and done.

As she guided the red pony around the curving road that skirted San Carmelita's gently rolling foothills, Savannah briefly found herself distracted once again by the view. To her right rose the brown, dusty, rain-starved cliffs, where only the most drought-resistant, native plants survived. Sagebrush, prickly pear cactus, and a few varieties of stalwart daisies and poppies clung to life there on those rocky slopes.

But to her left was the town—her town—her home for many years now. White stucco houses gleamed in the late-morning sun, picturesque with their clay, Spanish tile roofs and graceful drapings of crimson bougainvillea. Statuesque palm trees bent gracefully to the onshore flow of ocean breezes, their glimmering fronds rustling like a Polynesian dancer's grass skirt in the gentle wind.

In the distance lay the Pacific Ocean in all its splendor and grandeur, its diamond-dusted waves breaking against the city's pier, sailboats gliding in and out of the harbor, pristine beaches where children splashed with their families and chased their dogs.

All these things had lured a little girl from rural Georgia years ago. And the little girl, all grown up, had never gotten over the beauty of her new home. She would never take its charms for granted.

This sort of distraction she could take.

But once she turned the Mustang left and began to descend into town—more specifically, a not-so-great part of town—and head toward the police station, her moment of soulish rejuvenation was over.

Time to get down to business.

"Tell me again," she said, "why you want to question Carlos and Manuel again today."

"I already told you."

"I know, but I'd only had two cups of coffee and I was half asleep."

"Because they were acting suspicious last night. Extra nervous for a couple of innocent guys with an alibi."

"I noticed that, too. But I chalked it up to an immigration issue. I know, I shouldn't profile and all that. But it's the first thing that crossed my mind."

"Mine too. But Tammy texted me first thing this morning. She checked them out, and they're both here perfectly legal. Carlos Ortez was born and raised right here in San Carmelita. His parents, too. And Manuel Cervantes married himself an American gal five years ago. He even took the citizenship test last year and passed it. He's as legal as you can get."

"I hear that test is really tough. That most of us couldn't pass that if we had to."

"Tell me about it. Took me two years to get through U.S. history in high school, and even then I just squeaked through with a D."

"Then you want to know why they were acting hinky last night if it wasn't an immigration problem."

"Exactly."

"They're in trouble for being legal. Because they're bona fide citizens, they're murder suspects."

"Ironic, ain't it?"

"Okay. Are they both going to be at the station house?"

"Just Manuel. I couldn't get ahold of Carlos. We can go looking for him later."

"Once we're done with them, what's next?"

"The morgue."

"When did Dr. Liu say she'd be finished with the autopsy?"

"Between three and four this afternoon."

"Then you'll be clamoring to go over there about, what, one? Two at the latest?"

"Only if you think noon would be pushing it."

"I think if you go in there, three or four hours before she's finished, to do your usual nudging crap. It might be you that she'd be pushing."

He looked moderately alarmed. "What? You didn't bring any kind of bribe?"

"Of course. On the backseat."

He turned and saw the large, square, plastic container sitting in the middle of the rear seat.

Breathing a sigh of relief, he said, "Oh, wow, thanks. For a minute there I thought I'd have to pull in somewhere and try to score a box of Godiva chocolates."

"Heaven forbid."

He sat for a moment in silent contentment. Then suddenly he sat up straight, fully at attention.

"Wait a minute," he said. "How much does it cost for the ingredients to make a big container full of cookies like that?"

Savannah sighed inwardly, steeling herself for the next dip on the Dirk Roller Coaster Express. "Um-m-m. I don't know. About twenty-five bucks I'd say, give or take."

"Twenty-five bucks! Holy cow! Really?"

"Unless I use macadamia nuts, like these. Then closer to thirty-five."

His eyes narrowed. His forehead crinkled. His lower lip shot out.

Watching him, she nearly blew through a stop sign.

Her mental cogs whirred, but only for a moment. She was getting pretty good at this.

"We've got some of that Chantilly cream left over," she told him with a little elbow nudge and a sideways wink. "Whatcha say we put it to good use tonight?"

The clouds parted, and sunlight shone on his face. "You betcha, babe! Wow! Great idea!"

Chapter 6

In order to avoid the brass, who had fired her—thereby also avoiding the temptation to murder any of them for doing so—Savannah always snuck through the back door of the police station.

Although she was held in only the highest esteem by the rank and file of the SCPD, she was pretty sure that the suits were about as eager to run into her as she was them.

All parties involved would prefer to tippy-toe, naked and barefoot, through a field of poison ivy and cockle-burs.

Plus, the back entrance was the shortest way to get to the interrogation rooms. Just through the door, down a dark and depressing hallway, and to the left was an equally dark and depressing room that was little more than a cubicle.

Dirk fondly referred to it as the "sweat box."

"You wanna watch through a one-way mirror?" he asked her.

She shot him a look of disdain.

"Or would you rather climb in the ring with us?"

"Does Victoria's Secret have fancy bloomers?"

"Gotcha."

She took a seat inside Interrogation Room B and waited while Dirk went to the reception area to collect his interviewee.

At least *she* called them "interviewees." Dirk had other, more colorful names for them. Terms best not used in front of news cameras or defense attorneys.

As she sat on the hard, cold, gray metal chair and wished for a couple of warm, comfy cushions, she took a moment to contemplate the wisdom that had been employed when decorating this room.

The walls were covered with dingy and stained, white-in-a-past-life, acoustic tiles. They were the sort that one would normally only have the opportunity to enjoy on an old and badly neglected schoolroom's ceiling. Savannah supposed they had been installed—rather than, say, paintings of the bucolic, rural roads of Vermont—for soundproofing. But their primary purpose was probably to convey the message, "Go ahead and scream all you want, nobody's going to hear you."

In all of Savannah's law enforcement years, she could honestly say she had never witnessed an act of cop violence toward a suspect, beyond what was absolutely necessary to apprehend and control them.

But this room, with its gray walls, gray chairs, and gray table, had no doubt been designed to suggest to bad guys that they were very much in the hands of the law and therefore in danger of some serious unpleasantness.

So when Dirk marched his interviewee into the room, pulled out one of the metal chairs from the metal table, and gave him a moderately gentle nudge in that direction, Savannah wasn't surprised. Nor did she consider it strange to see that the gentle, affectionate teddy bear of a guy, who petted and cooed to her cats for hours on end at home, was wearing a scowl that would have intimidated a male rhinoceros during mating season.

It was all an act. And within these walls, Dirk had won far more than his share of Academy Awards.

For that matter, so had she.

"Have a seat over there, Manuel, my man," Dirk told him. "It's time you and I had a serious talk. Mano a mano."

Manuel sank onto the chair, leaned back, and folded his arms across his chest. His denim shirt and jeans—threadbare, stained, and ragged—were simple testaments to years of hard labor. From the high decree of sun damage on his handsome, young face, Savannah suspected that he had spent more of his life working outdoors than inside a restaurant kitchen.

Everything about his appearance bespoke poverty, except for the simple but shiny gold wedding ring on his finger. Pristine and without a scratch, it seemed out of place with the rest of his clothing.

"I don't know why we have to talk," he said to Dirk. "We already talked last night. I told you all I know. I know nothing."

"So you said before." Dirk pulled out the chair between Savannah and Manuel and sat down. He leaned back a bit and clasped his hands behind his head. Immediately, Savannah recognized the gesture. It was his pseudocasual pose, the one he used when he was the most stressed.

Detective Sergeant Coulter took his interrogations very seriously. Almost as seriously as food and sex—but not quite.

Dirk made no effort to conceal the fact that he was studying every aspect of Manuel Cervantes's appearance and demeanor. His eyes raked his possible suspect from head to toe, leaving nothing unscrutinized.

Fully aware of the attention he was being paid, Manuel squirmed on his chair and tightened his arms across his chest.

"Here's the thing," Dirk continued. "Something told me in my gut that you had a few more things to say to me. I think we have some unfinished business, you and me."

"Like what?" the young man asked.

"That's what we're here to find out." Dirk took his notebook from his pocket along with a ballpoint pen. He flipped it open and with great deliberation made quite a show of reading his previous notes.

Many times Savannah had watched him do this with a blank piece of paper. The thoughtful frown, the occasional nod, and more disturbing, the deeply troubled scowl while slowly shaking his head at something mysterious that seemed to bother him on a deep, soulful level.

"You told me last night that the three of you—you, Carlos, and that Francia gal—were in the alley together. You said that none of you left the others' sight. Not even for a minute."

Manuel uncrossed his arms and grabbed the sides of the seat he was sitting upon with both hands. Savannah looked closely and saw that he was, indeed, quite literally "white-knuckling" it.

She could certainly understand why Dirk was suspicious. An interrogator might not always know the exact truth, but there were some pretty clear, telltale signs that indicated you're being lied to.

Three of the most common indications are excessive fidgeting, avoiding eye contact, and more sweat on one's brow than could be blamed on the stuffy, overheated little room.

Manuel was exhibiting all three and more. His hands were shaking, and his deeply tanned face had taken on a pale, gray pallor.

"You might as well tell me the truth," Dirk said. "Because I know for a fact that you weren't all three out there together the whole time the chef was getting murdered. And you acting like you were—that just makes me all the more suspicious. Understand?"

Savannah never fail to be amazed by the ease with which Dirk could tell bold-faced lies to potential perpetrators. For a guy who stammered and stuttered when questioned about a broken water glass at home, for a fellow who turned red in the face when trying to hide any secret—even those completely innocent ones concerning birthday and Christmas gifts—Dirk could lie his bohunkus off on the job without the slightest twitch to give him away.

"I don't know what you mean," Manuel told him with less than convincing sincerity. "The chef, he was alive when we left the kitchen. He was eating the leftover food, like he always does. We went into the alley, around toward the side of the building. We smoked our cigarettes. When we came back inside, he was dead."

"Except that you weren't all three out there the whole time," Dirk said. "Either you're covering for someone else, or they're covering for you. Which is it?"

Frantically, Manuel glanced around the room, then

stared down at the floor, as though he wished it would open up and swallow him. "I know nothing. That is all I can say to you. I know nothing."

Dirk stood up so abruptly that Manuel jumped, startled by the sudden movement. "Then tell me about that earlier fight. The one we walked in on, where the pots and pans were flying around the room. What caused that?"

A brief look crossed the young man's face—fleeting, but potent. It was a look of pure rage that set off alarm bells in Savannah's head. She also noticed that he gave a quick glance down at the shining band on his finger.

A second later he had recovered himself, and he gave a casual shrug. "It wasn't a fight," he said. "It was just the chef getting mad. If he doesn't get what he wants, when he wants it, the way he wants it, he throws a fit."

Savannah couldn't help noticing that he was referring to his former boss in the present tense. That was a mark in his favor, as far as she was concerned. She had noticed that innocent parties had a harder time adjusting to the idea that someone they knew was dead.

Murderers seemed to have no problem in that regard.

They'd know all too well, because they'd been there when it happened.

"And what was the chef throwing a fit about that time?" she asked.

"Who knows? Who remembers?"

Again he refused to meet her gaze and gave an exaggerated shrug that suggested to Savannah that he did, indeed, know and remember all too well.

"You do," she said. "It would be better for you if you told us now. We're going to find out sooner or later. When somebody gets murdered we find out everything . . . sooner or later."

For the first time since he had entered the room, Manuel Cervantes turned to Savannah and looked deep into her eyes. The pain, fear, and sadness she saw in his went straight to her heart. Obviously, this young man was harboring secrets. But she had a hard time believing he was evil.

Evil enough to stab another human being over and over, then take a meat cleaver to his head? No, she couldn't believe it.

"You know, Manuel," she said as gently as she could, "we don't care about people's secrets, unless they have to do with this murder. The killing—that's all we care about, not people's personal lives. We know you have secrets. Everyone does. If we find out what they are from someone else, it's going to look bad for you. It would be much better if you tell us yourself."

"I cannot, senora," he said. "My secrets are not my own to tell."

Again he glanced down at his wedding band.

"What is your wife's name?" she asked him.

He looked startled, upset by the question. "Why? Why do you ask about my wife?"

She gave him her warmest, kindest smile. "Because you have a very pretty wedding band. I was wondering what nice lady gave it to you."

She cast a quick, sideways look at Dirk and saw the confused expression on his face. No doubt he wondered where she was going with this.

As Savannah had hoped, Manuel's manner softened in response to her kindness. A gentle sweetness filled his eyes when he said, "Celia. *Mi esposa*, her name is Celia."

"What a lovely name. How long have you and Celia been married?"

"Only two . . . oh . . . I mean . . . five years."

Savannah shot Dirk another look. This time she could practically see the antennae sprouting out of his head.

"Which is it?" Dirk snapped. "Two or five years?"

"Five years," Manuel repeated a bit too emphatically. "We've been married five years. She is a citizen. I'm a citizen now, too."

"So we've heard." Dirk walked over to the door and opened it. "Congratulations. Now you can vote and pay taxes like the rest of us. And if I arrest you for murder, you can serve your sentence here in a decent jail, where we feed you and everything. Not like where you come from."

Manuel wasted no time as he hurried toward the door. But just before he exited, Dirk stopped him, a firm hand on his shoulder.

"Don't you go anywhere, Manuel, my man. Now ain't the time for you to be takin' no vacations to Puerto Vallarta. You stick close to home until we've got this case wrapped up. You hear me?"

Manuel gave him a curt nod. "I hear you. I will stay."

"Good. See that you do."

Once Manuel had disappeared down the hallway, Savannah reached under her chair, retrieved her purse, and stood. As always she was happy to escape from the tiny room and the claustrophobia it induced. Tonight it had seemed especially hot, and she was eager to leave it and its stale air behind.

Joining Dirk in the hall, she said to him, "You were

pretty rough on that kid, considering that you don't have a doggone thing on him."

"I do, too, have something on him. He's lying to me. I can feel it. And you know how much I like being lied to."

"About as much as you like finding a big ol' juicy worm in the middle of your kosher dill pickle?"

He took her hand and led her through the back door of the station house. "No. About as much as I like finding *half* of a big ol' juicy worm in my kosher dill pickle."

Savannah parked the Mustang a block away from the Castillo de Ortez. Since she was feeling the ill effects of having taken a nap, rather than sleeping an entire night, she would've been happy to have parked closer. But the corner of Lester Street and Milton Lane was the busiest and most crowded in San Carmelita.

The so-called "Castillo" was the reason why.

The name, which translated to "Castle of Ortez," was a joke, as the "castle" was no more than a rickety, unsightly shack about 16 feet by 12 feet. But out of that tiny establishment came a cornucopia-like flood of some of the best tacos, burritos, and tostados to be had north of the Mexican border.

From eleven o'clock in the morning until two o'clock in the afternoon, a long line of hungry patrons stretched down the block, eagerly awaiting an inexpensive, nutritious, outrageously tasty lunch.

Often, when passing the Castillo, Savannah had chuckled to herself, thinking that the proprietors of this humble establishment must be giggling with glee on their daily trips to the bank. With the money made from this ridiculous little hovel, they were probably paying for a mansion with a breathtaking view of the ocean, perched high on one of San Carmelita's majestic hills.

As she and Dirk left the Mustang and walked along the nearly deserted sidewalk toward the taco stand, she said to him, "It was a good idea, waiting until after two to come over here. If we'd come at lunchtime, it would've been pert near impossible to have a meaningful conversation with Carlos."

Dirk sniffed. "You think it was a good idea because it was your idea. I wanted to come over here at noon when they were still serving and nab one of those burrito grandes things."

"You've been here a zillion times. You know how it works. It's a two-man operation. One guy—as it turns out, Carlos—works like crazy in the back, cooking and throwing everything together. The other guy shoves it out the window and collects the money. It would have been dangerous to drag that cook away from his grill at a time like that."

"Harrumph. I ain't afraid of that guy. I've handled dudes way bigger and meaner than him."

"I wasn't talking about him. I meant the crowds. Can you imagine the riot that would have erupted if you'd called a halt to all that cooking and eating?"

He thought it over for a minute, then nodded. "You're right."

She chuckled. "Oh my goodness, a husband admits he's wrong and his wife is right. What's this world coming to?"

"Don't be a smart aleck. Us guys admit that we're wrong way more than you gals do. Men apologize all the time. Women, when they are wrong, won't actually say the words."

Savannah opened her mouth to retort but swallowed

the denial. What he'd said was true; she had to admit it. At least in her marriage, the male of the species uttered those bitter words far more than she did. Not that it bothered her all that much. She had few twinges of conscience in that regard. After all, she only made an apology-worthy mistake about once a month. Usually in the throes of PMS. Where he, on the other hand, usually committed some transgression or the other about every ten minutes.

"No," he continued, "they won't give you an actual apology. They'll just be a little bit extra nice for a while. You know, make sure you have your favorite food to eat for dinner, and then you get laid that night."

Savannah gave him an affectionate grin and a nudge in the ribs with her elbow. "And you guys just hate that, huh? You'd much rather have a heartfelt verbal apology than good food and hot sex any day. Right?"

He laughed and slid his arm around her waist. "Now, now. I wasn't complaining. Just observing. It's not such a bad system, all in all."

As they neared the taco stand, the tantalizing aroma grew stronger and Savannah's appetite soared. Their full country breakfast was becoming a distant memory, and she was beginning to doubt whether her plan to arrive postservice had been such a wise one after all.

"Damn, that smells good," Dirk said. "You know, they probably have some leftovers."

"Don't you dare."

"Dare what?"

"Ask for a bribe."

"One little taco. A burrito maybe. . . ."

"No. I swear, I'll report you. You'll do five to ten in the slammer."

He took a deep breath, filling his lungs. "Hell, it might be worth it. Wonder if they have carnitas."

"We could ask."

They walked to the front of the stand, where the previously open serving window was now covered by a highly complex and decorative barrier—a piece of unfinished, exterior-grade plywood with the word CLOSED scrawled across it in red paint.

Dirk rapped on it. And when there was no response, he rapped again even harder.

Savannah could hear movement inside. Water running. Metal clanging. It briefly reminded her of the kitchen scene the night before, and she cringed. Most certainly she'd never be able to look into a restaurant kitchen without seeing that gruesome, traumatizing sight in her mind's eye.

"Police," Dirk shouted. "I can hear you in there, and I ain't goin' away. Open up."

After a longer than expected time, the plywood lifted a few inches, then was lowered. A young woman with an uneasy look in her dark eyes swept her black curls away from her face and twisted them into a haphazard bun at her nape.

As she fiddled with fastening the "do" with a couple of bobby pins, Dirk called out, "Carlos? You in there?"

"He's busy," the woman said, wiping the sweat from her face with a damp towel. "We're closed now."

"Yeah, yeah. We know that," Dirk snapped.

"We decided to wait until after you'd closed to drop by," Savannah said, stepping closer to her and giving her a sweet smile, "so as not to inconvenience you."

Someday, she was going to sit down and count every time she'd had to be extra nice to someone to make up for Dirk's grouchiness. Then she was going to charge him a dollar for each of those occasions and move to the Bahamas.

She might or might not bring him along with her, depending on how much he was aggravating her on moving day.

Dirk leaned his head through the window and shouted, "Carlos, I can see you, dude. What? You think you can hide in this cracker box? Get out here and talk to me."

The reply came in the form of much clanging and banging of metal. Savannah could hear the creaking of a water faucet being turned off.

A moment later, Carlos appeared beside the young woman. He was drying his hands and forearms with the much-stained apron he wore.

He gave Dirk a wary look. "I thought we were done talking last night," he said. "I told you everything I saw. I've got nothing else to say."

Dirk took a step to the right and opened a small, rickety door that led inside the stand. "Come along, and let's you and me take us a stroll through that park across the street. I'll betcha we can think of something to chat about. Like, say . . . global warming, the next presidential election, those Lakers."

"I don't have time to watch sports," Carlos returned, tearing off his apron and pitching it into a bin of dirty cloths.

"Then we'll come up with another topic of conversation," Dirk said as he motioned for Carlos to come through the open door. "You know, like, murder."

Dirk placed a companionable hand on Carlos's shoulder—one that Savannah was sure the younger man did not appreciate. Dirk was taller and heavier than most men, and he knew all too well how to use that to his advantage. "Intimidation" was a well-sharpened, oft-used instrument in any cop's toolbox.

Savannah knew why he was leading Carlos away to question him. It was so that Savannah could talk to the young woman. If she worked with him, she might have some useful information herself. They operated on the assumption that it was best, whenever possible, to get two interviews for the price of one.

But her possible interviewee was reaching down for the plywood again. Savannah quickly thrust her hand through the still-open window before the opportunity had passed.

"I should introduce myself," she said. "My name is Savannah Reid. And you are . . . ?"

Looking more than a little uncomfortable, the woman set down the plywood and shook Savannah's proffered hand.

"I'm Maria," she replied. "Nice to meet you."

The cautious, uneasy look in her dark eyes suggested the contrary. But she forced a smile, and it brightened her pretty face.

"You get really busy here at lunchtime," Savannah said. "I've dropped by many times and seen you guys working your butts off. It must be a tough job."

Maria shrugged. "You do what you have to. It can't be easy, you being a policewoman."

"I'm not a policewoman. Not anymore, anyway."

Maria looked confused. "But you're . . ." She pointed toward the park where Dirk and Carlos were walking. ". . . you're with him."

"I used to be a cop. His partner, in fact. Now I'm a private investigator. And I'm also Detective Coulter's wife."

Raising one delicate eyebrow, Maria gave her a little

smile and said, "That must be interesting, being married to a policeman."

Savannah chuckled and shrugged. "Well, you know what they say. 'Sleep with a cop, you'll always feel safe.'"

"So you both feel safe—you sleeping with him, him sleeping with you?"

Savannah thought it over and nodded. "Pretty much, I reckon."

The two women shared a moment of companionable silence. Then Savannah said, "What's it like, working here in this busy little taco stand with Carlos?"

"Oh, I do more than work with him. I'm married to him. And we own this busy little taco stand."

Savannah took a moment to digest this new information. Carlos Ortez wasn't just working here for a cousin or uncle. He was the owner—the guy who, according to her earlier estimations, could probably afford to live in a mansion on the hillside.

She could understand why he and his wife would choose to operate this stand by themselves. There was hardly room inside for more than two workers anyway. But why would Carlos be working as someone else's prep cook? Why subject yourself to a nasty boss like Norwood when you owned a successful eatery?

A taco stand might not be the pinnacle of the restaurant business, but it certainly seemed like a profitable establishment. Every day a lot of delicious food crossed that service counter and fed a lot of hungry, grateful people.

That sounded like success to Savannah.

"If you don't mind me asking," Savannah said, "how long have you two owned this place?"

"It belonged to Carlos's father and mother. When his father died seven years ago, his mother retired and turned it over to Carlos. I've been working here with him for two years."

"And how long had Carlos been part of Chef Norwood's team?"

A dark look crossed Maria's face. Savannah was fairly sure that she detected a look of strong dislike when she heard the chef's name mentioned.

"Almost a year," she answered. "A long year."

Savannah nodded. "I saw Norwood in action, screaming at his staff, throwing things, pitching a major hissy fit. It must've been really hard working for a guy like that."

Maria nodded and wiped her face again with the damp towel. Her eyes were no longer friendly, and Savannah got the idea that she was growing progressively uneasy with this topic of conversation.

"It was difficult. Very difficult," she replied softly.

"Then why did he continue to work for someone as abusive as Norwood? Holding down two jobs would have been exhausting even with a decent boss, let alone a guy like that."

"My husband is a hard worker. He always has been. It's one of the things I love and respect about him most." She waved a hand, indicating the shabby stand. "Do you think he wants to work here forever? To make tacos and burritos until he dies? No. My Carlos has dreams of being a chef, a real chef, a fine chef."

"And that was why he was working for Norwood?"

"Yes. Why else? He knew he had to start at the bottom and work up. He began by washing dishes. Then he moved up to kitchen steward and now prep chef. He has to learn how to run a restaurant. A *fine* restaurant, worthy of his talents. Not just a fast-food stand."

Savannah was surprised to see the young woman's eyes fill with tears.

"But as soon as he started working for the chef, Carlos realized that he wouldn't be learning anything from that man. Baldwin Norwood had nothing to teach anyone about cooking or anything else in life."

"What are you saying?" Savannah asked, trying to get her mind around this new accusation. No one had made any bones about the fact that Chef Norwood was a jerk, but this was the first time she had heard that he couldn't cook.

"I'm saying that the famous celebrity chef, Baldwin Norwood, couldn't prepare a decent meal if his life depended on it. He's a fraud."

Maria paused and swallowed hard. Savannah noticed that her hands were shaking as she twisted the towel. "Or should I say he *was* a fraud. I guess now he's a dead fraud."

"Well, I don't know about the 'fraud' part, but he certainly is dead. I don't know how much Carlos told you, but it was a terribly violent murder."

Maria nodded and began to tremble all over. "Yes, he told me it was awful. I'm sorry it happened."

Savannah's right eyebrow lifted a notch. "You're sorry? Why would you be sorry?"

Maria stared down at the towel in her hands, then across the street toward the park where her husband was walking with Dirk. "I just mean—even someone as bad as Norwood doesn't deserve to die like that."

"Who do you think might have done it?" Savannah asked. "If you had to guess, who would you say it was?"

Maria dropped the towel, reached for the edge of the counter, and grasped it tightly, as though to keep herself from falling. "I don't want to say," she replied. "I don't want to accuse anyone of something so terrible."

Savannah felt a surge of excitement welling up inside her. She had to remind herself not to press too hard, too fast.

As gently as possible, she said, "It's okay, Maria. Don't worry. This is just between you and me. I'm just going to ask you a simple question, and if you can answer it, it might help me a lot. Okay?"

Maria gave her a tentative nod.

"All right. Here goes. . . ." Savannah drew a deep breath. "Of all the people that Chef Norwood treated badly, whom would you say he treated the worst?"

Maria looked slightly relieved and offered a quick reply. "Oh, that's easy," she said. "He was awful to everybody around him. But the person he hated most was Francia Fortun."

"Francia? Why would he hate his sous-chef?"

"Because she was much more than his sous-chef. She was *the* chef. The food he served and called his own was made by her. Every bite of it."

"Really? But how? How could that be?"

Maria gave a dry, bitter chuckle. "Why do you think he went crazy any time someone other than his staff came into his kitchen? It was because he was afraid they would find out his secret. And his secret was: He couldn't cook. He screamed and shouted and strutted around, acting the part of the celebrity chef. He hated Francia because she was everything he claimed to be."

"And he couldn't fire her, because if he did—"

"—the world would find out that he was a fraud."

Savannah recalled everything that Ryan and John had said about Francia and how they had nearly hired her as their head chef. She considered how Francia must have felt when that golden opportunity was snatched away by her unscrupulous, abusive boss.

But there was the matter of the alibi.

"I see what you're saying," Savannah told her. "But your husband claims that Francia and Manuel were with him in the alley around to the side of the building, having a cigarette, when the chef was killed."

Maria glanced over toward the park, where Carlos and Dirk were finishing their walk and heading back toward the stand.

Savannah saw the young woman's love for her husband in her eyes as she watched him. But there was a sadness there, too.

"My husband is a good man," she said. "Sometimes he's too good."

"What do you mean?" Savannah asked.

"He's too loyal. He's a better friend to others than they are to him. And sometimes he gets hurt." Her eyes searched Savannah's, pleading, looking for reassurances. "Will you try to help him?" she asked. "I've tried to help you all I could. I answered your question. Please don't let my husband get hurt."

"I'll try, Maria," Savannah told her. "I'll do my best."

But even as she spoke the words, Savannah wondered if it was a promise she would be able to keep.

Chapter 7

Savannah supposed that there were more depressing places on God's green earth than the county morgue.

But she couldn't think of one.

In all the years she had been coming to this awful place—probably at least one hundred visits or more—she couldn't remember one time when her mission had been "festive" in nature.

The only times she had ever felt even a smidgen of something akin to joy inside that grim, somber, gray building were when she was walking out of it.

Dr. Liu didn't seem to mind living with the specter of death on a daily basis. But Savannah couldn't help feeling uneasy about being inside a building the very existence of which was to deal with one of life's most inevitable and least pleasant realities.

Then, to make things even worse, there was good old Kenny Bates.

Like the biggest green fly atop a dog pile, Officer

Bates manned the reception desk, doing his utmost to offend everyone who walked through the front door.

And he succeeded famously.

He flirted with every female who passed through, and his method of seduction was so crude and overt that Savannah wondered how he could have escaped a sexual harassment charge for so long.

Several years before, he had made the mistake of showing her the centerfold of a porn magazine and commenting at length about how much the model, who was displaying everything but her ovaries, resembled Savannah.

Savannah had cheerfully taken the magazine away from him, rolled it up, and beaten him half to death with it.

Since then his ardor toward her had, thankfully, cooled a bit.

He was even less charming with the males who passed through his front door, as he snapped, snarled, and seized every opportunity to establish his dominance over them. He protected the desk, the sign-in sheet, and its accompanying pen like an ill-tempered guard dog defending a junkyard from midnight marauders.

Savannah had seen homicide detectives more relaxed at a multiple murder scene than Kenny Bates was with his stinkin' clipboard and ballpoint.

That afternoon, as Savannah parked the Mustang in the morgue lot, Dirk reached back to the rear seat and grabbed the container of chocolate chip cookies.

"Don't want to forget these," he said. "We're at least an hour and a half earlier than she said to come."

Savannah reached over and snatched the container from his hands. "I baked them," she said, hugging it to her chest. "I get to be the one who gives them to her."

"Yeah, yeah, what you mean is, 'I wanna snag one of those for myself while we're walking up to the door.'"

He knows me way too well, she thought as she got out of the car, closed the door, and started across the parking lot toward the front of the building.

Of course, that was exactly what she had in mind. If he hadn't been so snippy about it, she would have offered him one, too.

But she didn't have to offer. No sooner had she raised one corner of the lid than he reached around her and shoved his big hand inside.

"If you're eating one, I am too."

"Okay," she told him. "But we probably shouldn't mention to Dr. Liu that she's short two cookies. We don't want to get the visit off to a bad start."

Long before they reached the front door, the pilfered cookies had been dispatched to confectionary heaven, and all traces of crumbs had been brushed from lips, chins, and the front of Savannah's blouse.

Dirk flicked his lower lip vigorously, then turned to Savannah. "Did I get it all?"

"Yes. Did I?"

He reached over and rubbed a spot of chocolate away from the corner of her mouth. "You're okay now. All evidence destroyed."

"Not all." She rummaged around in her purse until she found a pack of breath mints. "Here, have a couple of these. We can't walk in there reeking of chocolate."

"Good point. It's not easy, you know, being a criminal. You've gotta think of everything. It's so easy to slip up. You overlook one little thing like chocolate breath, and you're busted."

She laughed and popped a couple of the mints herself. "Does it ever occur to you that you and I are ridiculously afraid of Dr. Liu? I mean, I'm carrying my 9 mm Beretta, and you've got your Smith & Wesson. Call it a hunch, but we could probably take her in a pinch."

He shook his head vigorously. "No way. That woman has knives and saws and scalpels, and she knows how to dissect the human body in less than five minutes. No way I'd ever mess with her. Plus she wears all that leather. You gotta watch out for gals who wear leather."

"And here I always thought you liked my leather, undercover hooker miniskirt."

"I'm nuts about your leather miniskirt. And anytime you wanna put it on for me, I promise I'll watch out for you real good."

When they reached the entrance, Dirk held open the door, and Savannah preceded him inside.

The moment she stepped over the threshold, she glanced toward the reception desk, looking for Bates. She had to admit that she enjoyed the slideshow of ugly emotions that played on his face every time he laid eyes on her.

Hate. Lust. More hate. And in the end, settling back into unadulterated lust.

Since the moment she had beaten the tar out of him with his own girlie magazine, he had despised her. But he still wanted her. Oh so desperately.

And knowing that made her want to scurry home, grab a gallon of bleach and a box of steel wool pads from under the kitchen sink, head for the bathroom, jump in the tub, and scour herself from head to toe.

Perched on a chair that barely supported his overly robust physique, he sat at a desk positioned behind the reception counter. The instant he heard the door open, he jumped and turned off the computer in front of him.

Dirk chuckled. "Whatcha up to, Bates? Watching naughty videos on the taxpayers' dime, are we?"

"No! I was not! And you can't prove it!"

Dirk turned to Savannah. "Oh, well. Hell, I'm convinced. Aren't you?"

She nodded, a serious look on her face. "Absolutely. The plaintive denial of an innocent man wrongly accused. No doubt about it."

Her container of cookies clutched tightly to her chest, Savannah attempted to walk past the reception desk, ignoring Bates's precious sign-in sheet. It wasn't that she particularly minded scribbling a name and time on the paper. She just couldn't pass up an opportunity to irk Bates.

One of her life mottos was: Those who are easily offended should merely be offended more often.

Watching an idiot like Bates throw a conniption fit served as entertainment, when nothing better was available.

"Hey! Where do you think you're going? You're not getting past me until you sign that sheet."

Dirk grabbed the clipboard with its attached ballpoint pen. "Chill out, Bates, my man. You gotta learn to relax a little, hang loose, get a Zen thing goin'. You can't sit around all day, getting your dickey do in a twist over a little thing like a sign-in sheet."

Savannah nudged Dirk. "Here," she said. "I'll sign it. We don't want Officer Bates here to get all upset. When he's mad he swells up like a big old toad." She took the pen from him and shoved the cookies into his hands. "The buttons on the front of his uniform might start popping off, and we could get hit with a deadly projectile. And we can't be havin' that. I'm pretty sure

Saint Peter wouldn't let us through the pearly gates if we died that way."

She scribbled the time on the sign-in sheet. Then, on the corresponding signature line, she wrote, "Ura Wayne Cur" and shoved the clipboard back across the counter at him.

In all the years that she had been signing his sheet, using monikers of a low caliber, he had never noticed. And she couldn't help being mildly disappointed. After all, what was the point of insulting someone if they didn't even realize they'd been dissed?

Leaving Bates to his menial duties and his Internet porn, Savannah and Dirk continued down a long hallway toward the back of the building in the autopsy suite.

"I saw what you wrote on the sheet," Dirk told her, his eyes twinkling with affection and admiration. "You're a wicked woman, Van, if ever there was one."

She giggled. "Guilty as charged. But I'd rather be a wicked woman any day than a Wayne Cur."

They had reached the end of the hallway, and before them stood the oversized, swinging double doors that opened into the morgue's autopsy suite.

As always, Savannah's pulse rate quickened a bit at the thought of passing through those doors. More than once, she had seen things inside Dr. Liu's examination room that had haunted her for a long time afterward.

Some of the worst, most gruesome specters still paid her an unwelcome visit, from time to time, in the middle of a long dark night.

And, of course, there was added anxiety when she and Dirk were showing up at the morgue prematurely and unbidden.

As one of the fastest and most efficient medical examiners in Southern California, Dr. Liu didn't like being pestered. And Detective Sergeant Dirk Coulter was the biggest pest in the SCPD.

Even bearing a bribe of Savannah's best home-baked cookies, there was always a chance that you were taking your life in your hands when nudging Dr. Liu.

Dirk put one big hand on the left door, turned to Savannah, and said, "Ready?"

She nodded. "Get set."

"Go." He gave it a push, then stood aside for her to enter first.

This time, she wasn't altogether sure that his primary motivation was chivalry.

One quick glance told Savannah that Dr. Liu was right in the middle of the autopsy. Or more accurately—right in the middle of Chef Baldwin Norwood.

At the sight of a body splayed open, innermost organs exposed, Savannah felt her customary physiological reaction—the urge to deposit her most recently eaten meal in the sink on the other side of the room.

She would have been in good company had she done so. More than one big, tough cop had upchucked in Dr. Liu's sink.

But as always, Savannah flipped the switch from visceral to cerebral. She was here to learn everything she could about the untimely passing of Chef Norwood, not to make a fool of herself by losing her breakfast.

Shooting an annoyed look over the top of her surgical mask in their direction, Dr. Liu said, "Gee, I've been working for a whole half an hour. I wondered what was keeping you."

"Interviewing witnesses," Dirk snapped back. "Oh, and we slept for a couple of hours and gobbled down some breakfast. How about you, Doc? You probably got in a full night's sleep, right?"

"Two hours and thirty minutes," Liu replied dryly. "And my breakfast was four cups of coffee, which I drank in the car on my way here."

Quickly, Savannah stepped between the two of them and held out the container of cookies. "I come bearing gifts," she said.

Dr. Liu raised one delicately plucked eyebrow and looked at the offering. "Coming from you, I suppose I don't have to ask if there's chocolate in that box."

"Chocolate chip cookies. And not white chocolate, either. The real thing."

"With nuts?"

"Macadamia."

Dirk grumbled. "Thirty-five bucks worth, or so I just found out. You better like them, or just keep it to yourself."

The medical examiner fixed him with a long, piercing look, then turned to Savannah. "I see that being married to a good woman like you hasn't improved him much," she told her. "And I had such high hopes."

Savannah laughed. "Yeah, me too. But by the time they're in their forties, they're pretty set in their ways."

Stepping closer to the examination table, Dirk cleared his throat and said, "Are you two gonna hang around, cacklin' like a couple of hens, gossiping about me like I'm not standing right here? Or are we gonna talk about what happened to the chef, here?"

"What you're going to do," Dr. Liu replied, "is put on some gloves and a mask or step away from my table." To Savannah, she said, "You too. But first, feed me one of those cookies."

Savannah glanced down at the blood and gore on the

table, then at the organ that the doctor was holding in her gloved hand. She was pretty sure it was a gallbladder. "Really? Now?"

"I told you—I had coffee for breakfast. Black coffee. I could use something with a calorie in it. Okay?"

Savannah gulped. "Sure, Doc. Whatever you say."

Savannah opened the container, took out a cookie, and broke it into four pieces. She walked over to Dr. Liu, tugged the surgical mask down under her chin, and patiently fed her each bite.

Dr. Jennifer Liu never failed to amaze Savannah. Of course, holding a bloody gallbladder in one's hand was all in a day's work for a medical examiner. But the odors that accompanied an autopsy alone were enough to put Savannah off food for hours. Barbecued short ribs, in particular, could be off the menu for days.

There was just no getting around it—Dr. Liu was "special."

Once the cookie had been consumed, the doc's mask replaced, and Savannah and Dirk properly attired with surgical gloves and masks of their own, the grim business at hand resumed.

"Do we have a cause of death yet?" Savannah asked. "I mean, I feel silly for even asking, considering how many times he got perforated, but . . ."

"That's never a silly question," the doctor replied in her patient, kindly "teacher" voice, which was much gentler than her surly medical examiner voice. "You'd be surprised how many times the cause of death turns out to be something other than obvious."

"Yeah," Dirk said, "but this time? Come on. If it wasn't the stabs to his chest and belly, it had to be one of those cleaver whacks to the head."

"You would think so. But I'm not altogether sure."

Savannah looked down at the body, which, at least
for the moment, was no longer a human being to her
but an instrument that might lead them to an important
truth.

"Are you telling us that he wasn't stabbed to death?"
she asked.

"Stabbed, obviously. Seventeen times, in fact."

"That would make it: death by sharp force trauma."

Liu nodded. "Yes, most likely it was sharp force
trauma that killed him. One of those stab wounds actually
severed his abdominal aorta. And that may have led to
exsanguination."

"What do you mean *may have?*" Dirk said. "That
abdominal aorta thing—isn't that one of your main
blood vessels? I thought that was about the worst thing
that you could have cut."

"It is," Dr. Liu told him. "If it's severed you can
bleed out in twenty to twenty-five seconds. And his
was cleanly bisected."

Savannah shook her head. "Then what . . . ?"

"It wasn't his only potentially fatal wound."

"Don't tell me he was shot," Dirk said.

"No. But look at this." Dr. Liu led them to the head
of the table. "Once I'd washed away the blood, it was
visible."

She pointed to a large area at the base of his skull,
just above the lower edge of his hairline. The chef's
luxurious silver locks, of which he had been so proud,
mostly concealed it. But when she pulled the hair back
to show them, there was no mistaking the misshapen,
discolored area.

Savannah caught her breath. "Blunt force trauma?"
she asked.

"*Severe* blunt force," the doctor replied. "Enough to put somebody down, for sure."

"Enough to kill them?" Dirk asked.

"Absolutely," was Dr. Liu's reply. "I'll have a much better look, of course, when I open the head. But I could tell just by palpating the area that the skull is fractured. I'd be surprised if we don't have bone fragments in the brain."

"Wow." Dirk ran his gloved fingers through his own hair. "The perp must've been a pretty strong guy to do that."

"Or a mighty angry female," Savannah suggested. "Never underestimate what a woman can accomplish when she's got a mind to do you harm."

Dirk shot her an uneasy look. "Okay, darlin', I'll certainly keep that in mind." He turned back to Dr. Liu. "Do you have any idea what kind of weapon would leave that sort of bruise?"

"Not until I get under the skin and fat. Then I might be able to tell you."

"Okay," he said. "Is there anything else—like that's not enough?"

She nodded and gave him a perverse little smile. "As a matter of fact, yes. He wasn't stabbed with the bloody kitchen knife that Eileen's team collected at the scene."

Dirk's face fell. "Do you mean to tell me that we don't have murder weapons?"

"The cleaver you have might be the one that inflicted the sharp force trauma to the head. But the knife you recovered from the scene is a chef's fillet knife with a seven-inch straight blade."

"And . . . ?" Dirk prompted her.

"And the knife that made those wounds was closer to eight inches with a partially serrated blade."

"What does that mean, 'partially serrated'?" Savannah asked. "I mean, I know that a serrated blade is one of those bumpy ones, like a saw, that you cut bread and tomatoes and cakes with, but how can it be partially serrated?"

"The first six inches, the blade is straight. But the last two inches, closest to the hilt, are serrated," she explained.

"What's the point in that?" Savannah asked. "Why would you want a knife with both?"

"It's called a combo blade," Liu replied. "You have a sharp, straight blade to pierce with—"

Dirk interjected, "And a serrated edge to cut rope or fishing line or whatever with."

Dr. Liu gave him a sinister smile. "Yes, and the 'whatever' is a bit more ugly than rope cutting. Some believe that the serrated edge rips and tears, creating a nastier wound than just a straight blade."

"Is that true?" Savannah asked. "Does it?"

The M.E. nodded toward the victim. "In this case, it certainly did. Those wounds are as ugly as I've ever seen. Bunched, not scattered the way they are in most knife attacks. All in the area of the abdominal aorta."

"Hmmm," Savannah said. "They were going for the kill, that's for sure. Severing that particular aorta . . . would you say that was luck or some knowledge of the human body?"

Dirk sniffed. "Or knowledge of how to kill a human body?"

"Yes, and a determination to do so," Dr. Liu added. "Every thrust was the full depth of the blade."

Savannah felt a chill shiver through her spirit. "Would that rule out a woman? Could a female stab that hard?"

"Absolutely." The doctor plopped the chef's gallbladder onto a nearby scale. "Wound depth is a poor indicator of the amount of force applied. With a sharp-tipped weapon, it takes very little pressure to penetrate the human skin and tissues."

Savannah and Dirk watched in dejected silence as the doctor reached inside the body cavity for the next organ.

Finally, Dirk said, "I'm afraid to ask if there's anything else."

"I'm sure there will be, once I'm inside the head," Dr. Liu replied.

Savannah gulped. "Gee, something to look forward to."

"Until then, there's not much to see," the doctor told them. "Why don't you two toddle along and find somebody else to harass for the next couple of hours until I finish here."

Dirk grunted. "Maybe we should take those chocolate chip cookies with us. You know, just in case the next person we talk to is as grumpy as you and needs a little bribing."

Dr. Liu held up the glistening, bloody scalpel. "You touch those cookies, Coulter, you'll lose your fingers."

Dirk walked away, shaking his head. "Come on, Van," he said as he stripped off his gloves and mask and tossed them into a nearby bin. "We know when we're not wanted."

Savannah took off her gloves and mask and dropped them onto his. "It's more likely that *you're* the one who's not wanted. Not me."

As they walked toward the door they heard the doctor say, "Have your new wife teach you how to bake, Coulter. God knows, with a personality like yours, you need a saving grace."

"Grumpy," Dirk said. He always had to have the last word. "That gal may be hot in those leather boots and miniskirts of hers, but I'm telling you . . . she is grumpee."

"Yeah," Savannah agreed, "and she knows way too much about knives."

Chapter 8

"When I grow up someday, I'm going to live up here in this complex with Ryan and John," Savannah announced as she and Dirk made their way along the cobblestone walking path that wound between San Carmelita's most luxurious condos.

Perched at the top of the hills that rimmed the eastern side of the beachfront town, these exquisite units offered breathtaking views of the ocean and the mountains, as well.

When visiting up here, Savannah always had the feeling that, for a while, she was truly on top of the world—at least, her world. Of course, it was a silly, illogical thought, and she knew it. People who lived on hillsides were burdened with just as many of life's problems and stricken with just as many inevitable tragedies as those who lived in valleys.

But there was no denying the psychological boost of high living.

As they passed the natural rock pool with its surrounding lush, tropical greenery, Dirk said, "Must be nice to have a swim-up bar. That's what we need, babe. Let's install one in the upstairs bathroom."

She sighed. "Right now, I'd settle for a freshly scrubbed bathroom. Gran's gonna be here before we know it, and I can't have her see the utter filth and degradation we're living in right now."

"Filth? Degradation? Are you kidding? I've never lived so clean in all my life! You go hog wild if I hang a towel crooked."

She stopped in the middle of the walkway and gave him a quizzical look. "'Go hog wild'? Is that what I just heard you say?"

"Yeah, what about it?"

"That's a Down-in-Dixie phrase if ever I heard one."

"Gee, you think? Guess I've been hanging out with some Southern chick too long."

They continued down the path, past the tennis courts, toward the unit in the far corner. The one with the best view and the most privacy. Ryan and John's.

"By the way," she added, "I'll have you know that I do not go hog wild over crooked bath towels. I just get mildly perturbed when you wad one of my best towels into a ball and ram the whole shebang between the rod and the wall."

He chuckled as he reached over, wrapped his arm around her waist, and gave her a squeeze. "My darlin' girl, you have never, ever, in your entire life been 'mildly' anything. You're all the way or nothing. That temper of yours is an on-off switch, not a thermostat."

She smiled up at him. "But you love me anyway."

"I love you because . . ."

"Because?"

"Because it's so much fun to watch you blow your top and spew hot lava—especially when it's raining all over somebody I don't like, somebody who really deserves it."

"How about when it's falling on you?"

"I never really deserve it, so you always pull your punches with me—at least a little bit."

She slipped her arm around him and returned the squeeze. "Well, we can't have you feeling neglected. Next Friday night, I'll wrestle you to the floor and slap some cuffs on you."

He gave her a flirty grin and hugged her tighter. "Ooh, sounds like fun. It's a date. Maybe we should dust off the leg irons, too."

"Now you're talking."

They had reached Ryan and John's unit, which, although it was a condominium, was much larger than Savannah's house. Like Savannah's humble home, the entryway was draped with lush bougainvillea. However, theirs had lovely apricot- and copper-colored blossoms, rather than her traditional crimson.

Ryan and John always did things with a unique twist, all their own.

They walked up to the door, and Dirk gave it his standard, knuckle-cracking cop knock.

"It's awful quiet in there," Savannah said, when she didn't hear any response.

"I thought you called and asked if we could drop by about now." Dirk rapped again.

"I did, and they said now would be a good time. But I can't help worrying. You know this had to be really hard on them. To see their dream crash and burn like that. What an awful thing to happen to such nice people."

Dirk snorted. "It's almost always the nice people that awful things happen to."

Savannah would have enjoyed contradicting such a cynical point of view. But sadly, experience had taught her that his observation, dark though it might be, was all too accurate.

Dirk was about to knock a third time when they heard a lock slide, then another, and the door opened.

John stood there in a blue paisley robe of exquisite embossed silk. Beneath he wore pajamas that were sapphire satin. His hair, usually with every strand in perfect place, was slightly mussed.

He looked tired but pleased to greet them. "Ah, how lovely to see you, Savannah." He held out one hand to her and ushered her inside. "And you, too, lad," he told Dirk, though with a wee bit less enthusiasm.

No one tried to pretend that John and Ryan were as devoted to Dirk as they were to Savannah. Over the years they had been friends, the male trio had pretty much tolerated each other—and mostly because they knew that "tolerance" was what Savannah wanted and expected.

As a result, all three loved her enough to make the considerable effort to get along.

In the end, they had decided that compromise had its benefits. They had discovered that they had more in common than just the love of a transplanted, sassy Southern belle. They also enjoyed working a challenging case. And to their surprise, they worked well together.

Who really cared if Dirk swigged beer while they sipped chardonnay? Even if their idea of the perfect Saturday night was an art gallery opening and Dirk's an HBO boxing match, they could put their differences aside for the love of a good woman or to snag a bad guy.

John led them from the sunlit foyer into the dark coziness of the living room, which looked more like a reading room in an old British gentlemen's club. The heavy, masculine furniture was plush and inviting, suggesting how nice it might be to spend the evening enjoying one of those leather-bound, gilt-edged classics from the bookshelves.

But Savannah had less interest than usual in the comfortable living room, because she could smell something heavenly coming from the kitchen. Something that smelled vaguely like pancakes, only far more divine.

"Ryan is making us a late brunch," John said, "of cognac crepes. We'd be delighted to have you join us."

"Dear Lord above, that sounds heavenly," Savannah gushed. "But he's probably got just enough made for the two of you and—"

"I heard that," came a deep voice from the kitchen. "Don't be ridiculous."

They followed John to where Ryan was standing at the stove, expertly folding a crepe.

She tried not to notice how Ryan's black stretch microfiber T-shirt and matching lounge shorts showed off his magnificent body. She fought back thoughts like, *How can a man look so doggoned fit to eat just flippin' some pancakes?*

Mostly, she tried not to notice, because she was sure Dirk would notice her noticing. And that would make it harder for her to complain the next time she caught him noticing some bimbo crossing the street in some barely there short-shorts.

Ryan gave them a bright smile and handed a plate

with one of the amazing crepes to Savannah. "Do you really think, knowing you two were on your way over, that I'd just mix up enough for us? Sit over there at the bar and dig in." He nodded to Dirk. "You take a seat, too. Yours will be up in a minute."

"Wow! Cool!" Dirk was all smiles as he joined Savannah. "Now I don't mind it so much that we didn't get a free taco."

Savannah accepted a small, cut crystal pitcher from John and found it contained warm maple syrup. "What a treat," she said. "The chunks I see in the crepes, are they bits of pineapple?"

"Fresh pineapple," Ryan told her.

"And that amazing smell?"

"The cognac."

"You put it in the batter?"

He nodded, grinning. "Have a bite and tell me what you think."

She did. And had trouble not falling off the stool as every muscle in her body went limp with pure delight.

"Her eyes are rolling back in her head," Dirk observed. "That's usually a good sign."

"Exquisite!" Savannah said when she had finally regained control of her faculties. "Ambrosial lusciousness beyond compare!"

Ryan poured more batter into the pan and swirled a small, T-shaped rake over the mixture, spreading it thinly across the pan.

"If you don't mind me asking," Dirk said, watching in awe. "If you can cook like this, why don't you just run your own restaurant kitchen?"

Ryan laughed, but the sound was hollow and a tad bitter. "Owning a restaurant and being the master chef are two completely different matters. It's one thing to whip up a nice meal for family and friends, but to serve fifty hungry people a dozen or more different dishes all at once? No way."

John set Dirk's offering in front of him, and after one bite, his reaction was as enthusiastic as Savannah's. "Ryan, that's some awesome grub, dude."

Ryan gave a half-bow and then continued to cook as John poured everyone strong cups of coffee.

"I'm glad to see you guys doing okay today," Savannah said when she had polished off the last bite. "I've gotta say, I was a bit worried about you last night. I know that had to be plum horrible for you."

"Yeah," Dirk interjected with a mouth full of crepe. "Went right down the crapper, huh? I mean, as opening nights go, that had to be the worst of all time."

He looked up from his plate to see all three of them staring at him.

"Well? I'm sorry, but it was. Maybe except for the Titanic or—"

"Eat," Savannah told him with a kick to the shin. "Just hush and eat your food. Sheez."

He leaned over and put his mouth next to her ear. "But it's true," he whispered.

"And you're a nitwit, but the obvious need not always be stated."

Dirk looked at John and Ryan and rolled his eyes. "Man, no matter what I do, I'm always in trouble."

"Go figure," Ryan mumbled, handing John a plate.

"'Tis a lovely day," John said. "Why don't we relocate out to the balcony where we can enjoy the fresh air?"

They collected their plates and mugs of coffee and

exited through the French doors that led from the living room onto a spacious patio.

They settled at a wrought iron, glass-topped table with comfortable deep-cushioned wicker chairs.

"I hate to nudge the elephant in the room," Dirk said, "but have you two had time to think about the case yet today?"

"Think about it?" Ryan replied. "We've been working on it all morning."

"So true," John added. "We aren't still sitting about in our jim-jams because we had a leisurely sleep-in. We simply haven't had time to dress."

"And what did you come up with?" Savannah asked.

"Bloody little," John replied. "Why do you think I'm drinking coffee instead of tea? I need the caffeine to buoy me up a bit. I tell you, this is some tragic, depressing business."

Savannah reached over and patted John's forearm. "I was telling Dirk on the way here that I can hardly stand you two having your hopes dashed like that. I know how long and how hard you worked to put your restaurant together. And then to have that happen . . ."

"We aren't rolling up the welcome mat in front of the place just yet," Ryan said. "Obviously, out of respect for the chef, if for no other reason, we have to close for a while."

"Plus you've gotta get a new cook," Dirk piped up.

Again, he received stony stares.

He cleared his throat. "Stating the obvious again?"

"Yes," they replied in unison.

Ryan said, "That's sort of neither here nor there. We'd already decided before the murder that we had to find a solution to that problem."

Dirk chuckled. "Yeah, but not such a permanent one."

"Dirk!" Savannah kicked him under the table, and this time she didn't bother to hold back.

He yelped and said, "Okay then. Fine. I'll just sit here and keep my mouth shut and drink my coffee."

"That might present a problem," Ryan said.

"You may find yourself dribbling down the front of your shirt," John told him.

Savannah winked at him, reached over, and squeezed his hand. "But go ahead and try anyway. It might be entertaining to watch." She turned to Ryan. "If you two have been knocking your heads together about this mess all morning, you must've come up with something or the other."

"Mostly we were looking up phone numbers," Ryan said.

"Phone numbers?" Dirk asked.

Savannah stifled a chuckle. So much for Dirk's silent protest. How long had it lasted? Ten seconds? That had to be an all-time personal record for him.

"First," Ryan replied, "we checked out the dining-room staff, whom we've cleared because none of them were in the kitchen area when it happened. Then we scoured the list of diners."

"But you said, 'phone numbers,'" Savannah said. "What phone numbers?"

"From the reservation list," John said over the rim of his coffee mug. "Some of our guests were there by invitation, and of course we know who they were. But the rest had made reservations, and fortunately we asked for their phone numbers."

"Good goin'," Dirk said. "That was smart of you guys. Makes our job a lot easier."

Ryan sighed. "Well, we had a far more innocent reason at the time for asking. We had no idea that our reservation list might turn out to be evidence in a murder investigation."

"What did you find among your phone numbers?" Savannah asked. "Anything interesting?"

"Actually," Ryan said, "there were a couple of guests who were questionable. Not because they were there, but because they weren't."

"What's that supposed to mean?" Dirk asked.

"They were conspicuous by their absence," John told him. "They had made reservations but didn't show up."

"What's conspicuous about that?" Savannah wanted to know. "I'm sure restaurants have that happen all the time. People make reservations, and then their plans change. They aren't always courteous enough to call the establishment and let them know that they aren't coming."

Ryan nodded. "That's true. No doubt it's a common occurrence. But these reservations weren't made by the absentee guests themselves."

"Who made them?" Savannah asked.

John stroked the end of his lush, silver mustache. "Our victim, Chef Baldwin Norwood himself, made the reservations—apparently for people close to him, people with whom he wanted to share the experience."

"Do we know who they were?" Dirk asked.

"The first turned out to be Norwood's inamorata."

"Inamor-what?"

Savannah leaned toward Dirk and whispered, "I'm pretty sure that means his girlfriend."

Ryan nodded. "Their address is the same and has

been for quite some time, so we're assuming they're an item."

"What's this gal's name?" Dirk asked, taking his notepad and pen from his pocket.

"Perla Viola," John told him. "Forty-five years old."

"We'll sic Tammy on her," Savannah said. "By the end of the day you'll know what wine she drinks and the color of her knickers."

Dirk sniffed. "I'd be happy just to know if she has an alibi."

Ryan reached into his shorts pocket and pulled out his phone. He scrolled his thumb over it for a moment, then said, "The second no-show guest was a guy named Yale Ingram."

"Ingram, as in the big-wig entrepreneur guy, who lives out in that creepy old monstrosity of a mansion on Milton Hill?" Dirk said.

Ryan's eyes widened a bit. "Wow. I'm impressed. Do you know him?"

"Naw. But his ol' lady's called us a couple of times when he didn't come home from wherever as quick as she thought he ought to. Because he's a big shot, the chief would send us out to search the streets for him."

"Did you find him?" Savannah asked.

"Sure. It wasn't hard. I just checked out the expensive hotels in town and, sure enough, he was there, bumpin' some bimbo. A different bimbo each time, if I remember right."

John drained the last sip of his coffee and pushed back a bit from the table. "Did you inform the unfortunate wife of her husband's indiscretions?"

"Hell, no." Dirk sniffed. "I ain't as stupid as I look. Why should I put my butt in the sling just 'cause he's being stupid? That gal was scary—a real battle-axe. If I was him, I probably wouldn't come home any sooner than I had to, either."

"What's Ingram's connection to Norwood?" Savannah asked.

"Ingram was Norwood's business partner. Together, they owned a restaurant in Hollywood called Villa Nuevo," Ryan replied. "You may have heard of it."

"I sure have," Savannah said. "About a year ago there were articles about it almost every weekend in the *Times*, and stories on TV, too. It was the place to go for good food and celebrity spotting."

"Supposedly, the foremost reason why it was such a successful establishment was our talented Chef Norwood." A look of keen disappointment crossed John's face. "Why do you think we were so elated to have snared such a prize?"

Savannah recalled what Francia, Manuel, and Maria had said about Norwood being a fraud. Though she hated to tell her friends that they had been duped, she felt she had to under the circumstances.

But Dirk beat her to the punch.

"The funny thing is," he said, "you boys hired yourself a fake cook. We have it from the folks we interviewed, who worked with him, that ol' Norwood couldn't cook his way out of a paper bag. Not even a grocery sack."

"What?" they asked in unison.

"I'm afraid Dirk's right," Savannah told them. "His help told us that he was nothing but a sham—a celebrity chef whose staff did all of his cooking for him. Apparently, that's why he was so adamant about everybody staying out of his kitchen or else."

At hearing this news, Ryan and John looked even more dejected than before.

"I don't mind telling you," John said, "I'm somewhat disappointed in us. I thought we had better judgment." He turned to Ryan and slapped him on the shoulder. "We let that scoundrel bamboozle us most thoroughly."

"We did." Ryan nodded somberly. "I'd consider beating the crap outta him . . . if he wasn't already dead."

After a long silence, Dirk nudged Savannah and told her, "If I'd said that, you'd be kicking me under the table."

"Yes, I would."

"So, why aren't you kicking *him?*"

"He's not my husband."

Dirk sighed. "Gee. Lucky me."

Chapter 9

"I don't know how Eileen and her crew can stand to work in this part of town," Savannah told Dirk as she drove the Mustang into the area of San Carmelita that locals simply called "the industrial park."

Dirk gave her one of his long-suffering, patient husband sighs and said, "I don't know how I can stand to listen to you gripe every time we come down here about how much you hate . . . let's see now . . . oh, yeah, everything in sight. The buildings—"

"—big ol' cement block cracker boxes, that's all they are."

"The roads—"

"Y'all got a lot of nerve, talking about how bad Georgia roads are. Look at all these potholes. I'll betcha there are folks who've fallen into those holes and never been heard from again."

"The trees—"

"There *aren't* any trees. There's not one green living

thing in sight—unless you count those scraggly weeds growing up out of the potholes."

"And you bellyache about all of it every time we have to come to the lab."

"I do? Every time? Really?"

"Every single time. And for a gal who goes around preaching to *me* about how I need to focus on the positive and not gripe about annoying crap, you should take some of your own advice. As soon as we come into this part of town, your mood turns as black as that rainy night in Georgia they sing about."

Savannah nodded thoughtfully. "You know, that's true."

"What? Are you saying I'm right again? Wow! I'm on a roll."

"It's true that Georgia gets a bad rap. For our lousy roads. For our rainy nights. For Sherman's army marching across it and burning all those pretty mansions to the ground."

"Now, see? That's exactly what I'm talking about. If you were sitting on the beach right now, you'd be talking about Georgia peaches, Vidalia onions, and all the beautiful belles who come out of that fine Southern state. But no. The minute we drive down into the industrial area, it's potholes and rain and Sherman's army marchin' and burnin'."

She looked around at the rectangular, gray, mostly windowless buildings lined up, row upon row. Each was the same as the last.

Architectural design, or the lack thereof, at its worst.

The girlie-girl decorator in her rebelled at the thought of such ugly, soulless construction. Would it really have been all that hard to stick in a few more windows, attach flower boxes underneath them, and plant a few petunias, for heaven's sake?

A brighter, happier, more serotonin-enriched area of her brain whispered that the guys who operated their auto shops out of this park might not be the petunia-loving sort, but she ignored it. It was bad enough she had to argue with Dirk on an hourly basis. The last thing she needed was some pesky Pollyanna whispering in the back of her head and pointing out the errors of her logic.

Besides, they had arrived at the county crime lab. In moments they would be contending with Eileen, the Wicked Queen of the CSI.

Savannah was convinced that in a former life Eileen had been a Marine drill sergeant. One plagued with hemorrhoids, impacted wisdom teeth, and ingrown toenails who took it out on her troops.

Possibly even in this life.

Dr. Liu might have a bit of a mean streak that showed once in a while, when she was especially aggravated. But for Eileen, "mean" was an avowed lifestyle.

Figuratively speaking, Eileen ran a tight ship, and anyone who didn't meet her high standard was tossed overboard to the crocodiles.

To avoid suffering that fate, Savannah usually brought a container of freshly baked goodies, just as she did when visiting the medical examiner. But since she had already exhausted that currency with Dr. Liu at the morgue, she was concerned that perhaps she and Dirk would be staring into gaping crocodile maws before the visit was over.

"Damn. We don't have any more cookies," Dirk said, again stating the obvious, as they left the Mustang and walked up to the nondescript door, adorned with only the county seal, a security buzzer button, and a camera and speaker mounted above.

"I was just thinking that." Savannah scrambled to reach the button before Dirk. He had a tendency to push it far too long, virtually leaning on it for five seconds at a time. The nerve-jangling, ear-splitting racket was less annoying when it was only a tiny burst.

And most important, it didn't annoy Queen Eileen as much.

Eventually the speaker over the door crackled to life. "Hi, Savannah," said a halfway cheery voice.

Halfway was as cheery as Eileen ever got, so Savannah felt special.

"Hi, Eileen," she replied. "Could we come in for a few minutes? We need to talk to you about the Chef Norwood homicide."

"Tell Coulter I don't have anything yet. And when I do, I'll give him a call."

Savannah turned to Dirk, who was standing right beside her, fully able to hear every word coming from the overhead speaker. "Sorry, darlin'," she told him. "But she says—"

"Hell, I heard what she said." To the speaker, he shouted, "I ain't deaf, you know. And I'm the investigating officer, so show me some damn respect and open this door right now, in the name of the law."

Savannah turned to him, her eyes wide, eyebrows raised. "In the name of the law?" she whispered. "Really?"

But to her surprise the door opened, and Eileen was standing there, filling it with her massive presence, a bit of a smirk on her face.

"Woo-hoo," she said. "Look who's wearing his big-boy pants today."

Dirk pushed by her, inviting himself inside. "Yeah,

and I got a gold shield inside my big-boy pants. So don't give me any of your nonsense, woman. I've only had three hours of sleep and one meal in twenty-one hours, so I ain't in the mood for harassment."

Eileen turned to Savannah. "I thought you were supposed to be civilizing this grizzly bear now that you're married to him."

Savannah shrugged. "We're making a little headway with the table manners. But the rest of it comes and goes."

"Well? What's going on around here? How far have you got?" Dirk asked as he looked around the office area, with its cubicles where the CSI techs did online research and bookwork.

Eileen's cubicle was larger by a few square feet— the only physical evidence of her seniority. Standing six foot two and as massive in her girth as in her height, Eileen hardly needed any additional trappings of authority.

Eileen reached into the pocket of her white smock and pulled out a rubber band. She twisted her long, wildly curly silver hair into a bun and fastened it with the band. "All right, then, if you insist. Come on to the back," she said, "and I'll show you what we don't have."

"Gee," Dirk replied. "I can hardly wait to see it."

Eileen led them through the office area toward the rear of the building, which housed the laboratory. The large room had numerous, long tables, and its walls were lined with workbenches.

The equipment that covered those surfaces reminded Savannah of a mad scientist's "la-BOR-a-tory"—or so they had pronounced it in the horror movies of her childhood. Beakers and microscopes competed with all sorts of newfangled, meter-faced gadgets . . . equipment that Dr. Frankenstein wouldn't have known what to do with.

"Okay, you asked for it. So here goes," Eileen said as she headed toward a table where numerous items they had collected from the restaurant crime scene were spread. "First off, we don't have a murder weapon."

Savannah looked at the bloody fillet knife and cleaver. She couldn't remember when she had begun a homicide investigation with two murder weapons and ended up so quickly with none.

Dirk took a pair of surgical gloves from his pants pocket and offered them to Savannah. Then he took out a pair for himself and put them on. "Dr. Liu already told us that this knife wasn't the one used on Norwood. I guess she told you, too."

An indignant look crossed Eileen's face as she said, "No, I haven't spoken to Dr. Liu. Believe it or not, Coulter, I figured that out on my own."

Eileen pointed to the blade that was stained crimson from hilt to tip. "I've seen enough bloody knives in my time to tell the difference between a knife that was pulled out of a body and one that was dragged through a puddle of blood."

"And this one was dragged through blood?" Dirk asked.

"Or dipped in it," Eileen told him. "Either way, blood was deliberately deposited on this knife."

Savannah asked, "Are you saying it was deliberately bloodied as part of someone staging the scene?"

"I'm sure of it."

Savannah thought that over for a moment. "That's rather strange. With all the stabbing and the whacks with the cleaver, you'd think this was a rage killing, an out-of-control blitz attack. And yet the killer had the presence of mind to plant a fake murder weapon. That doesn't make sense."

"I was wondering," Dirk said, "why two weapons were used. If you've already stabbed a guy seventeen times in the chest and belly, why switch over to a cleaver and go for his head? Talk about overkill."

"Is there any chance that we have more than one killer?" Savannah asked Eileen.

"I doubt it," she said. "The prints are the same on the cleaver and the knife."

"You've got prints?" Savannah and Dirk shouted in unison.

"You said you've got nothin'," Dirk said, excited and annoyed in the same moment, "and now you're telling us you've got fingerprints?"

"I didn't say they were fingerprints. Not unless a cow left them."

"A cow?" Dirk was starting to lose it. "What the hell are you talking about, woman?"

Eileen gave him a satisfied smirk. "Your killer was wearing gloves," she said. "Leather gloves. And leather is nothing more than cow skin, and skin leaves a distinctive print—whether it's human or bovine."

After pulling on her own sterile gloves, Eileen picked up the knife and the cleaver and carried them over to a microscope. She situated the knife handle under the lens and motioned for Dirk to take a look.

"See those three oval prints," she said, "right there in the blood, clear as day."

He peered through the scope for quite a while, then said, "I think I see what you're talking about. But I wouldn't say it's all that clear."

"They're clear to an experienced eye, which you apparently do not have." Eileen tugged him away from

the microscope and motioned for Savannah to take a
turn.

Savannah looked for a long time, too, wanting badly
to see what Dirk had missed, if for no other reason than
that she could tease him about it later. But she had to
be honest. Granny Reid was on her way from Georgia,
so Savannah felt the need to get into her Truthful Good
Girl mode in preparation for Gran's visit.

Savannah's love and respect for her grandmother
had always brought out the best in her character—that
and the threat of a hickory stick vigorously applied to
her rear end out behind the garden shed.

"Oh, for heaven's sake," Eileen said, losing her patience. "And you two call yourselves detectives?" She
took the knife out of the scope. "Then there's no point
in showing you the cleaver. The prints are even less
pronounced on it. But you can take my word for it—
there are three prints on the cleaver that match the
prints on the knife. They were held by the same person,
and that person was wearing leather gloves."

"And if we brought you a pair of leather gloves,"
Dirk said, "you'd be able to determine whether they
were the same ones that left those prints, right?"

"Definitely."

"Can you tell us anything about the gloves?" Savannah asked. "Like if they were large or small, a man's or
a woman's?"

"I'm good, Savannah," she replied with a grin. "Not
that good. I can't do all of your work for you."

Eileen walked back to the table where the case evidence was spread and replaced the knife. As she was
slipping the cleaver back into its evidence bag, she said,
"You might be interested to know that, considering how
many times your victim was hit with that cleaver, there

wasn't much blood on it. Some skin, hair, and a couple of bone fragments. But not a lot of blood. I would've expected more on a weapon that was creating head wounds like those on Norwood."

"Hmmm . . ." Savannah said. "Are you thinking those injuries might have been postmortem?"

"I certainly am. I suppose Dr. Liu will know for sure after she finishes the autopsy. But most of the blood at the scene appeared to have come from the chest and abdominal wounds. And since the head bleeds profusely when it's cut, and this guy's didn't, I'm thinking his heart had already stopped beating before those final chops."

"That doesn't make a lot of sense either," Savannah said. "Why would you stab the heck out of your victim with your own knife that you had brought to the scene, only to then pick up a weapon of opportunity like the cleaver and go at the dead guy with that?"

Dirk ripped off his gloves and ran one hand wearily through his hair. "When it comes down to it, it makes no sense to commit a murder in the first place."

"That's true," Savannah agreed. "No matter what kind of situation a person finds themselves in, killing somebody is just gonna make it worse."

"I've been pretty pissed off at people in my life," Dirk continued. "Downright furious at times, for that matter. But I can't imagine being so mad at somebody I'd wanna take a cleaver to them."

"I can," Eileen said calmly, coldly. "People who come into my lab and ask a bunch of silly questions, and waste my time . . . I can imagine all sorts of implements of destruction that I would like to use on them. And in creative ways, too."

Dirk turned to Savannah, reached out, and took her arm. "What do you figure, darlin'? About time for you and me to skedaddle?"

"I reckon we should be making some tracks. Call it a hunch, but something tells me we've just about worn out our welcome."

Eileen grinned. But it wasn't a smile that warmed the heart. "Gee," she said. "You think?"

Chapter 10

"What's the matter, babe? You okay?"

Savannah closed the driver's door of the Mustang and leaned on its roof. For a moment, the ground under her feet rocked and rolled, and she had to struggle to keep her balance.

It felt like a five-point-two earthquake.

But having lived in Southern California for years now, she had experienced a hefty share of seismic activity, and she knew the subtle difference. This rocking and rolling was within her head. She wasn't sure if that was good news or bad. Was losing one's personal equilibrium preferable to a minor temblor?

"Van, are you okay?" Dirk asked again as he made his way around the front of the car to join her.

"Yeah, I'm okay," she said, her tone far less convincing than her words. "Why do you ask?"

"Because you're all pale and sweaty."

"It's a hot day."

"It ain't that hot."

Of course, he was right. Even in her driveway where there was no shade, it couldn't have been over 75 degrees.

Since when did a Southern belle, raised in the heat and humidity of inland Georgia, feel the heat of a typical, perfect day in Southern Cal? Especially for a tough gal who didn't consider herself the swooning type.

"I'm fine," she told him as she took a couple of tentative steps away from the car and toward her house. "I'm just tired, that's all. Not enough sleep. Not enough food."

He slipped his arm around her waist. "Not as young as you used to be."

She gouged him in the ribs with her elbow. "Boy, you could've talked all day and not said that."

He laughed and squeezed her harder. "Now that's my girl. We're gonna get you some food, a little bit of rest—"

"'Rest' meaning 'talk about the case.'"

"Knowing us, it'll probably come up. But then it's off to bed for both of us. We'll get a long night's sleep and wake up rarin' to go."

At that particular moment, Savannah felt so bone-deep tired that she couldn't imagine being "rarin'" to go anywhere or do anything. And that worried her a bit. Since when did the loss of one night's sleep make her feel like this—too tired to breathe?

Lately she had been feeling a level of fatigue that she had never experienced before, and she couldn't help being concerned. Okay, so she wasn't twenty years old anymore. But what was with this business of feeling like she was eighty?

While Dirk's supporting arm around her waist should have given her comfort, it actually heightened her concern. The last thing that she, or he, needed right now was for something to go wrong with her health.

Dirk had been absolutely devastated when she had been shot. And he had worried himself sick throughout her convalescence, neglecting himself terribly as he cared for her day and night.

She had been quite relieved when he had finally stopped fretting over her every sneeze and sniffle. Under no circumstances did she want to return to that dark place.

Forcing a bit of jauntiness into her step, she said, a tad too brightly, "You're absolutely right. There's nothing wrong with me that those fried chicken leftovers and eight hours of sleep won't fix."

Unfortunately, her detective husband was a bit smarter than was convenient for her. He gave her a searching, suspicious look as he unlocked the front door and ushered her inside.

Sometimes she envied those wives who complained about their husbands being clueless as to what was going on with them. Living with a guy like Dirk, she sometimes wished for a bit more "clueless."

As they stood in the foyer unstrapping their holsters and stowing their weapons, they overheard giggling coming from the living room area.

She had seen Tammy's bright pink Volkswagen Beetle and Waycross's orange General Lee Charger wannabe parked at the curb. So she knew that she and Dirk had to proceed into the living room with caution.

Tammy and her brother's romance had passed the adoring friendship stage and could now be classified as bona fide "hot and heavy." Both of them were incredibly shy, and they never would have indulged in public displays of affection. Their definition of "public" was any place with people other than themselves—and maybe a couple of cats.

From Savannah's position in the foyer, she could see the front living room window where Diamante and Cleopatra sat on their perch. She could tell by the ill-natured twitching of their tails that they disapproved of whatever was going on in there.

Di and Cleo couldn't bear to be ignored.

What was the point in having human beings around if they were focused on each other and you weren't being petted or fed?

"Boy, I don't know about you," Savannah said to Dirk, quite loudly, "but I can't wait to sink my choppers into those leftover chicken legs."

"Yeah, me too," he practically shouted. "You got any of that potato salad left?"

More snickering from the living room.

"Okay, okay," they heard Waycross say. "We know you're here. Sheesh. We got ears."

"And you can come in," Tammy added. "We're going over some figures."

Dirk waggled one eyebrow at Savannah and whispered, "No kidding. And we know whose figure your little brother's concentrating on."

They walked into the living room to find Tammy and Waycross cuddled on the sofa. But to their credit, they both had electronic tablets on their laps and appeared to be doing some sort of work.

"What figures are these that we're perusing?" Savannah asked. "My business bank account?"

"Afraid not," Tammy replied. "I hate to mention it, but there's not much in your business bank account to peruse at the moment. We haven't had a case—at least not a paying case—for a long time."

Savannah collapsed into her comfy chair and prepared herself for the onslaught of attention-starved felines. In three seconds they had filled her lap, a purring mass of glossy, ebony neediness.

"And this case isn't going to be any different," she said with a sigh. "It's not that I'm not happy to work for love rather than money. It's just that the electric company stopped taking love as a payment. Let this be a lesson to you two young people: self-employment, following your dream, fulfilling your life destiny. . . . It ain't all it's cracked up to be."

Tammy giggled. "Now you don't mean that, Savannah, and you know it. What would you do if you couldn't sleuth for a living?"

Savannah sighed. "Well, before the past twenty-four hours, I might've said that I'd like to be a chef. But after that mess last night, I'm put off by restaurant kitchens for the rest of my life."

"Me too." Waycross shuddered. "Did you guys find out anything worth tellin' there at the morgue or the lab?"

"Nothing to write home about," Savannah said. "Kinda feel like we spent a hundred dollar bill's worth of energy and got a nickel in return."

Waycross gave her the same searching and concerned look that Dirk had given her earlier. "What's up, sis? You're lookin' a mite peaked around the gills, if you don't mind me sayin'."

She did mind him saying. If there was anything

worse than having your husband fret over you, it was having the whole family fret at once.

"I'm fine," she snapped. "I'm just worn to a frazzle. Once I catch my second wind, I'm going to go scare up some dinner."

"No, you aren't," Dirk said. "You're going to sit right there while I scare it up—whatever the hell that means. And then you're gonna sit right there and eat every bite of it. Then you're gonna go to bed, point your toes to the ceiling, and snore for hours on end."

As Dirk stomped away into the kitchen, Tammy and Waycross watched, their mouths open, eyes wide.

"Wow!" Tammy said. "Get a load of ol' Dirk-o, taking charge like that."

"Boy, howdy," Waycross added, chuckling. "Who died and made him Captain Domestic?"

Savannah would have chuckled along with him, but with her world spinning around her once again, the humor of the moment was lost on her. Having Dirk wait on her hand and foot might have been a lovely luxury had it not reminded her of her former convalescence.

Yes, Dirk's words had been light, even mildly humorous. But she could hear the fear in his tone. The last thing she wanted was to have her husband worrying about her.

Dirk was a practical guy. And if he was worried about her, she had to at least consider the possibility that she should be worrying about herself.

Once their impromptu living room picnic was finished and the dishes cleared, Savannah, Dirk, and Waycross sat, enthusiastically munching on what remained of Dr. Liu's chocolate chip cookies. The ever-health-conscious Tammy nibbled, rather than gobbling like her companions.

Savannah couldn't help noticing that Tammy's scruples in that department had slipped just a wee bit since she had fallen for Brother Waycross. He, in typical Reid family tradition, had never met a dessert he didn't like. Therefore, most meals ended with some sort of decadent culinary delight.

Once in a while, Savannah saw Tammy sampling his banana split, tasting his pecan pie, or indulging in a lick of chocolate frosting.

Savannah had always respected Tammy's stoic self-control, but she couldn't help but think this was a step in the right direction. While she didn't think everyone needed to become a total dessert glutton like herself, she did believe a bit of culinary indiscretion from time to time was good for the soul.

Having been lectured for years by her young friend about the ills of sugar, flour, and salt, Savannah couldn't help taking a perverse delight in seeing Tammy walk on the wild side once in a while.

"Have another cookie, Tams," she told her when she saw her lick the last bit of chocolate off her forefinger.

"No, thank you," Tammy replied. "That half of one was more than enough for me."

Oh, well, Savannah thought with an internal sigh. *There's still room for improvement*.

Savannah reached behind her chair and took out the two-by-three-foot poster board that she liked to stash either there or under her bed, depending on where she was when working a case. After taking a pack of Post-its and a pen from her end table, she laid the board across her lap and began to scribble on the bits of paper.

"What are you doin' there, babe?" Dirk watched her, wearing his Concerned Husband face. "I thought you were going to bed right after dinner."

"Why? So we can lie there and talk about the case?" She shook her head. "No, thanks. I want to get it all out— put it here on the board—so I won't have the details running around my head like a bunch of crazy, chattering monkeys when I'm trying to doze off."

On one of the tiny leaflets, she wrote the name of the first suspect that came to mind. "Francia Fortun," she said as she placed the paper in the upper-left-hand corner.

"She has an alibi," Dirk said.

"Yeah, the same alibi as this other one that I'm writing right now." Savannah scribbled the name "Manuel Cervantes" on another leaflet and stuck it in the corner next to Francia's. "When Francia and Manuel were giving us their alibis, I caught a whiff of something rotten, like a roadkill skunk. Both were lyin' to beat the band. I might not be able to prove it, but I know it. So they're up here in my Suspects Corner."

"Be sure to stick Carlos Ortez up there, too," Dirk told her. "He gave me the same story, word for word, as the other two. You don't get three versions of an event to jibe like that unless it was rehearsed."

"Innocent folks don't need to rehearse nothin'," Waycross said.

"Exactly." Savannah looked at the trio of posts in the corner. "But if one or more of them did it, we're not going to be able to prove it unless we can break that three-way alibi."

"Who else do you have as a possible suspect?" Tammy asked, slightly wistful, as she watched Waycross down the other half of her cookie in one bite.

"Ryan and John seem interested in a couple of guests who were invited to the dinner by Norwood himself but didn't show," Dirk observed.

Savannah nodded. "That's true. Ryan and John seemed to set great store by the fact that they weren't there."

"Why?" Tammy asked. "If they weren't there, how could they have done it?"

"I don't know exactly what Ryan and John are thinking," Savannah said. "Maybe that they snuck in the back way or something."

"Is that possible?" Waycross wanted to know. "If those three people on your board really were out back smoking, wouldn't they have seen anybody comin' through the back door?"

"Not necessarily." Dirk reached down, scooped Cleo up, and put her on his lap. "They don't claim to have been right by the exit. Supposedly, they were around the corner a bit, not in sight of the rear entrance."

"Who were these people that didn't show up?" Tammy said. "And how are they related to Norwood?"

"The first one," Savannah said, "is Yale Ingram—a superrich dude who was his business partner in another restaurant. Apparently Norwood left Ingram's establishment to work for Ryan and John."

Tammy's fingers flew over her tablet's screen. "Right. I've got him here. You weren't kidding about him being rich. He's even got a place here in San Carmelita up on Milton Hill. And you oughta see this picture of it. It's gorgeous—an old Victorian beauty."

Savannah turned to Dirk. "Isn't that the one you called 'a creepy old monstrosity'?"

Tammy was outraged. "Creepy? Monstrosity?" She shook her head. "And this from a man who used to live in a house trailer."

It was Dirk's turn to be miffed. "I'll have you know, that's a mobile home. And before you make fun of it, remember that your boyfriend there is living in it right now."

Waycross laughed and jostled Tammy playfully. "He's gotcha there, puddin'."

"It's a mobile home now," Tammy conceded, "because Waycross has it all neat and tidy, the way a home is supposed to be. When you lived in it, it was just a house trailer. And by the way, I think Mr. Ingram's Victorian mansion is breathtaking. It's my dream home."

"If your dreams are nightmares, I suppose," Dirk grumbled as he fed Cleo some nonchocolate crumbs from his cookie.

Savannah ignored the squabbling as best she could. She had learned sometime back that trying to referee these fights between Dirk and Tammy was a thankless job. Occasionally, she yielded to temptation and tried to broker peace between them—mostly by threatening to stick them in opposite corners of the room, their noses pressed to the wall for lengthy time-outs.

But mostly she just left them alone to fight it out and, if worse came to worst, she would be nearby, ready to apply tourniquets or spray the fire extinguisher.

"When you guys get tired of discussing the finer points of Gothic mansion versus manufactured housing architecture, you let me know," she told them, "and we can get back to business."

"That's right," Waycross said. "I believe you said there were two people who didn't show up that night after the chef invited them. Ingram and who else?"

"A gal by the name of Perla Viola," Dirk replied after consulting his pocket notebook. "Ryan says she's like the chef's main squeeze or something. Norwood and her, they've got the same address."

"What else do you know about her?" Tammy asked, making a point to address the question to Savannah, rather than Dirk.

"Not much," Savannah answered. "Why don't you get on that for us, sweet pea? Find out all you can about her." She turned to Dirk and flashed him a too-bright smile. "Wouldn't that be nice, Dirk, if Tammy did that for us?"

"Yeah, yeah, whatever," was the lackluster reply. "But try to get it right this time, would you, fluff head?"

Savannah's last thin thread of patience snapped. "What's the matter with you, boy? Don't go calling her names like that."

He shrugged. "Fluff head, sweet pea, puddin' . . . All just terms of endearment, right?"

But Tammy wasn't ready to wave any white flags of peace. "No, wait a minute. I wanna know what you meant by that, Dirk-o. What did you mean, 'try to get it right this time.' Are you suggesting I gave you some bad information or something?"

"Well, since you brought it up—" Dirk began.

"I didn't bring it up. *You* brought it up," Tammy barked back. "So explain yourself."

Savannah sighed, feeling more exhausted by the moment. "Yes, by all means explain yourself, dear husband of mine. But be nice, or I swear I'll use that extra cream we've got for tomorrow night's dinner."

Tammy wrinkled her pert nose. "Ew-w-w. That better not mean what I'm afraid it meant."

"What I was referring to," Dirk said, "is that information that you gave us about Manuel Cervantes. You said he's been married five years to a woman who's a U.S. citizen."

"Yes? So?"

"It isn't true."

"How do you know?"

Savannah decided to join the affray. "Because we asked him how long he'd been married, and he acted weird, very suspicious, about it. Plus his wedding ring is brand-new. Not a scratch or mark on it in spite of all the hard work he does. You don't get that many calluses on your hands and not get your ring scuffed a bit in the process."

"Maybe he doesn't wear his ring when he's working," Waycross offered gently. "Brother-in-law Butch always takes his off when he's overhauling an engine. Of course, Vidalia thinks it's so that he can flirt with the waitress at the Chat 'n' Chew Café around the corner from his garage."

"Yeah, well, Vidalia's a ding-a-ling, and if you tell her I said that, I'll snatch you bald. You hear me, boy?"

Waycross grinned and nodded. "Can't say as I disagree with you none on that score. Vi is a few watts shy of a night-light. That's for sure."

Tammy ignored them as, once again, her nimble fingers slid over her tablet's screen. "I'm sure that the background search I did on him was accurate. But based upon *your* misgivings, *Savannah*, I'll certainly recheck all the data. You know I take great pride in giving you only the most accurate facts. Your trust in me—"

Savannah held up a hand to halt the flow. "Okay,

okay, darlin'. I have no doubt that you'll do exactly that. Don't worry about it. Everybody makes a mistake once in a while."

She glanced over at the clock, then picked up the remote control and flipped on the TV. "I don't know about you guys," she said. "But I'm going to watch the headlines on the evening news. And once that overly perky weather girl comes on, I'm going to bed."

"Good idea," Dirk said. "A good night's sleep and you'll be a whole new woman."

Savannah wasn't nearly as optimistic as he sounded. Lately she'd been having trouble falling asleep and remained awake throughout the night. Maybe that was why she was so tired, but she didn't think so.

Fortunately, she didn't have long to worry about it, because the evening news had begun. And the subject matter of the lead story was all too familiar.

"The investigating officers of the San Carmelita Police Department remained tight-lipped today about their investigation of the murder of celebrity chef Baldwin Norwood," said the perfectly beautiful female newscaster with the perfect hair, perfect makeup, perfect teeth, and perfectly low-cut blouse that showed only the tiniest glimpse of perfect cleavage.

"What investigating officers?" Dirk said. "I'm it. Me, myself, and I."

The news commentator continued to deliver her story. "As we reported to you on the noon news, no suspects have been named in the brutal homicide that occurred last evening in that lovely, little seaside town. The bloody and vicious attack took place in the kitchen of ReJuvene, a chic, new restaurant that had just celebrated its grand opening in the mission district of San Carmelita. We take you now, live, to San Carmelita where our own Desiree Haddrell reports to us from the magnificent home of Chef Norwood and his longtime companion, Perla Viola."

The scene changed to a stretch of beachfront homes that Savannah instantly recognized as one of the more posh areas of town. A mishmash of all sorts of architecture—mostly gaudy, a bit overstated—this neighborhood boasted everything from glass and steel contemporary structures, to Wall Street Tudor, to Italian villas, Spanish haciendas, and even the occasional French chateau.

A young blond reporter stood in front of a stunning Mediterranean mansion, a professional smile pasted on her face and a microphone in her right hand. The evening onshore wind was brisk, and she was having a difficult time keeping her full skirt down and in place with her left hand, while her hair whipped across her face, the ends of it getting stuck in her mouth.

"Yes, this is Desiree Haddrell. I am here at the Norwood mansion, where no one is answering the door. But earlier this afternoon we did catch a glimpse of Perla Viola, longtime girlfriend of the chef, as she was leaving this beautiful home that they have shared for the past fifteen years. When we asked her for a comment, this is what she said . . ."

Again the scene changed, and it was daylight outside the mansion. Desiree was in hot pursuit of a smartly dressed woman in a stylish business suit and outrageously high-heeled pumps, who was racing toward a super-charged V8, silver Jaguar in the driveway.

In those high heels, Perla didn't stand a chance. Desiree intercepted her before she could get the automobile's door open. Shoving a microphone into her face, the reporter said, "I'm sorry for your loss, Ms. Viola. Could you comment on Chef Norwood's tragic demise."

Perla Viola whipped off her designer sunglasses and faced the camera, a fierce light burning in her eyes.

Savannah thought she was going to rebuke the intrusive reporter, maybe feed the cameraman his equipment, make a statement about how callous the press could be when dealing with grieving people.

But Perla Viola had other things on her mind, and quite a different statement to make.

"All I have to say about Baldwin Norwood's murder is . . . You get what's coming to you in this life. And when karma bites you in the ass, sometimes it tears a great big chunk out and spits it at you."

Even Desiree seemed a bit surprised at this unexpected response. She stammered for a moment, then said, "Excuse me, Ms. Viola. But are you saying that Chef Norwood got what was coming to him?"

"No," was the curt reply. "He got a *little piece* of what was coming to him. I suppose we'll all have to be satisfied with that."

The on-scene reporter signed off and the desk anchor concluded the story by saying, "The owners of ReJuvene, Ryan Stone and John Gibson, were also unavailable for comment."

Quickly she moved to another story, as those who were watching the broadcast in Savannah's living room sat silently, staring at the television screen. No one said anything for a long time as they digested what they had seen and heard.

Finally, Tammy said, "Ho-ly cow!"

Waycross nodded. "Appears she ain't all that broken up about her honey's tragic, untimely passing."

"No kidding," Dirk said. "Considering that she was mad enough to spew bile right there on camera for everybody to see, I guess we'll be adding her to our tally of suspects."

But Savannah was a few steps ahead of them. She had already written "Perla Viola" on a Post-it and was rearranging the ones she had previously affixed to her board. "You can bet your lily-white hiney on that," she said. "I just moved Ms. Viola to the top of my list."

Chapter 11

The next morning, after nine hours of fitful sleep, Savannah forced her protesting body out of bed. Still wearing her pink flannel Minnie Mouse pajamas, she plodded downstairs, following the scent of freshly made coffee.

Bless his little pea-pickin' heart, she thought, realizing that her husband was already up and had brewed that life-giving elixir.

He was pretty darned good at it, too. As with most of his vices, Dirk's motto was, "More is more." And the coffee he brewed, using twice as many beans as instructed on the can, had the power to fuel cruise ships to the Bahamas or launch a satellite into outer space.

It was nearly strong enough to enliven a morning-despising gal like Savannah to full wakefulness.

Not quite, but almost.

Three mugs of it, diluted with a little half-and-half, and she could usually manage to speak a coherent sentence.

When she entered the kitchen, Dirk was bent over the cat dishes, filling them to the brim. She couldn't help noticing that her girls, Di and Cleo, were entwining themselves around his ankles in the most ingratiating manner.

It was disgusting really, how they sucked up to him just for some food.

Of course, they had done that to her every morning for years, before he had come along. And for some reason, back then, she had thought it irresistibly adorable. All that purring. All that rubbing. The goo-goo eyes gazing upward with rapt adoration.

It just had to be love. Once-in-a-lifetime love.

Fickle, ungrateful, rotten, worthless beasts.

"Hey, girls," he practically shouted, far too cheerfully for Savannah. She figured no one should be that chipper before, say, nine o'clock in the evening. But he continued as enthusiastically as ever, "Diamante, Cleopatra, look! It's mo-o-m-my! Say, 'Good morning, mommy!'"

Savannah opened the refrigerator door and gazed with blurry eyes at its crowded contents, trying to identify the quart carton of half-and-half. "Bite me," she grumbled.

Silently, she cursed him further for having placed his own brand of coffee additive in front of her half-and-half . . . not only obscuring it but requiring her to actually have to move his stupid creamer crap aside to get to her stuff.

Why the hell did I ever marry him? she thought. *I never used to have to move everything in the dadgum icebox around just to find my half-and-half.*

Another, less annoyed, kinder voice inside her head suggested, *Yes, but if you hadn't married him, you would've had to make your own coffee this morning. And that's a lot harder than just locating a carton in the refrigerator.*

Oh, shut up, she told the sweeter voice. *What the hell do you know?*

As she poured a generous dollop into her Mickey Mouse mug, she could hear him still talking to the cats, but, thankfully, now under his breath.

"I know. I know," he was whispering. "Mommy's a bit of a nasty bitch in the morning. But she gets better as the day goes on. And we love her anyway. Don't we? Yes, we do-o-o."

Fortified with three mugs of Dirk's superoctane coffee and a couple of raspberry Danishes from the Patty-cake Bakery, Savannah was primed to take on the day—or at least slog through it.

The first item on the "to do" list was a visit to the home of the recently departed Chef Norwood and the not-so-shy-and-retiring Perla Viola.

When they arrived at the address on Harbor View Drive, Savannah had to admit that the sprawling Mediterranean mansion was even more impressive in person than it had been on television last evening. Although the neighboring houses were expensive and oversized, the walls of the Norwood mansion towered over them.

Unlike Savannah's tiled roof, which seemed to always be in need of some sort of repair, this roof and everything else about the house appeared to be in perfect condition. Ornate iron work accented the home's graceful lines, enhancing its windows, doors, fences and gates, and balconies. Scarlet bougainvillea and white oleander hung in lush profusion over stone walls, while overhead palm trees sparkled in the morning sunlight.

As she parked the Mustang in front of the house, Dirk said, "Not bad, for a world-famous chef who couldn't cook his way out of the frying pan—or so it's been rumored."

"No kidding," she replied. "I'm probably a heckuva lot better cook than he was, and nobody ever offered me a house like this."

Dirk opened the car door to get out. "Yeah, but before you get too jealous, remember, he's dead."

That was true, she reminded herself as she remembered how Chef Norwood looked, lying on Dr. Liu's autopsy table. There had been nights when she had actually prayed to God, before falling asleep, that when it came her time to go toes up, He would let her kick off from natural causes.

She would much prefer to bypass the good doctor's scalpel and scales altogether and head straight for the mortuary.

"You're thinking about the autopsy again, aren't you?" Dirk said, giving her a searching look as they left the car behind and headed up the sidewalk toward the mansion.

She shook her head, amazed and not a little unsettled by his uncanny ability to read her mind. He'd always been pretty good at it, but since they had gotten married, it was getting downright scary.

Two shall be one, indeed.

"And now," he said, "you're thinking how annoyed you are that I knew what you were thinking. That's what you're thinking. I'm right, huh? And now you're thinking that you're getting really bent out of shape because, lately, I've been right a lot."

"If you really must know," she told him, "I'm thinking that if I had just gone ahead and murdered you the first time you annoyed the hell outta me, I could've served my sentence and been out by now."

He laughed. "Timing's everything, babe. Timing's everything."

A few moments later, they were sitting in the formal living room of the mansion, a room that—with its soaring three-story ceiling, twenty-foot-tall ficus trees, fern pine and assorted palms, concert grand piano, sparkling travertine floors, and circular, wrought-iron staircase—was positively breathtaking.

Except for the haphazard pile of luggage stacked in the middle of it.

Dirk leaned close to Savannah and whispered, "Looks like a baggage conveyor belt at LAX threw up in here."

"Sh-h-h, I hear somebody coming," she said, leaning over to look down the hallway.

Ten minutes ago, a maid had ushered them inside and seated them in the living room, where they had been waiting, not all that patiently, for the mistress of the house to make her appearance.

Yes, Savannah was sure that she heard movement, a door opening, keys jingling. And she realized the sound was coming from the foyer, not the center of the house.

A moment later, a female who was maybe in her late teens or early twenties walked into the living room. At first, she didn't see Savannah and Dirk sitting on the sofa. She walked over to a desk in the corner of the room, set her purse on it, and tossed some keys into a copper bowl.

Her face, rather plain by Hollywood standards, was somehow appealing in a fresh, unaffected way. She wore no makeup but had large Bambi eyes and a pretty complexion—except for a rather pronounced sunburn.

Her long brown hair was pulled back and fastened with a tortoiseshell barrette. Her simple jeans and ivory blouse accented her nice figure.

But her expression was one of extreme sadness, pain, and exhaustion.

It occurred to Savannah that this girl looked like every other family member she had ever seen who had lost a loved one to homicide. They all had a certain look about them: a haggard face; a dejected body posture; a slow, almost mechanical way of moving from one place to another, as though sleepwalking.

Walking through a nightmare that never ended.

As the girl turned, she saw Savannah and Dirk and was startled. "Oh," she said. "I didn't realize we had company."

Savannah stood, and so did Dirk.

"We aren't company," Savannah told her. "No cause for alarm."

Dirk took out his badge and showed it to her. "I'm Detective Sergeant Dirk Coulter from the San Carmelita Police Department. And this is Savannah Reid. We're just here to ask a few questions about Chef Norwood. And you are . . . ?"

She walked over to them—in that stiff, wooden manner—and held her hand out to Savannah. "I'm Umber Viola." She hesitated. "I would say it's nice to meet you, but under the circumstances . . ."

"We understand." Savannah shook her hand and found it cool and moist. "Not very many people are happy to meet us."

"Especially me," Dirk said. "Most people hate me the minute they meet me. But I don't care. I'm used to it."

Umber appeared to think that over for a moment, then she said, "That must be rather nice, actually . . . not caring what people think of you. I wish I could be like that."

Dirk cleared his throat. "Saves a lot of time and energy."

"But on the other hand," Savannah added, "he hardly ever wins the Miss Congeniality title in the beauty pageants he enters."

Again the look of sadness crossed the younger woman's face. She looked down at her simple ballet flats and said, "I wouldn't know. I don't enter a lot of beauty pageants."

Savannah gave her a soft, sympathetic look. "I don't either."

Waving a hand toward the sofa, Savannah said, "Can you join us for a minute? We're here to speak to Perla Viola. And she's your . . . ?"

"Mother."

Savannah couldn't help noticing that there was a lot of pain spoken in that one word. And having seen Perla Viola in action, she wasn't surprised.

Yes, the crime of murder brought out the worst in many people. But Savannah's instincts told her that the woman who had freely spewed her bitterness at the television camera last night habitually did so in everyday life. She appeared to be well practiced at the fine art of rage.

Savannah couldn't imagine that it had been a lot of fun being Perla Viola's daughter.

When they were all seated—Savannah and Dirk next

to each other on the sofa and Umber on a side chair—
Dirk pointed to the avalanche of baggage in the center
of the room. "Are you guys getting ready to take some
sort of vacation, or did you just get back?"

Umber opened her mouth to speak, then closed it, as
though reconsidering what she was going to say. She
thought about her answer long and hard.

Too long. Too hard. And Savannah made a mental
note of the extended hesitation.

"Um, yes. Well, maybe," was the tentative reply. "My
mother . . . she was thinking that it might be good for us
to get away and—"

"Who the hell are you?"

The angry, authoritative voice boomed through the
room like the warning shot of a cannon fired over a
ship's bow.

All three of them turned to see Perla Viola rush into
the room, looking like someone who had just escaped
from the set of a zombie movie.

Unlike the immaculately groomed, perfectly coiffed
lady on last night's television news, this woman was a
disheveled mess.

Her hair stood practically on end. The front of her
white cashmere cardigan was stained with what appeared to be red wine, as were her otherwise snowy
palazzo pants. Her mascara, smeared liberally beneath
her eyes, made her deep, dark circles look even worse.
On her feet were red, high-heeled slides, adorned with
ostrich feathers, of a style that Savannah had seen only
in old movies.

Savannah picked up on three important facts within
the first two seconds of being in the woman's company.
One, Perla Viola wasn't doing so well. Two, she was as
mad as a bull that was in the process of becoming a

steer. And three, judging from the way she was wobbling on those slides when she walked, she just might be a heavy drinker.

"Why are you talking to my daughter?" She marched over to the sofa and stood not two feet from Savannah, hands on her hips, glaring down at her. "I never gave you permission to speak to my child."

As Dirk reached into his pocket, once again, to pull out his badge, he turned to Umber and said, "Ms. Viola, would you please tell me your age?"

In the presence of her mother, Umber Viola seemed to visibly shrink inside herself, becoming more of a frightened little girl by the moment. She stared down at her hand in her lap, and nervously toyed with her fingers. "I'm, uh, eighteen, sir."

Dirk stood, took a step toward Perla and flipped his shield open, sticking it directly under her nose. "I'm Detective Coulter with the SPCD. And it appears that your 'child' is, in fact, of legal age. Therefore, I don't need your permission to talk with her. And right now we're having a little chat about you having a pile of luggage in your living room. I hope you aren't planning any trips in the near future. Because until this case is solved, you aren't going anywhere."

Perla whirled on her daughter. "What did you say to them?"

"Nothing!" Umber looked like she was about to burst into tears. "They asked me about the suitcases. They wanted to know if you were going on a trip. I told them that maybe, but just maybe, you were thinking about it."

Perla stared down at her daughter for what seemed like a very long time, then turned to Savannah. "What if I am? You can't keep me here against my will just because you're investigating a murder. It's not like I'm a suspect or anything, right?"

Savannah had taken an instant dislike to this woman. She couldn't help it. And she didn't feel the need to hide it. She rose and took a step closer to Perla until the women were almost face to face, though even in her extremely high heels, Perla was still considerably shorter.

Savannah stared her down with the glacial blue laser stare that she had perfected during her years on the force.

"Of course you're a suspect," Savannah said in a voice that was ominous in its softness and total lack of intonation. "In fact, you're the victim's live-in girlfriend, so you're our number one suspect. It's always the spouse or the lover or the ex-lover who did it," she said. "Heck, everybody who watches crime shows on TV knows that."

Perla Viola gave a little gasp, and her mouth dropped open an inch. She took a step backward, wobbling on her slides.

Savannah couldn't help experiencing just a little twinge of perverse satisfaction when she saw the anger and arrogance leave the woman's face, to be replaced with genuine fear.

But finally, she seemed to recover herself. She ran her fingers through her mussed hair, then crossed her arms defensively over her chest. Lifting her chin a notch, she said, "You're mistaken. I didn't kill Baldwin. If you watched last night's news report, and I'm sure you probably did, then you know that I'm not all torn up about his passing. But I guarantee there are a lot of people who aren't exactly in mourning today. He was a bad guy, a total piece of crap. The world's a better place without him."

Still sitting on her chair, Umber suddenly leaned forward, placed her hands over her face, and began to sob.

Briefly, Perla's eyes and manner softened as she looked down at her daughter. Her tone was far less sharp when she said, "There may be one or two people who are grieving him, but not many. Baldwin Norwood made a lot more enemies during his life than he did friends. That's for sure."

Savannah wondered at the lack of sensitivity that would allow this woman to say such things about a man in the presence of someone who obviously loved him and was in pain over his passing.

But then, sensitivity didn't appear to be high on the list of Perla Viola's priorities. Something told Savannah that virtues like kindness were ranked well below other things like designer luggage, haute couture shoes, and getting one's way in almost every circumstance.

Taking another look at the pile of suitcases, Savannah noticed a couple of boxes in the mix—standard cardboard boxes affixed with packing tape.

Somehow, Perla Viola didn't strike her as a woman who traveled the world, staying in five-star hotels and yet living out of cardboard boxes.

"Is it a vacation you're planning," Savannah asked her, "or something a bit more permanent?"

"None of your damned business" was the sharp reply as Perla snapped back into Ugly mode. "If you two have any more questions to ask, I suggest you talk to my lawyer. I'm done with you."

She reached down, put her hand on her daughter's shoulder, and gave her an exceptionally rough shake that had to hurt, considering her sunburn. "And that goes for you, too. Don't you say another word to them.

These people aren't interested in finding out the truth about Baldwin, which was that he was the slime of the earth and deserved whatever he got. They just want to solve a high-profile case so that they can get their faces on television and maybe some sort of promotion in their dead-end jobs."

In an instant, Dirk had snatched her hand away from Umber. He squeezed her wrist tightly as he said, "That wasn't very nice, lady. Or smart. Because when you say ugly things like that, it just makes me want to get to the bottom of things that much faster."

Savannah gave her the full benefit of the blue lasers once again and added, "And as nasty as you are, lady, I can't help but hope that when we do get to the bottom of this particular septic tank . . . we find *you*."

Perla wrenched her arm out of Dirk's grasp, but the fight seemed to instantly disappear from her. She sank onto a nearby chair, drew a deep breath, and said, "Okay, what do you want to know? Ask me and get it over with."

"That's better," Dirk said, but he remained standing.

So did Savannah. "Where were you two," she asked, "the night before last?"

"At the Pantages in Hollywood," came the quick reply. "We went to see *Phantom*."

Savannah raised one eyebrow. "You hadn't seen *Phantom* yet?"

Lifting her nose several notches, Perla said, "Of course. Many times. It's a new production. We know the director personally."

"You'd better hope it doesn't start raining in here," Savannah muttered. "You'd be in danger of drowning."

"What?"

"Never mind."

Dirk shot Savannah a quick grin, then said to Perla, "And I suppose you have tickets for this play you went to?"

"I'm sure they're still in my evening bag."

"And the *Playbill*?" Savannah wanted to know.

Again, the nose hitched a notch higher. "We attend the theatre regularly. We've no need to hoard souvenirs like plebeians. However, I might have inadvertently brought it home. If I did, you're welcome to it. You can keep it as a souvenir, if you like."

Savannah turned to Dirk. "Since she's down on the souvenir hoarding rabble, I reckon she wouldn't be all that impressed with your goldfish bowl full of Dodger Stadium tickets, huh?"

His feathers sufficiently ruffled, Dirk glowered at his number one suspect. "If you know what's good for you, you'll go round up those ticket stubs, gal. And make it snappy."

Chapter 12

Savannah and Dirk couldn't believe their good fortune when, upon revisiting the morgue, they found the reception desk deliciously, delightfully deserted.

"What luck!" Dirk exclaimed as they hurried by Bates's deserted post without signing his precious sheet. "Remind me to buy some lottery tickets later. Maybe the stars have shifted in our direction."

"Maybe he ate one too many bags of those chili cheese chip things he's always munching on, got all strangled on it, and keeled over dead from a heart attack," Savannah said with an evil grin. "He might have lain there on the floor behind that desk for Lord only knows how long, kicking and squirming around before he finally gave up the ghost." She sighed, savoring the image. "I reckon it's too much to ask for—it not being my birthday or Christmas—but one can always hope."

She gave him a sideways glance as they hurried down the hallway toward the back of the building. He looked a little surprised, and not in a good way. Maybe even a bit alarmed.

"What?" she asked. "You're shocked?"

He shrugged. "Well, it's a little harsh, don't you think? Hoping that the guy kicked off? Chokin' on a chili cheese chip, no less."

"Oh, for heaven's sake. You didn't think I actually meant that, did you? I was just kidding."

"Really?"

"Of course. Sorta."

"That's what I thought. You know, Van, I love you to pieces, but you're one helluva scary broad."

"Why, thank you, darlin'. That just might be the sweetest, most romantic thing you've ever said to me."

"And the fact that you think that was a compliment doesn't exactly alleviate my concerns."

Savannah breathed a little sigh of relief as they passed the double swinging doors of the autopsy suite. Thankfully, Dr. Liu had told them to meet her in her office.

With the more gory aspects of the doctor's duties fulfilled, she would be at her desk, filling out the endless reams of paperwork that an autopsy generated.

But when they knocked on her door and were invited inside, Savannah found her not up to her elbows in folders and forms but staring at a computer screen.

Progress, in the form of carefree, efficient technology, had finally found its way into the county medical examiner's realm.

"This damn thing!" Dr. Liu slammed her hand down on the keyboard. "I hate it! I just spent the last four hours writing the report on Norwood, and this stupid machine crashed and ate it."

Savannah felt her pain. Not everyone had a Tammy Hart to come to their rescue at times like this.

The doctor turned to Savannah. "You wouldn't happen to have a sledgehammer in your purse, would you?"

Savannah pulled back the lapel of her linen jacket, exposing her holster and weapon. "No, but if you're serious about mass destruction, my Beretta would probably do the job."

Dr. Liu shook her head, drew a deep breath, and pushed back from her desk. She reached into a drawer, pulled out a red-and-orange-striped scarf, and tied her hair back with it. "Have a seat," she told them. "And if you're hungry, help yourself to some of those cookies you brought me." She pointed to the container that was sitting on top of the file cabinet.

"No, that's okay," Savannah said, her courteous Southern upbringing coming to the fore, in spite of the fact that her mouth was watering at the thought. "We brought them for you."

Dirk nabbed the box. "I'll have some. I'm starving."

"No, you won't," Savannah told him. "Those are hers. We've got six dozen at home."

"Well, 'at home' ain't doin' me no good here, now, is it?" He dug in, grabbing one chocolate chipper for each hand.

Two seconds later, he was happily munching away, leaving Savannah to plot where she would hide the cookies when they returned home. She decided she would stash them with her hoarded chocolate bars in the cupboard over the washer and dryer.

She had quickly learned that a woman had to take preemptive—and sometimes retaliatory—measures when living with an omnivore like Coulter.

With rapt attention and morbid fascination, Dr. Liu watched Dirk devour the cookies in record time.

"So what do you have for us, Dr. Jen?" Savannah asked.

"What?" The doctor seemed mesmerized by this display of pure, unadulterated gluttony. Then she shook her head, as though trying to snap out of her reverie. "Oh, I'm sorry. I was just remembering a special I saw on the National Geographic Channel last night. It was about a pack of wolves living in Yellowstone Park."

She picked up a notepad from her desk and looked it over. "Baldwin Norwood. Manner of death: homicide. Cause of death: blunt force trauma to the head."

"That wound you showed us at the base of his skull?" Savannah asked.

Dr. Liu nodded. "I do believe so. When I examined the head I found not only the fractured skull that I was expecting but a tramline contusion as well."

"What's a tramline contusion?" Dirk said, shoving a third cookie into his mouth.

"It's a unique bruise caused by a sharp blow from a long object like a baton, or even a belt or rod. But judging from the crushing of the skull, I'd say it was something very hard and cylindrical."

"Something cylindrical?" Savannah asked. "Do you mean like a lead pipe?"

"A tire iron?" Dirk suggested. "Maybe a baseball bat?"

Dr. Liu reached over and took the container from Dirk's hands. She stuck it into her desk drawer for safekeeping.

"Yes," she said, "something exactly like those items would do it. A tramline bruise actually looks like two bruises, running parallel to each other, with a white area in between. When something long and hard strikes the flesh, the object pushes blood out of the area it contacts, leaving it white. The blood is pushed to either side with such force that it ruptures the blood vessels, creating the dark lines of bruising."

Savannah nodded, remembering several of those bruises that she had seen over the years. Sadly, she had seen them at times on victims of child abuse. She could hardly stand to think what circumstances had led to those wounds.

"Do you have any idea what sort of weapon might have been used on Chef Norwood?" she asked.

"Not precisely," Dr. Liu replied. "But I would guess that it was about 25 millimeters wide."

Dirk's brow furrowed. "How many inches would that be?"

Dr. Liu gave him a condescending smirk. "For you backward, nonscientific types who were absent the day they covered that in high school, it's about an inch."

"Gee, thanks," he replied. "I guess."

"You may also be interested to know," Dr. Liu continued, "that his blood alcohol content was .113. Considering his size, that would indicate he had consumed the equivalent of seven drinks."

"Drunk as a skunk," Savannah observed.

"Yes, and his liver showed signs of acute alcoholism."

Dirk brushed some crumbs off the front of his Harley-Davidson T-shirt. "This bruise you say he got on the back of his head . . . Was it straight across, like perpendicular to his spine? Or was it at an angle?"

Dr. Liu nodded thoughtfully. "I knew you would ask that. It was straight across. And that's a little puzzling. Assuming that the perpetrator snuck up behind him and delivered the blow, you would expect it to be at an angle. Considering the chef's size, the killer would have almost certainly been shorter. It would have been awkward to deliver a blow straight across like that."

"Even if, somehow, the person who hit him was much taller," Dirk said, "it seems like there would be at least a bit of an angle."

"Unless," Savannah added thoughtfully, "he was bending over at the time. Both Manuel and Francia said that the last time they saw him, he was bent over the counter, shoving leftover food into his face. It was some sort of ritual for him after a dinner service."

"Yes," the doctor agreed. "That would account for a perpendicular wound. And if he was absorbed in his eating, as your witnesses suggest was his habit, he probably never saw it coming."

"How sad," Savannah observed. "What an awful way to go."

Dirk said, "Oh, I don't know. Getting whacked on the back of the head while you're shoveling gourmet food into your mouth . . . all with a .113 buzz on. I can think of worse ways to go."

"Like choking to death on a chili cheese chip?" Savannah asked.

"Exactly."

"So, Chef Norwood probably got whacked in the head before he got stabbed or tenderized with the cleaver," Dirk said as he and Savannah walked from the morgue across the parking lot to the Mustang.

"Then what was all the rest of the attack about?" Savannah mused aloud. "You give somebody a skull-fracturing blow to the back of the head. Just to make sure they're dead, you stab them a bunch of times, going for the abdominal aorta. And to cap it all off, you give them some finishing chops with a cleaver."

"Brutal. That's for sure."

"Overly brutal. Three different weapons used. When have you ever seen that? It's almost always one. Who stops to change weapons in the middle of a murder?"

"Darrell Holladay. He used a knife *and* gun. Remember?"

"Yeah, but Darrell was crazier than a fresh-sprayed roach. And he had just found his brother-in-law in bed with his mother."

As soon as they were inside the Mustang, Savannah continued to press her point. "The Holladay killings were crimes of passion enhanced by mental deficiencies caused by familial inbreeding."

"And who's to say that this wasn't a crime of passion? Considering how gruesome it was, I always figured it *was* personal. Highly personal."

"But three weapons? There has to be a reason for that."

Dirk reached into the glove compartment and pulled out a small plastic sandwich bag filled with cinnamon sticks. He pulled one out and stuck it in his mouth.

Sometime back, Dirk had stopped smoking. And one of his most successful tools had been cinnamon sticks. He seldom resorted to using these fragrant crutches anymore. But Savannah had noticed that when he was trying to figure out something complicated—like a murder case, the directions on a microwave popcorn box, or what to get her for her birthday—he would reach for the cinnamon sticks. Apparently, they helped him think.

"All those stab wounds, clustered there in the chest

and belly region, that's a little unusual," Savannah remarked.

"True. Most victims have at least a few punctures in odd places and some defense wounds, too."

"It makes sense that there wouldn't be any defense wounds if the blow on the back of the head took him out first."

Dirk sucked a few "draws" from his cinnamon stick. "But if you've already got the guy down with a smack on the head—a nasty, fatal smack—why pick up a knife to finish the job?"

"A knife is more personal. Frankly, more vicious. More hands-on than, say, a baseball bat."

"And there's something else. That abdominal aorta thingamajig that Dr. Liu was telling us about. Not just everybody knows about that vein being so important."

"Artery."

"What?"

"You called it a vein. The abdominal aorta is an artery. Dr. Liu said so."

"Vein, artery, what's the difference?"

"Arteries carry the blood from the heart out into the body. Veins bring the blood from the body back to the heart."

Dirk shook his head and rolled his eyes. "Veins, arteries. Millimeters, inches. I've had quite enough of prissy, know-it-all females for one day."

"And you apparently missed that biology class, too. What did you do, boy, play hooky all the time?"

"If you don't mind, I'm trying to make a point. Not just everybody knows how important that particular blood vessel is—or that you could kill somebody in seconds if you cut it."

"That's true. I'd say that the average person would go for the center of the chest, the heart."

"But there were so many stab wounds right there over the aorta that it looked deliberate. The killer was going for that particular spot. And I'm thinking chefs know a lot about meat and what's what inside an animal. That might translate to knowing about humans, too."

Savannah nodded, giving him her most serious, wifely, I'm-Hanging-Breathlessly-On-Every-Word-You're-Saying look. "If you think about it, that's a solid lead. All we have to do is find somebody who wasn't playing hooky that day in biology class."

"Smart-ass."

She giggled and leaned over to give him a kiss on the cheek, but her cell phone rang, startling them both.

"Good news maybe?" she said hopefully.

"Hell, at this point I'd take any kind of news."

"It's Tammy," she said, looking at the caller ID.

Dirk sighed and grumbled something under his breath: "Bimbo . . . probably found a new recipe for celery juice."

"Hello, Tamitha," Savannah said. "I'm in the car with Dirk and you're on speakerphone, so don't call him any names."

"Hi, Savannah. Hello, Pee Pee Head," was the reply.

"How mature," Dirk shot back, "for a gal who's a few macaronis short of a tuna casserole."

"Okay, okay," Savannah said, smacking Dirk on the knee. "What's up, sugar lump?"

"You questioned a woman named Maria Ortez, right?" Tammy asked.

"Sure. She's Carlos Ortez's wife. I talked to her there at their taco stand. Why?"

"She called here just a minute ago and asked for you."

Savannah shot Dirk an excited look. He perked up and even removed the cinnamon stick from his mouth.

"She did? That's great! I mean, it could be great, depending on what she wanted. Did she say?"

"She said she wants to talk to you right away. But she doesn't want her husband to know."

"Did she say where?"

"Yes, she said she would be at the northeast corner of the park that's across the street from their stand. She said she'd wait for you until ten-thirty, because that's when her husband's going to arrive, and she has to help him get ready for the lunch crowd."

"Call her back for me and tell her I'm on my way. I'll be there in five minutes."

"There's just one thing, and she was really adamant about it."

"What's that?"

"She said she'll only talk to you. Just you. She said specifically for you not to bring Dirk-o."

Dirk visibly swelled. "She called me Dirk-o?"

"No. Actually she called you 'that obnoxious police detective.' I thought I'd soften the blow a bit."

"How kind of you."

Savannah was already starting the Mustang and putting it in gear. "Thanks, babycakes. Call her the instant we hang up."

"You got it."

As Savannah peeled out of the parking lot, the red pony's engine whining, she told Dirk, "Hang on to your knickers, darlin'. It's gonna be a bumpy ride."

Chapter 13

Savannah found Maria Ortez exactly where she said she would be, in the northeast corner of the park. She was sitting on a bench in the shade of a giant fig tree.

As Savannah hurried up to her, dodging Frisbees tossed by children and a couple of teenagers who were ripping through the park on skateboards, she noticed that the young woman looked scared and sad. Much as she had before, during their earlier interview, only worse.

Though she felt sorry for her, Savannah couldn't help being a bit optimistic. More than once she had cracked a case with evidence supplied by scared and sad informants.

It was the nature of the crime. Homicide was a frightening, depressing business, and there was no way getting around it.

The instant Maria saw Savannah, she jumped to her

feet and glanced around nervously. So did Savannah. If
Maria didn't want her husband to witness this meeting,
neither did Savannah. The last thing she wanted to do
was cause this young woman problems with her husband, whom she obviously loved very much.

When she and Maria met halfway in the center of
the park, Savannah said, "Would you feel better if we
were sitting in my car? It might be a bit more private
there."

Maria thought it over for a moment, then nodded.
"Yes, okay."

"It's right over here. Let's go." Savannah led her to
the Mustang at the edge of the park. She unlocked the
door and seated her inside.

Once settled in the driver's seat, Savannah lowered
the windows so they could benefit from the cool ocean
breeze.

"I was very pleased to hear you wanted to meet me,"
Savannah said, giving her a friendly smile. "Thank you
for calling."

"I had to," Maria replied. "I can't stop thinking
about it. I can't sleep. I'm so worried."

"Don't you worry, sugar. You did the right thing by
reaching out. After you and I talk, I'll betcha you're
going to feel a whole lot better."

She reached over and patted Maria's hand. She was
gripping the seat cushion as though it were some sort
of life preserver.

Savannah said, "Now you just take a deep breath,
relax, and tell me what it is that's bothering you so bad
that you can't sleep."

Maria closed her eyes and shuddered. "I'm so afraid,"
she said.

"I know you are. But you're doing the right thing anyway, even though you're afraid. That takes real courage. I'm very proud of you for being so brave."

As the seconds ticked by and Maria said nothing, Savannah began to worry. Her fear might be too much for her, after all.

"Maria," she said softly. "If you know something about that night, you have to tell someone. This is a very serious situation. A person lost his life at someone else's hands. It doesn't get any more serious than that."

Finally, Maria spoke. "I don't know anything about that night—the night the chef was killed. But I know what happened three nights before that. And it might have something to do with him dying. It might. I don't know for sure."

"Okay. You're doing fine. Please go on."

"And my husband thinks so, too. But he won't tell you himself, because he's afraid that he'll betray his friend."

Savannah could feel her pulse rate quickening. "Which friend?"

"Manuel Cervantes. He and Manuel have been friends for a long time. They're like brothers. Carlos would never do anything to get Manuel in trouble. And he would get very angry with me if he knew I told you this. Can you keep it a secret? The fact that I told you. Can you not let my husband find out?"

Savannah hesitated before answering her. She certainly did not want to lose this lead. But she couldn't lie to this woman with the soft, innocent, trusting eyes.

"I promise you that I'll try very, very hard not to let him find out. And, depending on what you tell me, I probably can. But either way, like I said before, this is murder. And bringing the killer to justice is the most important thing here. Your husband seemed like a good man to me."

"He is. He's a very good man."

"And he seems to love and respect you."

"He does. Very much."

"Then in the end, even if he finds out, he should understand and forgive you for doing what you think is best. Right?"

Tears filled Maria's eyes, but she nodded. "Yes. He will."

"So, tell me what happened four days ago."

Maria pushed her dark curls back from her forehead and cheeks and took a deep breath of resolve. "The chef had a meeting at his house—the big, fancy castillo down by the water."

"Yes, I know the place. I was there this morning."

"He told Carlos and Manuel to be there. And Francia. There were three servers, a bartender, and a busboy, too. I don't know their names, except for one server, Celia. She's Manuel's wife."

"That's okay. Go on."

"The meeting was to talk about the new restaurant. They had all been working together as a team at Villa Nuevo. But Chef Norwood told them that they were finished there and moving to ReJuvene. Most of them weren't happy about that. They liked working for Mr. Ingram. He's a very nice man—different from Chef Norwood. But wherever the chef went, they went."

"I understand. Please continue."

"They talked about the new restaurant, how it's a lot smaller than Villa Nuevo and how they would need to manage with a much smaller staff. Everything went fine at the meeting. But afterward—there was trouble."

"What kind of trouble?"

Maria's face flushed, and she stared down at her lap as she continued, "The chef sent Celia to the cellar to get him some more wine. Then, as soon as she had gone, he said he needed to go to the bathroom. He was gone only a minute or two when Carlos and Manuel heard Celia scream."

"Hmmm. Not good."

"They ran down to the cellar and saw Chef Norwood had one hand over her mouth and the other hand up her blouse. She was trying to get away from him, but he was very big, and she's a small woman."

Savannah tried to hide her excitement when she said, "I can imagine. What happened then?"

"Manuel tried to hit the chef, but Carlos stopped him."

"I should think most men would try to hit someone who was doing that to their wife."

"Yes, but Manuel has to be careful. He isn't . . ." Her eyes searched Savannah's, looking for understanding.

"He isn't legal."

"Right. Chef Norwood was a powerful man. He was rich. He was famous. And Manuel is an illegal worker with no papers and no money. He sends every penny he makes to his family in Mexico because they would starve without it. All he has in the world is his pretty new wife. And yet, the chef would take her from him, too."

"I understand why that would make him very angry." Savannah felt a sinking, sick feeling sweep through her. "And how did this awful situation resolve?"

"It didn't. Chef Norwood just laughed at Manuel, at his anger, at Celia for crying. He told him that as his patron, his boss, he should have gotten his 'right of the first night' with Celia before their wedding."

"What a hateful thing to say."

"And to such a proud man as Manuel, who loves his wife so much. It was a horrible insult—to him and to his Celia."

Suddenly, it felt hot inside the Mustang. Savannah felt as though she couldn't breathe, as if all the air had been sucked out of the vehicle, leaving the two women inside to suffocate.

She could feel her pulse pounding in her temple and a pain in the back of her head. The same area where Norwood had been hit.

More than almost anything in her career, she hated it when a case took a turn in a direction that she hadn't anticipated and didn't want.

Why did Lady Justice have to point her accusing finger at a nice guy like Manuel? Some might even say that he had an understandable reason to hate Norwood. Certainly, that didn't justify a murder, but . . .

Why couldn't her number one suspect remain Perla Viola?

Savannah turned slightly in her seat to better scrutinize the young woman sitting next to her. Maria's eyes were filled with tears, and she was still trembling like an oak tree's last leaf of the season.

Why had she stepped forward at this time and in this way? Savannah wanted to think it was because she was a virtuous soul, one who couldn't bear to see a killer get away with taking a life. And yet she seemed to care very much about Manuel and worried about what might happen to him.

"Maria . . . ?" Savannah asked, her eyes searching

the other woman's, trying to see her soul. "Why are you telling me this?"

The young woman started to cry in earnest, deep sobs that seemed to come from a place very deep in her spirit. "I think it was wrong, me telling you. I should have done it for the right reason—to get justice for Chef Norwood. I wish that was why, but it isn't."

"Then what is the reason?"

"Because I'm afraid for my husband. He didn't tell you or your policeman all of the truth. He didn't say that he saw Manuel walk away and go back into the kitchen that night. He wants to protect his friend. But *I* want to protect *him*. Carlos is my world. My everything. I couldn't live without him. And I was so afraid that when you found out he was lying, you would arrest him and take him from me."

"Okay. That makes sense. I understand now."

"And if he gets into trouble later, for helping his friend, you'll remember that I helped you, right? You'll remember and not hurt him."

Savannah reached into the backseat and produced a box of tissues. "I'll remember," she told her. "And I'll make sure that the authorities remember, too. Try not to worry."

Maria took the proffered tissues and blew noisily into them. "Thank you, Savannah."

"You're welcome, darlin'. You still did the right thing. And who knows, maybe you'll be able to sleep tonight."

When Savannah dropped by Harbor Beach Park to pick up Dirk, he was doing pretty much exactly what he had been doing when she had left him there to go meet Maria. He was playing with kids and dogs.

She pulled into the parking lot, cut the key, and sat there in the car, watching him for a while.

"That's my *husband*," she whispered, wondering at the words. "*Husband*. Wow, I have one of those now. Go figure."

In spite of the warm day, he was still wearing his battered, leather bomber jacket. She knew it had to hinder his style a bit as he tossed a bright yellow tennis ball down the beach where half a dozen eager kids and a couple of black retrievers waited anxiously to catch it. Even from this distance she could see the sweat on his brow, and she knew he would be more comfortable if he peeled the coat off and dumped it on the sand.

But he wouldn't. And she knew why.

If he removed his jacket, the children would see his gun and holster. So Dirk would suffer the discomfort rather than alarm the little ones.

Yes, that was her husband.

Even if he was known among the adult citizenry of San Carmelita as a grouch, curmudgeon, and all-around grumpy guy, every kid and every animal in town that knew him loved him. And that mattered a lot more to Savannah than his sullied reputation among the disgruntled grown-ups.

"Kids and dogs can always tell whose heart is pure and whose ain't," Granny had always said. And Savannah agreed with her, except for the amendment that Diamante and Cleopatra had insisted upon: kids, dogs, *and cats* can tell.

She sat quietly in the car a bit longer, watching as the retrievers returned the ball to him over and over, and he sent it soaring again and again. As she enjoyed the brief respite from the day's stress, she massaged the back of her neck, willing the pain to leave.

Since when did she get headaches?

She tried to remember if she had ever had a period like recent days when they had been less the exception and more the rule. Like everyone else, she might get sinus pain when the Santa Ana winds blew or a neckache if she slept in a funny position.

But this, like the dizziness, was a new development. And she didn't like it one bit.

Go to the doctor, dummy, a voice whispered deep inside her mind—in fact, close to the region of her headache pain. *It might be something serious. You need to find out what it is.*

"It's nothing," she whispered back. "I'm tired. I haven't gotten enough sleep lately. My best friends had a murder take place in their kitchen on opening night. Duh. Is it any wonder I'm not feeling my best?"

But as she sat there, watching Dirk run effortlessly up and down the beach, she felt the leaden, aching fatigue in her own legs. It hadn't been that long ago when she could have run right beside him. But not now. Something was different about her body. Something was going on.

And if the ol' bod didn't knock it off soon, she just might have to listen to that nagging, headachy voice and make an appointment with her doctor.

"You're probably low on iron, or B-12, or B-52, or some darned thing," she told herself. "Pop a few pills, and you'll be good as new."

She climbed out of the car and began to make her way across the sand toward Dirk. But as she reached the halfway mark between the parking lot and the waterline, the dizziness returned with a vengeance.

She had to stand still and wait for the world to stop spinning around her.

"What in Sam Hill is going on?" she muttered as she tried to keep her balance.

As though from far away, she heard Dirk calling out, "Savannah? Savannah?"

Suddenly, the beach seemed to tilt sharply upward. And the next thing she knew, it had hit her on the right side of her face. Sand filled her mouth, and she could taste its salty dampness. She blinked, trying to get it out of her eyes.

Her vision blurred, and her lids stung.

Faintly, she could hear Dirk's deep voice shouting, "Savannah! Van, are you okay, baby? Savannah!"

Then she couldn't feel, hear, or see anything at all.

Chapter 14

When Savannah regained consciousness, she had no idea how long she had been out. But Dirk was shaking her, a circle of children surrounded her, and a black retriever was licking her cheek.

"Honey, what happened?" Dirk was asking. "Can you hear me? Are you unconscious?"

What seemed like one hundred thoughts raced through her mind. Was she unconscious? No, she could hear him. So, of course she couldn't be unconscious. Though she was pretty sure that she had been just a moment before.

But was she going to tell Dirk that?

She looked up at his face, bent over hers, and saw the abject horror in his eyes.

"I fell down," she told him. "No big deal. I just tripped on something and fell down."

She struggled to sit up, and he helped her.

"You tripped?" He glanced back over the path she had walked—a path that was relatively smooth and clear of any debris. When he turned back to her, he didn't look very convinced. "What did you trip on?" he asked.

She could hear the suspicion in his voice.

"Oh, I don't know. A piece of seaweed or something. No harm done, really." She brushed the sand off her cheek and tried to smooth her hair back into place.

One of the little girls leaned down, peering at her. When they were finally almost nose to nose, the child's big blue eyes filling Savannah's vision, the youngster said, "Wow, lady, you've got sand in your mouth."

"Yes, I do," Savannah replied in a less than cheerful tone.

"Ew-w-w," the little girl said, screwing her face into a grimace. "You shouldn't eat sand. My mommy says that sand is icky and dirty. Seagulls poop on it."

Savannah spit out the offending grit. "Thank you," she said, "for telling me that."

"You're very welcome," replied the well-mannered child as she backed away.

Savannah turned to Dirk and held out her hands to him. "I would really like to get the hell out of here now," she said, "if you could maybe give me a hand up."

"Good idea." He rose to his feet, grabbed her hands, and hauled her up.

As Savannah turned and made her way gingerly across the sand back toward the parking lot and the Mustang, she heard the helpful girl behind her chattering away.

She was gleefully telling her companions, "I heard that lady say a ba-a-ad word. She said, 'H–E–double hockey sticks.' My mommy says that's a bad word, and I'm not supposed to ever, ever say it. Nope. Not even if Daddy says it all the time."

* * *

"I'm just gonna have to bite the bullet and get another car," Dirk said mournfully as she pulled over to the curb in front of ReJuvene to drop him off. "And I can't stand to even think about it."

"I know, darlin'," she told him. "But you live in Southern California, not New York City, and you're a grown-up. You have to own a vehicle."

"I just want my Buick back."

"Your Buick passed away, sweetie. It went to Automobile Heaven, where all good cars go when they die."

His bottom lip protruded, and she could swear she saw it tremble a bit. "I don't want any other car. I could never feel the same way about another car as I did about my Skylark."

"You just have to go to a used car lot and pick out something, honey. Anything. I'm not going to keep toting you around everywhere."

Yes, the lower lip was definitely trembling.

She reached over and patted his hand. "You must find the courage to start anew, sweetheart." Flashing him a sarcastically sweet smile, she added, "Don't worry. You can learn to love again."

He bailed out of the Mustang and closed the door a bit too hard. Sticking his head through the open window, he said, "Yeah, yeah . . . make fun of me all you want, but heaven forbid anything happens to this jalopy. You'd have it buried outside your bedroom window and plant daisies on its grave."

She sat, watching, as he stomped up to the restaurant door and disappeared inside. Through the windows she saw Ryan and John greet him.

The three men were going to search the kitchen for the mysterious cylindrical object that had felled Chef Norwood. Meanwhile, she was going to see if she could locate Manuel's wife, Celia. Tammy had done some research and told Savannah that Celia was performing maid service at San Carmelita's infamous Blue Moon Motel.

Savannah wasn't particularly looking forward to driving all the way out to the hot sheets establishment located in the boondocks on the edge of town. She would have preferred to have gone home, crawled into bed, and attempted to sleep off her headache.

But she did what she could for the man she loved. Even when he jinxed her car and she didn't particularly like him.

When the three men inside the restaurant turned in unison to wave good-bye, she fluttered her fingers at them, then turned to pull out into traffic.

Carefully.

Very, very carefully.

She made absolutely certain there were no cars or bicyclists or marauding skateboarders hurtling down the road that might sideswipe that glistening red paint.

"Dadgum his hide for even thinking something like that," she mumbled to herself. She had decided, the moment he had uttered those fateful words, that if she was in any sort of accident, even a minor fender bender, within the next year, it would be all his fault.

"Hex me, will ya?" she grumbled.

Plant daisies on the red pony's grave, indeed. How dare he insult her that way!

If and when that sad day ever arrived, it would be roses. Great big red ones!

As a town that thrived on tourism, San Carmelita had more than its share of hotels, motels, and B&Bs.

Most were charming and safe and enjoyed a good reputation in the community.

The Blue Moon Motel was not one of those.

It was definitely not what one would call a family establishment. Newlyweds did not book suites with fireplaces and whirlpool bathtubs for two at the Blue Moon. When a family's matronly aunt came to visit for a week, they would never consider treating Aunt Bessie to a room at the Blue.

Not unless Aunt Bess was in the habit of supplementing her social security check with a bit of hanky-panky for hire on the side.

At one time, Savannah might have considered luring her new hubby out to the Blue Moon and plunking down a few bucks for an hour of pseudo-sordid romance. It never hurt to liven things up on the home front with a bit of novelty from time to time.

But a few months back, she had been present when Eileen and her CSI team were searching for blood spatter in one of the rooms. They had used an ultraviolet lamp to illuminate bodily secretions. Seeing nearly every one of the room's surfaces light up with some sort of suspicious splattering, Savannah had hightailed it out of there and vowed never to return.

Since that day, she had not set foot in a no-tell motel.

For that matter, she hadn't felt especially comfortable in a five-star resort, either.

Romantic getaways were ruined for her forever.

When she arrived at the Blue Moon, there were only a few cars parked in the lot. Apparently, the lunch crowd had already come and gone. She wasn't all that sorry to have missed them, as she lived in mortal fear that she would run into someone she knew.

She could just imagine the awkward, stuttering, bumbling exchange that would follow.

"Oh, um, hi, Pastor Arnold. Fancy running into you here . . . you and your lovely, young bookkeeper. Yes, it just so happens that I'm here without my spouse, too. But I'm working a runaway teenager case. No, of course I wouldn't dream of mentioning this little encounter to Mrs. Arnold—formidable lady that she is. Then I'd be working a murder case, huh? Ha, ha."

When Savannah parked the Mustang and walked across the lot to the office, she took her time. Her headache had abated a little, and the sense of dizziness was gone, but she didn't want to tempt fate.

No, she had a strict personal limit when it came to falling flat on her face in public: Once a day, that's it, that's all.

And she had filled that quota.

Once inside the office, she found a scraggly haired, shaggy-bearded fellow sitting behind the counter. He was staring with rapt attention at a TV set that was just out of her line of vision.

Judging from the moans and groans coming from the television, she was glad that it was out of sight.

She started to prop her elbows on the counter, then thought better of it and crossed her arms over her chest instead. "Hi," she said. "You wouldn't happen to have a brother named Kenny Bates, would you?"

He turned his face toward her, but his eyes were still glued to the TV screen. "What? Kenny who?"

"Never mind." Wanting his full attention, she decided to risk contagion and slammed her fist down on the counter. "Hey! Reckon you can tear yourself away from that fine movie classic you're watching there?

Hell, it's not like you don't know how the story ends, right?"

He jumped. His eyes widened. "Yeah. Jeez, lady, chill out. You must be needing that room bad."

"What I need is to talk to an employee of yours, a Celia Cervantes," she said, whipping out her private investigator ID and passing it quickly under his nose.

She used the same casual, flipping motion that she had always used when displaying her badge. Only a bit faster. While she would never commit the crime of impersonating a police officer, she certainly didn't mind if Mr. Scraggly here got the wrong impression.

"I need to interview her," she told him. "I won't take much of her time or interfere with her work."

He started to shake his head. "No. I don't know what you think she's done. But Celia's a good girl, one of my best workers. And she hasn't done anything against the law. I think you'd better leave."

Savannah shook her head and made a *tsk-tsk* sound. "Now, now. Don't be like that—all contrary and prickly. There's no call for it. I've no doubt that you run a very classy, law-abiding business here. I'm sure that everybody you hire to change the sheets and scrub the toilets around here—they've all got green cards. And I'm sure you pay them at least minimum wage and do all that withholding employer paperwork that Uncle Sam requires. I'm sure if I was to check into all those particulars, everything would be in order and up to snuff. Right?"

He began to mess with the clutter on the counter, picking up some rubber bands and thumbtacks and stashing them in a drawer, putting away a stray key, tossing an empty candy wrapper.

Finally, he said, "Okay, she's cleaning room one-three-two. Go talk to her, if you just have to. But she needs to get that room ready in the next fifteen minutes. Somebody's asked for it, special."

"Aw-w-w, now ain't that just plumb romantic? Somebody renewing sweet acquaintances?"

"Naw. The guy just comes alone and uses it by himself. He likes it 'cause the TV's a little bigger and the picture's a bit sharper than the ones in the other rooms." He gave her a crooked smirk. "You know, not everybody comes here because they're needing company. Some people are just looking for a bit of solitude."

Savannah quickly jotted a mental note to herself: *Do not touch anything in that room. Consider it a biohazard zone.*

"Thank you," she said far more sweetly than she meant. "You have a nice day now, hear?"

As she was going out the door, she thought she heard him say, "Hey, officer? I didn't catch your name."

She ignored him and kept walking.

She found Celia Cervantes in room 132, as predicted, bent over a bed, stripping the sheets.

Probably in her early twenties, Celia was the epitome of a South American beauty with her glossy black hair and dark, exotic eyes. Although she was curvy in all the right places, a quick appraisal of her body told Savannah that her slender figure was not so much "fashionable" as it was the result of a lot of hard work and not a lot of food.

Savannah stuck her head through the open door and said softly, "Celia?"

The woman jumped, seeing her for the first time. It occurred to Savannah that Celia Cervantes's strings were strung pretty tight.

Not surprising under the circumstances.

Half an hour ago, Savannah had received a call from Tammy, who had told her—quite apologetically—that she had been mistaken about Manuel and Celia being in the United States legally. A bit of deep digging on Tammy's part had revealed that they were illegals who, like many others in their circumstances, were using the identifications of family members.

In their case, distant cousins—Manuel and Celia Cervantes on "Celia's" side of the family.

Tammy uncovered the fraud when she found out that the real Manuel and Celia had been deceased for over a decade and were buried in a cemetery in Los Angeles.

Looking into the young woman's eyes, Savannah saw a depth of sadness and wisdom that was beyond her years. Savannah couldn't help wondering what her real name was and what stories she had to tell.

Experience had taught Savannah there was no point in asking.

For all practical purposes and as far as Savannah was concerned, this young woman standing in front of her was Celia and her husband was Manuel. Savannah would leave the rest up to the law enforcement agencies whose responsibility it was to deal with these situations.

For a long moment, Celia just stared at Savannah with fear-filled eyes. Then she said, "I am sorry. I cannot talk to you now. I have to work."

"I understand," Savannah told her. "I already spoke to your boss, and he said I could talk to you."

Celia turned away and bowed her head. "He says that to you, but when you leave, he will say different to me."

She pulled the bottom sheet off the bed, wadded it into a ball, and shoved it into a large, canvas laundry bag. "If I don't finish my work fast, he will find another woman to do it faster."

Forgetting about her former resolutions, Savannah stepped into the room and made her way past the cheap chest of drawers with its much-ballyhooed television sitting on top, and around the foot of the bed to the other side.

She grabbed one edge of the sheet and began expertly tucking it under the mattress.

"What are you doing?" Celia asked her, an astonished look on her pretty face.

"Helping you do your work fast so that you don't get in trouble for talking to me."

Celia watched as Savannah executed a perfect hospital corner in three seconds.

As Savannah reached for the top sheet and began to spread it, she said teasingly, "What? Do you think you're the only one who knows how to make a bed? The only one who's ever done this sort of thing for a living?"

Celia didn't reply, so Savannah continued to smooth and tuck sheets and talk. "When I was a girl, my grandmother and I cleaned people's houses, did their laundry—whatever they wanted us to do—just so we could make a little extra money and feed all my brothers and sisters. There were nine of us. Ten, counting Gran. So, I know how it's done. And if you need me to, I'll scrub down the bathroom for you, too."

Celia said nothing as she put the finishing touches on her side of the bed. But when Savannah grabbed the pillows and began slipping on the cases with record speed, she could be quiet no longer. "I know who you are," she said. "My husband told me about you. He said you are a big, tall lady, *muy bonita*, with blue eyes and dark hair. He said you are the policeman's wife."

Savannah chuckled as she fluffed pillows and tossed them onto the bed. "I guess that about sums me up in a nutshell. Thank you for the *bonita* part."

"Why do you help him?"

Savannah shrugged. "He's my husband. I help him. He helps me. But mostly, I just try to keep him out of trouble. *Comprende*?"

Flashing a beautiful smile, Celia laughed. *"Si."* But just as quickly her smile faded, and she added, "My husband. I want to keep him out of trouble. But it is not easy."

"I know. Chef Norwood wasn't an easy boss. I'm sorry that he was so rude to you and your husband. You didn't deserve to be treated like that."

Instantly the young woman's eyes filled with tears. "I never told him I liked him. I did not like him. Why would I? I have a husband. A very handsome husband."

"I'm sure you did nothing to encourage Norwood. Men like him don't need encouragement. They don't care if a woman wants them or not."

"I don't understand. Why do they want someone who doesn't like them?"

Savannah sighed. "It isn't about attraction. It's about control. They don't care if someone likes them as long as that person does whatever they tell them to. He didn't want your love. He wanted your fear. It made him feel big and powerful."

"But he *was* big and powerful. So why would he hurt me? Why would he hurt Manuel?"

Savannah thought back over every sociopath and narcissist that she ever had the misfortune of dealing with. They were her least favorite creatures on earth. But long ago she had uncovered their secret, and having done so, she would never fear them again.

"Deep inside," she said, "they know that they're weak— weaker than most people. And the only time they feel strong is when they hurt and control someone else. They need other people's fear the way a vampire bat needs blood. They feed off fear. They don't worry about whether it's right or wrong. They do whatever they want to get whatever they want. And by doing so, they grow stronger, while their victims feel weaker and weaker."

She could see a light of understanding ignite in the younger woman's eyes as she took in her words. "I think you are right," she said. "I have known others like the chef. They like to hurt, to cause fear and pain. They are animals."

Diamante and Cleo's sweet faces flashed across Savannah's mental vision. "Oh, they're worse than animals. Much worse."

Grabbing a dusting cloth, Celia began to polish the top of the nightstand. Savannah took another rag from the supply cart parked beside the door and tackled the chest of drawers and the television.

"I was a police officer for a long time," she told Celia as they dusted. "And I saw a lot of jerks like that. Some of them had done terrible, terrible things to innocent folks—children, old people, the sick, the poor—anyone smaller or unable to defend themselves."

She took a moment and drew a deep breath before continuing. "Some of the things they did were so horrible that I actually wanted to kill them. I hate to admit such a thing, but it's true. Of course I never did. It's against the laws of God and mankind to take another's life. But I did think about it from time to time. And I can understand why someone else might be tempted to do the same."

Her eyes searched Celia's to see if the subtext of her words was registering on the other woman.

It was. Celia Cervantes, or whatever her name was, was an intelligent, street-savvy woman. And she knew exactly where Savannah was headed with this line of conversation.

Turning her back to Savannah, she busied herself arranging and rearranging items on the supply cart.

"Celia, I know that Chef Norwood attacked you in his wine cellar. I know that he said terrible things to Manuel. I know how insults and machismo and all business are very important to a man like your husband, to men in his culture. The men I grew up with in Georgia, that sort of thing is very important to them, too. You don't insult them, and especially their family, without paying a price for it."

Celia grabbed a squirt bottle of cleaner and a rag and rushed into the bathroom. She slammed the door behind her.

But Savannah had seen more than her share of closed doors in her day.

She wasn't about to let a little thing like having a door slammed in her face stop her.

Gently she pushed it open a few inches and shoved her foot into the crack. "What I'm trying to tell you, Celia," she said, "is that I'm wondering if your husband—"

Celia jerked the door open and stood, her hands on her hips, staring defiantly up at Savannah. "I know what you are wondering. You are wondering if my husband killed the chef. You are wondering if he is a *matador*—a murderer. And I am telling you, he is not."

A picture of indignation and rage, the young wife's eyes blazed as she defended her husband. Her courage and passion touched Savannah's heart.

If all husbands and wives defended each other with this much zeal, she thought, *there would be far more successful marriages in the world.*

"Celia," she said, "I understand that you—"

"No, *senora*. You do *not* understand." Celia began to cry. "I'm sorry. I know you have a good heart. I can tell. But you do not understand what it is to be me. You do not understand what it is to be my husband. You do not understand what it is to have no power, to have to do everything bad men—and women—tell you to do."

The "Big Sister" in Savannah welled up, filling her with compassion for this woman and her situation. She tried to reach out to her, to hug her, but Celia stepped backward, avoiding any embrace.

"You must believe me," the distraught young woman continued. "I know my husband. I know that, like you said, he wanted to kill the chef. But if he was going to do that, he would have done it the other night in the wine cellar, when he saw him hurting me. If he did not do it then, he did not do it later."

Savannah considered her words for several moments. They had the ring of truth about them. And if ever she had believed someone was telling her the truth, as they knew it, it was this woman, who seemed to have no pretensions whatsoever about her.

"Okay," Savannah said. "You're telling me that your husband is innocent, and I believe you. But somewhere there is someone—probably someone you know—who took another human being's life. And I can't stop until I find out who did it."

Celia wiped her tears away with the back of her hand and nodded. "I understand. It is your work. Important work." She gave Savannah a faint smile. "You helped me with my work. If I can, I will help you with yours."

"Good. Thank you. I appreciate it, because I need all the help I can get right now."

"What do you want me to do?"

"I want you to tell me who killed Chef Norwood."

Celia gave her a small, bittersweet grin. "Is that all?"

Savannah chuckled. "Okay, I believe you when you say your husband didn't do it. But he has to have some idea about who did. And since the two of you are so close, I'm sure he must have shared his opinion with you. Would you share it with me?"

"I would if I could. But he doesn't know. He told me so." Celia turned and began to squirt generous amounts of cleaner on the mirror, the toilet, the sink, and shower.

She continued, "My husband thinks the killer is someone who was there at the chef's house that night, the night he attacked me and insulted us. Everyone was there, and they saw what happened to me. They saw how angry my husband was."

"I don't understand what you're saying, Celia," Savannah said. "Do you think someone murdered the chef because he attacked you and insulted Manuel?"

"No. I think everyone there had a reason to kill him. And someone wanted to very badly. When they saw what happened—with the chef and me and my husband—they thought it would be a good time to do it."

"Because it would be blamed on you or your husband."

"Right."

That, too, rang in Savannah's head like a church bell at noon. She had learned to always trust those "dings" in the back of her mind. They seldom proved to be wrong.

"Thank you, Celia," she told her. "You've helped me a lot, and I sure appreciate it."

Celia smiled brightly. "You're welcome. I'm glad." Then she sobered and added, "Your work, *senora*, it is much harder than mine. All I have to do is clean this mirror, this sink, this toilet. But you . . . you have to find out who took a man's life from him. A man *everyone* wanted to kill. *Senora*, you have the hardest work of all."

Chapter 15

When Savannah walked through the restaurant's front door to pick up Dirk, she felt as though she had stepped into some kind of macabre crime scene reunion.

A quick glance around the dining room told her that almost everyone who had been in attendance on the night of the murder had returned for some sort of meeting.

Ryan and Dirk sat at the bar on stools, facing the dining area. About a dozen chairs had been placed in front of them in a neat line. On those chairs sat the majority of Savannah's suspects: Francia Fortun, Carlos Ortez, Maria Ortez, Manuel Cervantes, and several of the servers, whom she recognized as waiters and waitresses from the fateful dinner.

She couldn't help thinking that it looked like the perfect lineup.

Unfortunately, they had no eyewitness to make an identification.

Ryan was speaking to his impromptu audience, and

it sounded as though he were a coach giving them a locker room pep talk.

"I can't tell you how much John and I appreciate each and every one of you showing up like this at a moment's notice," he was saying. "Frankly, after what happened here, we didn't know if we should open the restaurant even if we could. But then we talked to Francia and Manuel and Carlos, and they got in touch with the rest of you, and your enthusiastic response ignited a spark of hope in us that maybe, just maybe, we could do it."

Savannah stood quietly off to the side, listening as her friend continued his speech. Her heart ached for him. She knew the anguish that he and John had been through, and yet they were lifting themselves up off the floor and preparing to battle again.

Knowing them as she did, she would have expected nothing less. But it was still satisfying and inspiring to watch it happen.

Once Ryan had finished speaking, John added his encouragement and praise for the staff's support. Then, speechmaking aside, the meeting became an informal question and answer as they discussed the practical matters of reopening.

Savannah couldn't help but notice that Francia appeared to be in fine form, enthusiastic—gleeful even—as she assumed the fallen king's crown. She was obviously the heir apparent and seemed to be having no trouble at all fulfilling the role of master chef.

Not seeing Dirk anywhere in the room, Savannah quietly made her way to the kitchen and slipped inside.

At first she didn't see him there either. But a rattling of pots and pans caused her to look down, and there he was on his hands and knees, head stuck inside a giant cabinet.

There was another volley of metal hitting metal, and she heard him curse under his breath.

For a moment she allowed herself to enjoy the view. Dirk's derrière in a pair of snug jeans had always been one of her favorite scenes. They might both be older than forty, but he still filled out his Levi's nicely, and she was still plenty young enough to enjoy the fact.

She did, however, resist the urge to give him a pinch or a pat. From the waves of blue language rolling out of the cabinet, she had the feeling he wasn't in a "friendly pinch" or "love pat" sort of mood.

"Hey, cutie, whatcha doing down there?" she asked, squatting beside him and peering into the cabinet.

"What do you suppose I'm doing?" he snapped. "I'm looking for a cylindrical rod." He pulled his head out of the cupboard and looked up at her. His hair was messy, his face was red, and his brow deeply furrowed. "You know, in other words, a murder weapon."

"You haven't found one yet?"

She grinned and gave him a wink. There was hardly anything he loved more than being asked a stupid question when he was in a bad mood. So she did it as frequently as possible.

After all, what was the point of having a mate if you couldn't annoy the daylights out of that person on a regular basis?

He snorted. "Of course I found it—a lead pipe with blood and hair and brain matter stuck on it. Somebody had pitched it behind the refrigerator. But just for fun I kept looking. You know how much I love standing on my head and poking around in dark places."

"Did you check the ballroom for a wrench?"

"Yeah, smart aleck. And the conservatory for a rope."

She reached down and ran her fingers through his hair, semistraightening it. "Well, as long as you were thorough, we'll give you an A for effort."

With a grunt of exertion, he rose and made an act of dusting off his knees. "An A, huh? And what does that get me?"

She raised one eyebrow and puckered her lips. "Oh, you might be surprised. I know how to reward a good boy with a good grade."

He bent down and nuzzled her ear. "It might be more fun if we pretend I was a bad boy and you punish me."

"I thought we saved stuff like that for Friday nights."

He sighed. "We're going to have to change our naughtiness schedule around a little bit. I talked to your brother Waycross about an hour ago, and he says your grandma is on a plane headed here right now. We might have to postpone some of our more adventurous stuff until after she leaves."

Savannah nodded thoughtfully. "That's true. We'll definitely have to reschedule Monkey Jungle Love Night."

"Much, much too noisy, with her right down the hall." For a second, he looked a bit pensive. "That *is* where she's staying, right? My man cave's gonna be a guest room for a while, I guess."

"Yeah. Sorry, sugar."

"Hey, anything for Granny. She is the best."

"I thought she wasn't supposed to get here until tomorrow at the earliest."

"Me too. But Waycross said she pulled one of her 'Poor Ol' Widder Woman' routines at the standby counter, and they let her on board an earlier flight."

Savannah laughed. "And knowing Gran, she probably

got to sit in first class, too. When is her flight coming in? We'll have to go to LAX to pick her up."

"She's getting in about seven." He glanced at his watch. "About four hours from now. But Waycross and Tammy already volunteered to go get her."

"More like they called dibs on the privilege."

"Yes, Granny's a pretty popular gal in these parts."

Savannah glanced around and saw several objects lying on the counter near the sink. "Are those the fruits of your murder weapon search? Your most likely suspects?"

"Not really. They're the right shape, but I've pretty much ruled them all out."

Picking the items up, one by one, he explained his reasoning. "Here we've got a rolling pin, which would be perfect except that it's too wide."

Savannah nodded. "Dr. Liu said it was probably an inch. That sucker's three inches, at least."

He picked up a turkey baster. "Way too light."

"You couldn't beat a housefly to death with that thing."

He showed her a pepper mill and the soap dispenser. "Same with these gadgets. They're the right shape, but they're way too fragile to get the job done."

He showed her another strange item that looked like an enormous screw of some sort. "And I don't even know what the hell this thing is."

"A pineapple corer."

"Seriously? And how do you know something like that?"

She shrugged. "I'm a woman. We know everything."

"And if you don't, you just make it up on the spot."

"We have been known to get creative from time to time—when the situation calls for it."

She searched the kitchen for anything that he might have overlooked. But if there was something that Detective Dirk Coulter was good at, it was processing a crime scene.

And looking good in a pair of jeans.

And inventing new uses for Chantilly cream.

There was also his ability to surrender something as precious as his man cave for a beloved grandmother, without registering much of a complaint.

Savannah decided that maybe she'd keep him after all.

"Did you look outside yet?" she asked him.

He gave her a blank, brainwave-free stare, not unlike when he asked her where they kept the ice cubes. "Outside?"

"Yeah. You know, you walk over there, and you open the door, and you step out there, where there's no roof over your head—just sky and birds and trees. That's called 'outside.'"

His eyes narrowed as he gave her his best Clint Eastwood, gunfight-at-high-noon glower. "You know, Reid . . . you can be a real smart-ass sometimes."

She turned and headed for the rear door, making sure to put a little extra Southern belle sashay in her step as she walked. "And I've heard that sometimes bad guys stash murder weapons and interesting stuff like that. . . . Are you ready for it? Here it comes. . . . That's right, boys and girls! *Outside!*"

She took one more sashay-enhanced step.

His hand connected with her backside.

"Ouch!"

* * *

Having spent a bit of time in alleys while a beat cop, Savannah had never failed to be amazed at how different they were from the heavily traveled streets and byways of an ordinary American town.

In tidy communities, heaven help you if you tossed a candy wrapper on the sidewalk. But only a few yards away, you could dump everything from decrepit mattresses to old Studebakers, to a dead body, in an alley, and it might go unnoticed for ages.

Except by the street people, who found and put society's castoffs to good use.

A discarded tee-shirt might double a homeless man's wardrobe. A worn chair gave a less fortunate person an alternative to sitting on cold cement. And a rusty length of pipe, left over from a plumbing project, could provide a modicum of self-protection to someone who had no walls and no locked doors or windows to keep them safe from the criminal element.

After half an hour or more of searching along rusty fences and in smelly garbage bins and behind rotten boards, Savannah decided that if a murder weapon had been stashed here in the alley, somebody had absconded with it.

So much for my "Let's Find It Outside" theory, she thought, as her headache returned and her limbs started to tremble with fatigue.

"So much for your know-it-all idea about finding something out here," Dirk told her as she tried to rub some evil-looking, green mystery stain off the palm of her left hand.

She groaned and resisted the nearly overpowering urge to smack him . . . with the stained palm, of course.

If there was anything more annoying than Dirk's oc-casional rude comment, it was when his words echoed her own self-incriminating thoughts.

"Yeah, well, I have to admit that we didn't come up with anything good out here, like that deadly turkey baster you found in the kitchen."

"Do you guys mind if I ask what you're looking for?" said a male voice behind them.

Savannah turned around and saw the same homeless fellow they had encountered the night of the tasting. He was walking toward them, limping as he had been that evening.

By daylight, she could get a much better look at him. And she realized he was younger than she had thought when first meeting him. Before, she had judged him to be in his fifties, possibly even his early sixties. But now she could see that he was closer to forty. Though it was obvious that at least some of those forty years had been tough ones.

His skin was deeply lined and spotted from sun ex-posure, and his beard and hair were liberally sprinkled with gray. His pants were desert camouflage, not just dirty as she had originally thought. But it was difficult to tell the original color of his badly faded T-shirt. On his feet he wore sneakers, the fronts of which were wrapped with duct tape.

Then she realized that he was scrutinizing her attire and Dirk's as closely as she was his.

He snickered behind his overgrown mustache and said, "You two clean up pretty good. And you look a lot younger in the daylight."

Savannah laughed, remembering that the last time

he had seen them they had been dressed in their under-cover, senior citizen garb.

Dirk glanced down at the camouflage pants. "Marines? Afghanistan? Pre-2000?"

The man nodded.

"Is that where you got the limp?" Dirk asked.

Savannah cringed, but the guy didn't seem to take offense. He just gave another solemn nod.

"I'm Dirk Coulter." Dirk extended his hand. "This is my wife, Savannah. It's nice to meet you."

Shaking Dirk's hand, he said, "I'm Otis Emmett."

"Thank you for your service, Mr. Emmett," Savannah told him, offering her hand as well. "I appreciate what you did, and especially your sacrifice," she added, nodding toward his lame leg.

"Thanks," he replied, returning her handshake without enthusiasm. "It's nice to hear that somebody does."

He was beginning to look uncomfortable with the topic of conversation, so she decided to change it. "You asked what we're searching for," she said. "Frankly, we're trying to find the murder weapon. You must've heard what happened to the chef in that restaurant the other night."

"Of course we did. That's all we've been talking about."

"We?" she asked.

He waved his arm wide, as though indicating the alley in both directions. "We who live back here. There're lots of us. But most stay hidden when people like you are out here."

Feeling a bit uneasy, Savannah glanced around. She couldn't help wondering who was watching at that moment, who might've been watching for the past half hour as they made fools of themselves, searching and finding nothing.

"What kind of weapon are you looking for?" he asked. "Maybe I can help you find it. After all, this is my home—so to speak."

"A cylindrical object, about an inch wide," Savannah replied.

"Something heavy and hard enough to do some substantial damage," Dirk added.

"That's weird," Otis said. "We heard he was stabbed to death."

A guarded expression crossed Dirk's face.

Savannah knew that look. Most cops played their cards close to their vests. Dirk kept his in a safe in his back pocket. He gave away only what he absolutely had to in the course of an investigation.

While it wasn't her natural inclination to leave a single word unsaid, she had to agree that his method was best.

"Yeah," Dirk replied. "If you happen to see a big bloody knife lying around somewhere, we'd like to know about that, too."

Savannah took a step closer to Emmett. "I'll bet you see a lot that goes on back here in this alley, don't you?"

He gave a curt nod.

"As a military man, you're a trained observer. I'll bet not much of anything gets past you."

"Yeah, but what I see, and what I hear . . . I keep to myself. I stay out of trouble that way."

"I can understand that," Savannah said. "But you traveled all the way to Afghanistan to fight for freedom and justice. A man like that doesn't stop fighting for those precious things just because he comes home."

Otis looked down at his feet and shuffled from one mismatched, duct-taped sneaker to the other. "I guess that's true. What do you guys want to know?"

"Absolutely everything that you saw or heard that night," Dirk told him. "We'll take anything you've got."

"But first," Savannah said, "why don't we go inside out of this hot sun. I've got a sudden hankerin' to buy one of this country's war veterans a drink."

"Sorry it's just a beer," Savannah told Otis Emmett as she and Dirk sat across from him at a table in the corner of the restaurant. "But they aren't set up to serve food just yet."

She was keeping her voice low, so as not to interfere with Ryan and John's continued staff meeting.

Otis closed his eyes, savoring a long draft of the beer in a frosty mug. Then he licked the foam off his mustache and said, "Don't worry about that. I'm just so happy to have this. I don't remember when anything tasted this good."

"I'm glad you're enjoying it," she said. "There's another where that one came from, once you're finished."

"But sooner or later you're gonna have to tell us what you saw," Dirk interjected. "Ain't nothin' free in this world, you know."

"Yes," Otis said. "I know that all too well."

"Then let's hear it." Dirk pulled his notebook and pen out of his jacket pocket. "Everything you've got."

Otis drained the glass, settled back in the booth, and began, "You're going to want to hear what happened the first night they all showed up here. The night I met the two of you, and you were wearing those funny old clothes."

Dirk bristled a bit but didn't say anything. Savannah knew he was taking offense at having his mother's gift, the flannel plaid shirt, called "funny" and "old."

She would remember this the next time he insisted on wearing it out to dinner. Her argument would go something like: "Even a street person made fun of that shirt, Dirk. You aren't going out with me, dressed like a homeless lumberjack."

"You're referring to the night of the tasting," Savannah told Otis.

"I didn't get to taste anything."

"It was an audition, of sorts, for Chef Norwood, to show the new owners—those two fellas sitting there at the bar—what he could do."

"Well, whatever the reason they were here, some stuff went down that night that might have led to what happened later."

"What did you see?" Dirk asked, obviously growing impatient.

"I saw that chef—the big, tall, fat guy—just outside the back door, pushing himself onto a pretty young woman. I heard her tell him that she had just dropped by to give her husband some bus fare so he could get home later. But the big guy was trying to kiss her, trying to feel her up. And it was obvious she didn't want anything to do with him. It was disgusting."

Otis reached up and ran his fingers through his matted beard, as though combing it. "I was just about to go over and tell him to leave her alone when that guy over there came out of the door and told him to stop or else."

"Which guy?" Savannah asked, anticipating the answer.

"The tall, skinny Mexican kid, sitting at the end of the row."

Savannah and Dirk turned to look, but she knew he was referring to Manuel.

So Manuel had pulled the chef off Celia more than once. Savannah noted the fact that neither of them had mentioned that.

Liking both of them as much as she did, she hoped their little omission wasn't indicative of anything too incriminating.

"Okay," Dirk said. "That's good to know. What else?"

"There was another argument even before that," Otis continued. "The big guy had it out with some fancy dude. I don't see him over there."

"How did that go down?" Dirk asked.

"It was before the rest of those workers got here. The only ones here were those two guys you say own the place and the chef. Then some rich poser type pulls up back there in the alley in a fancy Mercedes. He gets out and goes through the back door. It wasn't half a minute before I could hear the chef and him arguing like crazy."

"They were yelling?"

"No, more like hissing under their breath. I figured they didn't want the others to hear them."

"But you heard them," Dirk said, cutting him a suspicious look.

Otis grinned. "Okay, I'll admit it. I sorta worked at hearing them. I was back by the rear door checking out the car when I heard this pissed-off whispering talk, so I had to check it out. I'm the curious type."

"Me too," Savannah said. "I understand completely. Please continue."

"The fancy guy was saying something like, 'This is why you left me? You're deserting me and our business when it's in trouble? In trouble because of you, that is. And you're doing it for *this* dump?'"

Savannah felt her blood pressure rise at the term "dump." ReJuvene was a beautiful restaurant. Who did that guy think he was anyway?

Actually, she had a theory about who he was.

"Did you catch a name?" she asked.

"Yeah. The chef called him 'Yale' as he was leaving. He didn't stay long at all. Yale . . . that's kinda a hoity-toity name for a dude, don't you think?"

"Not especially," Dirk said, "but if you think so, when I have a son, I won't name him Harvard or Oxford."

"Did anything else happen that first night?" Savannah asked Otis.

Something crossed his eyes, something she couldn't quite put her finger on, but before she had a chance to analyze the moment, it had passed.

"Other than the fact that they wouldn't give you a handout," Dirk said.

"Yeah, that." Otis shrugged. "Whatcha gonna do? Some people are generous and buy you a cold beer. Some people wouldn't give you the mud scrapings off the bottom of their shoe. Go figure."

"Then let's go on to the night when Norwood was murdered," Savannah said. "Please tell us everything you heard and saw, and don't leave anything out."

"That's the funny thing about it," Otis said. "I didn't see much that night. There was one little squabble, some yelling, cursing, and a couple of pans flying. But that was about it . . . until . . . you know . . . afterward."

"Tell us about the squabble," Savannah said.

"I heard the chef yell at somebody. You could tell it was him, because he had that deep, unusual kind of voice. He always talked like he was being interviewed on television or reading the news, you know?"

Savannah chuckled at this simple but accurate description of Chef Norwood's pretentious delivery. "Yes," she said, "we know. Go on."

"I sneaked over to the door and listened to see what was up." He blushed a bit. "I know it's not very classy to eavesdrop like that, but without TV or the Internet, we don't get a lot of entertainment on the streets."

"So you sneaked up to the door, and what did you hear?" Dirk said, growing impatient.

"I heard the chef yelling at that guy, Manuel. He was chucking pots and pans at him and telling him that if he didn't like working for him, he could get the hell out. Then some other people came into the room and put a stop to it."

"Yeah, we were some of those people," Dirk said. He glanced over at the staff. "But the people in the kitchen wouldn't tell us what the fight was about or who was involved. Norwood just ordered everybody out of 'his' kitchen."

"What happened next?" Savannah said. "Please try to remember everything you saw and heard from that argument with the pots being thrown until—"

"Until that other chef gal started screaming bloody murder?" Otis interjected.

"Yes. Exactly."

"Nothing. I mean, nothing important. I guess they were just cooking and serving and all that. After a while, three of them came outside to smoke."

"Which three?" Dirk asked.

"The two Mexican guys over there and that chef gal with all the crazy tattoos."

"They stayed out there how long?" Savannah asked.

"Oh, I don't know. Long enough to smoke one cigarette. Then the gal went inside."

Savannah perked up. "She did?"

"Yeah. I heard her say she had to go to the bathroom. And that's when the tall Mexican kid came over to me and asked me if I was hungry . . . if I'd like something to eat. He said he felt bad that they hadn't given me anything that first night and he wanted to make it up to me."

"And he went inside by himself?" Dirk asked.

"Yeah, but don't go thinking anything suspicious about my buddy there. I walked right to the door with him. I could see inside, all the time, he was making me up a big takeout container, and he didn't kill anybody."

"Could you see Chef Norwood through that open door?" Savannah asked.

"Yeah, I saw him, but he was facing away from me, and he didn't see me. He was all absorbed with shoveling food into his mouth."

"So Manuel made you a container of food, and the chef was still alive at that point," Dirk reiterated, "and that Francia gal was in the bathroom and Carlos was still standing outside?"

Otis nodded. "Having a second smoke."

Savannah glanced around the room, recalling the scene from her point of view. "And the two servers and a busboy were in here, cleaning up, and so was the bartender."

"Everybody's accounted for," Dirk said, dejected.

"Okay," Otis continued, "then this guy you're calling Manuel came out with my dinner. I sat down on the other side of the alley on that old tractor tire. I was eating it and thinking it was about the best food I'd ever ate in my life when all hell broke loose with that screaming. Man, that gal has a set of lungs on her!"

Savannah recalled the sound—all too well. The memory of those shrieks still caused her skin to crawl and her headache to pound.

She pressed her forefingers to her temples. "Then you're absolutely sure that nobody, nobody at all, walked in or out of that back door between the time that you saw Chef Norwood standing there alive in the kitchen and when you heard Francia scream?"

"Absolutely sure. I'd stake my life on it." He stopped to drain yet another drop from his beer mug. "I was pretty excited about that dinner. It was the best I've had in years. But if anybody had walked through that doorway, I would've seen them."

"How can you be so sure you would have noticed?" Dirk asked.

"Because I was watching that door like a hawk. I was afraid the chef would come out and see me eating his food and try to take it away from me. I had to make sure that didn't happen, because I was dying to taste that raspberry pie thing."

"You and me both," Savannah said with a sigh. "You and me both." She turned to Dirk. "Whatcha say, big boy? Does our new best friend, Otis, deserve another beer?"

Dirk jumped to his feet. "Another cold one for the best—and only—eyewitness we have in this stinkin' rotten case. And while I'm at it, Otis, my man, I'll see if I can round you up some pretzels."

Otis smiled broadly. "Now you're talkin'. And if you can score me some peanuts, I'd take those off your hands, too."

Chapter 16

"Van, are you sure you feel okay?" Dirk asked her when they were heading home from the restaurant. "I don't mind driving if you aren't up to it."

He reached over and placed his hand on her thigh. "And I'm not just trying to finagle a way to drive the Mustang either."

She gave him a suspicious sideways glance, but the sincere look on his face told her that he was seriously concerned.

"Don't fret," she told him. "You know I can't stand it when you fret."

He gave her leg a squeeze. "Babe, I passed the 'fret' stage a couple of days ago. Now I'm starting to get worried. You're tired all the time. You're cranky all the time. You've been dizzy a lot. And today at the beach you did a serious face plant in the sand. Something's wrong."

She groaned and shook her head. "Dirk, how many years have you known me? During all of those years

I've been tired and cranky. And how many times have you called me a 'dizzy broad'?"

"That was a term of endearment, and you know it. I want you to go to the doctor and get checked out."

"No."

"Why the hell not?"

"Lots of reasons. I don't have time to right now. We're working this case. And now Gran's here, and I need to entertain her. Your mom and dad are coming for a visit next month, and I need to repaint the living room and kitchen before that. But most of all, I don't go to the doctor unless I'm sick. And I'm not sick—except maybe sick of having people worry about me when they don't need to."

She turned the Mustang down her street, but she pulled over to the curb several houses before hers.

Turning in her seat, she faced Dirk directly and gave him one of her icy stares—specifically designed to strike terror in the heart of the staree.

"Now you listen to me, you worrywart husband of mine. I want you to stop this right now. We're almost home, where Granny is going to be waiting with open arms. I haven't seen her for a month of Sundays, and I want this visit to be really nice for her and us. So don't you dare mention a word of this again until after she has left. I don't want her to hear you get all in a tizzy about nothing. You hear me?"

He matched her, stare for stare, and said, "I promise you that I won't say anything in front of her, 'cause I don't want to worry her either. But if you and me are in a room by ourselves, all bets are off."

Before she knew what he was doing or could fend him off, he had grabbed her and nailed her with one of his best, knee-wobbling kisses.

When he finally let her come up for air, he said, "I listened to you. Now you listen to me. I put a wedding ring on your finger, girl. A pretty damned nice one at that."

She glanced down at the gorgeous diamond on her finger. There was no denying that one. When it counted, stingy, cheap ol' Dirk had broken character and forked over the big bucks. She had to give him that.

"That affords me certain privileges," he continued. "And before you make some unladylike, silly joke, it's not just between the sheets that I get to exercise those husbandly rights."

As he paused for a breath, Savannah debated whether to reach up and yank out a wad of his hair or to grab him, hold him tight, and ask him for another one of those kisses.

Before she could decide, he recovered his wind and continued his speech. "I've got only one of you, Van," he said. "While, most of the time, that's more than enough, I do want to keep the one I've got for as long as I can. So get that pretty little butt of yours to the doctor and find out what's going on with you."

She sighed and shook her head. Then she drove the Mustang back onto the road and headed for home.

"You're plumb crazy, you know," she said as she pulled into their driveway.

"For wanting my wife to go to the doctor when she needs to? That makes me crazy?"

"No. That makes you a sweetheart." She reached over and chucked him under the chin. "But calling my overly curvaceous, abundantly proportioned butt 'little' . . . boy, that makes you nuttier than squirrel poo."

* * *

When Savannah stepped into her living room, all hell broke loose.

Actually, the screaming, the running, the outflung arms, the grabbing and the grappling, the free-flowing of tears—it was all just Savannah greeting her grandmother and vice versa.

A bystander who wasn't familiar with the overly rambunctious, spirited customs of the Reid family's womenfolk might have thought it was a reenactment of the First Battle of Bull Run.

As a child, one of Savannah's favorite things in the world was to have her grandmother pick her up and twirl her around in a circle while both laughed uproariously. But over the years—and neither of them could remember the exact moment it had happened—their roles had reversed. It was now Savannah who did the picking up and twirling.

But the hysterical giggling and the tight, lingering, loving hug that followed were the same.

Dirk, Tammy, and Waycross stood quietly by, smiling and waiting for peace to be restored. Long ago, they had learned not to interfere with this ritual.

It was a matter of self-preservation. Amidst all the running, screaming, twirling, and hugging, one could get hurt.

When they were finally finished, Gran turned to Dirk and opened her arms to receive him. He, too, gave her a hearty hug, though it would have registered a bit lower on the Richter scale.

"Why, darlin', just look at you!" she said, as she placed her soft hands on his cheeks and turned his face from side to side, checking him out. "I swear, you get handsomer every day. Seems that being married to my granddaughter has done you a good turn."

"It sure has, Granny. But I'm getting fat eating her good food three times a day."

"Aw, hush that nonsense. People make way too much of a fuss over that weight business. When I was a girl, the old-timers used to say, 'You need an extra ten pounds on your bones, just in case you get sick.' If you get too skinny, you might blow away in a windstorm."

Savannah glanced over her grandmother's figure, which, even under the billowing, floral-print caftan, appeared quite rotund. And looking down at her own ample curves, she did a bit of quick math and decided that the Reid family could survive several bouts of the bubonic plague without worrying about cyclones and such.

A bit weary from the exertion of grandma-whirling, Savannah felt the sudden need to sit down in her comfy chair. But good, old-fashioned Southern hospitality demanded that some sort of refreshment be served before the hostess's hind end was allowed to touch a chair of any kind.

"How about a big, tall glass of sweet tea, Gran?" Savannah asked her. "And some chocolate chip macadamia cookies to go along with it. I know you like pecans better, but I baked them to bribe a medical examiner, and she's not from Georgia, poor girl."

Gran smiled up at Savannah, her bright, young eyes sparkling in an old, wise face. "You know me too well, sugar. I never met a cookie I didn't like."

Savannah turned toward the kitchen a bit too abruptly, and once again the floor beneath her began to tilt a bit. She hesitated only for a second, but that was long enough for Dirk to take notice.

"Hey," he said, reaching for her arm. "Let me go get that tea and the cookies. You girls have got a lot of

catching up to do. So sit down over there, make yourselves comfortable, and get to it."

Savannah looked up at him and, for a moment, she
just stood there, loving him with her eyes—not just for
his offer of help but for covering for her with Granny.

"Why, thank you, darlin'," she said. "Aren't you just
the sweetest thing? Grab yourself an extra cookie for
payment."

He chuckled as he walked away. "Why do you think
I offered to do it?"

"Now there's the Dirk-o we know and love," Tammy
said as she and Waycross settled close to each other on
the sofa.

Savannah couldn't help noticing that Granny noticed. But that was to be expected. Gran had raised two
children of her own and nine grandchildren besides.
Over the years she had perfected the fine art of super-
vising young people. And part of that skill was knowing, at all times, who was doing what with whom in the
Romance Department.

Wasting no time, Savannah made her way back across
the room to her rose-print, chintz-covered chair. She sank
into it gratefully and waited for the inevitable onslaught
of black furriness. It didn't take long for her lap to be
filled with cats, both of them begging for attention.

Granny walked over to her, reached down, and scooped
up Cleo. Then she strolled over to the unoccupied end of
the sofa and sat down.

As she stroked the cat's glossy head, she said to Savannah, "These two"—she nodded toward Tammy and
Waycross—"have been filling me in on the case you're
working on now. Sounds like a doozy."

"I won't lie. It's a bit of a stumper."

"Then tell me all about it—don't spare any of the gory details—so's I can figure it out for you."

Savannah gave her grandmother a searching look and realized that she was completely serious. More than once, Gran in her infinite wisdom had solved a case for them, or at least found evidence that was instrumental in wrapping it up.

Far be it from her to disregard this offer of assistance. Why not avail herself of such valuable services, when the price of said services was a glass of sweet tea and a handful of chocolate chip cookies?

At that moment Dirk arrived with a tray loaded with the goodies. Only for a moment Savannah held her breath as he walked across the room and set his burden on the coffee table.

Yes, he was getting better and better at this domestic stuff. No doubt about it, and of course, as his wife and trainer in all such matters, she took credit for his improvement.

After all, when she had met him he had owned one plate, one fork, a spoon, and a Swiss Army knife. Platters and serving bowls were unnecessary, as he ate everything out of whatever packaging it had been in when he'd purchased it at the grocery or convenience store.

As he began to distribute glasses of tea, napkins, and cookies, Savannah told him, "Granny wants to help with our case."

"Of course she does," he said. "Why do you think she came out here? Just to see our ugly mugs?"

Granny nabbed two cookies, then held them close to her chest to keep them away from an overly curious Cleo. "Now, now," she said. "You know that your ugly mugs will always be my first priority. But a murder case, especially one that's nigh to impossible to solve, that does run a close second."

She looked over at Savannah, then Waycross, with a light of pride shining in her eyes. "My family, we're good at this crime-solving stuff. It runs in our blood. We have a fierce sense of justice and a heap of nosiness besides. And that makes us good detectives."

"Does that go for me, too?" Dirk asked.

Granny smiled. "Reckon it goes double for you. Not only are you part of the family, but you actually chose to be—not like these knuckleheads who just got born in. No offense, y'all."

Waycross reached over and patted his grandmother's hand. "No offense taken, Gran. Now, let Savannah go over that list of suspects on her board, and you can tell us who done it."

"You're right. It's a dadgum stumper," Gran said an hour later, as they all stared at Savannah's poster board, which was now lying in the middle of the coffee table next to the empty pitcher.

The bits of paper with the various suspects' names had been moved around from one corner to the other and shifted from one column to the next.

Now that Otis Emmett had established alibis for Manuel Cervantes and Carlos Ortez, they had joined Perla Viola in the lower-right-hand corner.

Squinting at the board—because she would never admit that she needed glasses—Granny frowned and said, "Are you sure that Viola gal passes muster? 'Cause you know as well as I do that the murderer is almost always somebody the victim is sleeping with or slept with. . . .

Not that a lot of sleeping goes on in those cases. 'Sleeping' is just what they call fornication these days."

She cast a quick, suspicious glance at her grandson, sitting next to her.

Quickly, Savannah put her hand over her mouth, hiding a smirk. With Waycross's cheeks flushing as red as his hair, there was no doubt that he had the look of a fornicator about him.

And Tammy's nervous tittering was equally incriminating.

Savannah half-expected Granny to produce a hickory switch and give them a tanning out behind the barn. Or the garage, as the case might be.

Dirk, having watched the silent exchange, again came to the rescue. "I checked out Perla Viola's alibi. It's solid. She and her daughter were at that play in Hollywood— that *Phantom* thing. I called the theater and had them check the ticket numbers. They were used. And the *Playbill* she gave me had this extra paper stuck inside it, saying that one of the main parts was being played by a different gal that night. The theater manager told me that was the only night that particular insert was given out. So, no doubt about it, she and her daughter were there."

Tammy stared down at her tablet in her lap while her fingers flew over its screen. "Yes, that's right. That night the character Carlotta was played by the understudy."

Savannah smiled, thinking that her little friend was trying way too hard. She still felt bad about having given them inaccurate information about Manuel and Celia and was attempting to make up for it. Tammy was a perfectionist when it came to her passion, and her passion was "sleuthing."

But judging from how close she and Waycross were sitting on the sofa—hip to hip and thigh to thigh—Savannah more than suspected that "sleuthing" might have slipped to second place on Tammy's priority list.

That was just peachy keen, fine and dandy, with Savannah. But time would tell whether it was all right with Granny.

"What about this guy who went to Yale?" Waycross asked.

"He didn't go to Yale," Savannah replied. "His *name* is Yale."

"He might've gone to Yale," Dirk interjected. "He certainly has enough money."

"We're going to interview him tomorrow." Savannah took a drink of her ice tea, wishing that its invigorating frostiness would alleviate her headache. So far, it hadn't. And neither had the aspirins she had snuck earlier. If it didn't let up at least a little bit, she wasn't going to feel like eating supper with the rest of them. And that would be an all-time, record-breaking first that everybody was bound to notice.

"I'm not expecting much from that face-to-face," she continued. "Yale may have had a falling out with Norwood, but all we've got is him showing up for a few minutes at the restaurant kitchen, having a brief argument, and then leaving. Nobody saw him anywhere near the restaurant the day of the murder."

Dirk agreed. "We'll talk to him, go through the motions. No stone unturned and all that. But we've got no real reason to think it was him."

"That leaves you with this Francia person," Gran said, pointing to the bit of paper with the sous-chef's name on it.

"Yes," Savannah said. "That leaves us with Francia.

When you track everybody there that night, she was the only one who had both motive and opportunity."

"You're right. It seems everybody had a motive," Tammy replied. "But Francia was the only one unaccounted for when the murder actually occurred."

Dirk popped half a cookie into his mouth and chewed it as he said, "That's the second rule of homicide investigation—right after Rule Number One: The spouse/ex-spouse/lover did it. Rule Number Two: It's the one who reports it. And boy, did she ever report it. That gal should get a job screaming for horror movies. She's got screeching down pat."

"Now that you mention it," Savannah remarked, recalling her conversation with Francia right after the murder, "she seemed pretty calm when we were talking at the table."

"Maybe all that screamin' and hollerin' was just a show," Gran suggested. "Wouldn't be the first time in the history of the world that a guilty person pitched a ungodly fit just so's they'd look innocent."

Savannah nodded. "Ain't it the truth."

Two hours later, when supper had been cooked and eaten and the dishes done, Tammy and Waycross said good-bye and left Savannah, Dirk, and Granny to themselves.

Although Savannah was enjoying her grandmother's company enormously, she couldn't help being relieved when Gran suggested an early turn-in.

"I'm sorry," she said, "but I'm still on Georgia time and it's three hours past my bedtime. I'm liable to turn into a pumpkin any minute now."

"Of course, Gran. That's fine," Savannah said, rising

from her chair and placing Diamante on the footstool. "Let me walk you up to the guestroom. There's been a few changes in it since you were here, and I'll have to show you where the extra quilts are now."

Granny rose, set Cleo next to her sister, and walked over to Dirk.

When he stood, she gave him a peck on the cheek. "Thank you for giving up your . . . what do they call it, a 'man cave'? . . . for me. I sure 'preciate it."

"Any time, Granny. It's nothing, really."

"It is, too. It's a matter of privacy and solitude. Both of those things are precious and in low supply these days. If you get a hankerin' while I'm here to be by yourself, you just kick me out and run right in there. I'll understand. You hear?"

Dirk pulled her to his chest and gave her a bear hug. "Don't you worry about that. I'll be fine. I'm just so glad you came to visit us."

Savannah watched them, enjoying the obvious and genuine affection between them—the two people she loved most in the world. What a joy it was for her, to have them not only like each other but love one another. A blessing, indeed.

Once Gran had said good night to Dirk, Savannah led her up to the spare bedroom.

Gone were the frilly curtains, the girlie bedspread, and the fluffy alpaca rug. A simple daybed and a throw rug with the Dodgers symbol had taken their place.

Instead of framed floral prints on the wall, there were shelves lined with Harley-Davidson memorabilia. Not expensive collectors' items. Just ashtrays and shot glasses and a few cheap snow globes with motorcycles in them instead of Christmas scenes. But they were Dirk's treasures. And Savannah knew that Gran would appreciate them as such.

"I hope you're comfortable," Savannah said. "The daybed isn't nearly as soft as my old mattress was, but—"

"Stop your frettin', sweet pea," Gran told her. "I'm so tired, I could fall asleep standin' up, here and now."

"Then I'll leave you be. If there's anything else I can do for you . . ."

"Just one more thing, so's I can get a good night's sleep with a clear mind."

"What's that, Gran?"

Granny stepped closer to Savannah, reached up, and placed her hand on her granddaughter's forehead, as she had done so many times when Savannah was a child.

"What you can do," Gran said, "is tell me what's amiss with you."

Savannah put on her best "innocent" look and said, "Nothing. Why do you ask?"

"I ask because your face is pale as a haunt and you've got dark circles under your eyes. I spied you rubbing your temples earlier this evenin', and I know that's means you got a headache. Plus you're moving slower than you used to. In my book, that adds up to somethin' or the other bein' wrong."

Savannah gulped and tried her best to look straight into her grandmother's bright blue eyes and not blink.

It wasn't easy, lying to Granny, for more reasons than one.

In the first place, standing there in the soft, golden light of the lamp, Granny's silver hair glistened like a halo around her head. More than once, when Savannah was a girl, she had truly believed that her grandmother might be an angel in disguise. And she certainly looked like one now, as she gazed up with love and concern at her granddaughter's face.

Then there was the second reason. Above all things, Granny Reid had impressed upon her offspring the necessity of telling the truth at all times. Especially when they were speaking to their grandmother. Because if there was anything Granny hated, it was being lied to. And if there was one reason why she would take you behind the barn and switch you until you danced an Irish jig, lying was it.

Therefore, between the love and respect she had for her grandmother and the fear instilled at such an early age, Savannah could scarcely let the words pass her lips. But she managed to, knowing it was for Granny's own good in the long run.

Any minute now, Savannah believed that whatever was going on inside her body and knocking her off kilter would straighten itself out and she would be back to normal. And then all this worrying would have been for naught. Until then, the less her family knew about what was going on inside her, the better.

Granny nodded thoughtfully, then said, "Okay. It's plain as the nose on your face that you don't want to tell me. And since you ain't a youngun no more, I can't rightly force you. So I reckon I'll wait until you're ready to talk about it."

Savannah fought back the hot tears that sprang to her eyes. She gathered Granny in her arms and gave her a tight, long hug.

"Thank you, Gran," she said. "I love you."

"I love you, too, my brave, strong girl . . . all the way to the moon and the stars and then back again."

*   *   *

When Savannah left her grandmother in the guest room and went downstairs to take another couple of aspirins, she was relieved to see that Dirk had already gone upstairs to their bedroom.

For what she needed to do next, she wanted a bit of privacy.

On the way to the kitchen, she scooped up her cell phone from the end table beside her comfy chair and shoved it into her jeans pocket.

As soon as she had downed the aspirin with a half-glass of milk, she made her way to the downstairs bathroom at the rear of the house.

After glancing around one more time to make sure that Dirk was nowhere nearby, she ducked into the bathroom.

She scrolled down the list of numbers in her phone until she found the one she was looking for, and she called it. It took about five rings before there was an answer.

"Dr. Dalano's answering service. May I help you?"

Savannah took a breath and plunged into the cold, dark water of the deep end. "Yes, um, this is Savannah Reid. I'm one of Dr. Dalano's patients. I need to come in and see her as soon as possible."

"Is this an emergency?"

Is this an emergency? The question raced over and over through Savannah's mind, causing her fear factor to rise several degrees.

Finally, she said, "No. I don't think so. Not like an emergency room kind of emergency. But I do need to see her. Tomorrow, if she can fit me in."

"Then I think the best thing for you to do is to call

the office tomorrow morning and schedule an appointment," the operator told her.

"Would it be possible for you to just give her office the message? Maybe they could text me at this number and tell me what time to show up."

"I'll forward your message to their receptionist, Ms. Reid. You can expect to receive a text from her tomorrow."

"Thank you. I appreciate it."

As soon as she gave the operator her phone number and wished her good night, Savannah felt her knees suddenly go so weak that they wouldn't hold her. She sat down abruptly on the toilet.

In an instant, it felt as though every molecule of oxygen had left the room and she had nothing to breathe. Her heart began to pound as she struggled for air. Her hands shook violently as she reached into a nearby cupboard, pulled out a washcloth, and wet it in the sink. Pressing it to her face, she shuddered and, for the second time in the past five minutes, fought back tears.

"What's happening to me?" she whispered. "Good Lord in heaven, what's going on inside me?"

As she had expected, no deep, celestial voice boomed an answer from up above. Nor did her body send any discernible reply from deep inside.

Gradually her heart rate began to slow, and her trembling stopped. She could breathe again, and the cold, wet washcloth felt good against her face.

Once again, she decided to send a message skyward. "I don't mind telling you, I'm a little worried about this. And I try not to bother you about stuff that I can work out on my own, seeing as how you've got famines and wars and a lot bigger fish to fry than my measly concerns. But so far, I'm not doing so hot with trying to handle this one alone. So tomorrow, if you've got the time and are so inclined, I'd sure appreciate a little help."

As before, there was no rumbling, thunderous reply. And for that, she was somewhat grateful, because, no doubt, such a thing would have sent her right over the edge.

But as Savannah hung her washcloth to dry on the towel rack, picked up her phone from the edge of the sink, and left the tiny bathroom, she felt much better than she had when she'd entered it.

Booming voice or not, something deep inside told her that her request had been heard and would be answered.

Whatever this strangeness in her body might be and whatever happened as a result, she would get through it.

Her husband loved her. Her grandmother loved her. And her family loved her—both the ones she had been gifted with biologically and the ones her heart had chosen.

With all that love and some help from up above, she was bound to make it through.

Chapter 17

"Granny was pouting something fierce when we left. Did you notice?" Savannah asked Dirk as they exited the 101 Freeway and drove inland toward the small, rural community of Twin Oaks.

"No kidding. I thought she was going to 'pitch a hissy fit,' as you Confederates call it, when we were walking out the door." Dirk reached into the glove compartment and pulled out his baggy of cinnamon sticks.

"I know. I feel so guilty. Deserting your own grandmother after she's traveled three thousand miles just to look upon her loved ones' faces. What kind of granddaughter does a thing like that? Lower than a snake in snowshoes—that's me."

Dirk shot her a quizzical look. "Do you really believe that she was pouting because she is not going to get to see your face for a few hours?"

Savannah shrugged. "Well, yeah. I guess so. Why?"

Laughing, he stuck the cinnamon stick in his mouth. "You goofy girl. I'm sure your grandma loves that sweet mug of yours, but I guarantee you that's not why she was in a foul mood this morning."

"Then why?"

"Because, my darling, she overheard us saying that we were going to question a suspect. And she would've liked to have tagged along."

Savannah rolled up the Mustang's window as the stink of the oil fields replaced the fresh scent of the ocean. On either side of the highway, big black pumps bobbed up and down, drawing oil from deep inside the earth to the surface.

To Savannah, they looked like colorless, oversized versions of the wonderful bobbing bird toy that Waycross had won for her many years ago when a carnival had passed through their hometown. She had loved that little guy, which she had named Dippy, with his red body and bright yellow hat. For hours she had watched in delight as he dipped his beak into a glass of water, then happily rocked back and forth.

One swipe of the family cat's paw had sent Dippy flying off the kitchen table. He had crashed on the floor, breaking into a hundred pieces, staining the linoleum tiles with the mysterious red fluid from inside his body, and creating Savannah's first "blood-spattered" crime scene.

She still missed Dippy. But if for some delightful but highly unlikely reason the oil industry decided to remove those hideous pumps, she certainly would not miss them.

As she followed the sign that indicated the turnoff for Twin Oaks, Savannah allowed her mind to drift back to her disgruntled grandmother, though it bothered her to do so.

For as long as she could remember, Savannah had

wanted nothing more than to give her precious granny everything she had ever wanted—and even a few things she hadn't. When Savannah had been about five years old, her heart's dearest dream was to grow up, become a princess, and give Granny a diamond-encrusted tiara.

As an adult, Savannah looked back on that lofty goal and realized that, at the time, Granny would've been much happier to receive a larger vehicle to haul the hoard of children she was raising. Or better yet, two extra bedrooms and another bath.

"But we can't bring her along every time we interview a suspect," she said, appealing her case to Dirk.

"I know," he said. "It's just not practical."

"I mean, she's not a cop. For heaven's sake, she's just a civilian."

They shot each other a quick, uncomfortable look and decided to change the subject.

Of course, Savannah was a civilian, too, yet she felt she had every right to tag along on Dirk's official business. And if it hadn't been for the fact that she helped him solve most of his cases, she was sure the SCPD brass would have called a halt to it ages ago.

"How long did Tammy say that Francia's been living out here in Twin Oaks?" Dirk asked, blowing cinnamon-scented breath in her direction.

"Six months," Savannah replied, happy for the change of topic. "Apparently, she moves around a lot, living first with one friend or relative and then another."

"Unstable." He nodded. "I like that in a suspect."

"Stop it. In this economy, lots of people are shuffling from one place to another, crashing wherever they can. It certainly doesn't make them cold-blooded murderers."

"Hey, I'm trying to be optimistic here. Aren't you

always hasslin', telling me I oughta look on the bright side?"

"I apologize most profusely. How insensitive of me. Here you are trying to raise your consciousness and improve yourself as a spiritual being by deciding that people who move around a lot make good homicide suspects. Whatever was I thinking?"

He sat quietly, staring at her for a long time. Silence reigned in the Mustang's interior—heavy and intense.

Finally, he said, "I've made a decision, Savannah."

"Woo-hoo. What is it?"

"I've decided that I'm going to start charging you five dollars for every smart-ass comment you make at my expense."

She thought it over for a while and said, "Okay. I can live with that. But I think I should get some kind of discount when you do something really stupid first and you totally deserve it. How's about two bucks for those inspired by pure dumb-nuttiness?"

He held out his hand, palm up to receive his fine.

Instead she slapped it and said, "Put it on my tab, boy. And you'd better be starting that tally on a long, long piece of paper."

The numbers on the crooked, rusted mailbox told Savannah and Dirk that they had arrived at 412 Twisted Oak Road, Francia Fortun's most recent crash pad. After Savannah turned onto the dirt road, they found themselves driving through a deep and lush orange grove.

Quickly, she put her window back down and breathed in one of her favorite scents in the world . . . that of sun-warmed citrus trees. The perfume of their fruit and deli-

ciously fragrant blossoms lifted her spirits like few
things could.

No matter how many times she entered a grove, she
would never get over the wonder, the beauty of it all.
The dark green leaves, the bright, succulent fruit, those
star-shaped white flowers, the peaceful quiet and solitary feel of the place . . . all combined to make an orchard one of Savannah's most cherished spots on earth.

"Don't you just love driving through an orange or
lemon grove?" she asked the love of her life. "I have to
tell you, for me, it's like a spiritual experience."

"Not really. I've found too many dumped bodies in
orange groves. When I'm in one, I can't help looking
for the next one. Sorta ruins the overall experience for
me. Know what I mean?"

She shot him a dirty look. "Yes. As a matter of fact.
I know exactly what you mean."

At the end of the dirt road, they came upon a small,
quaint farmhouse with a wraparound porch and some
flower baskets hanging on either side of the door. The
baskets were overflowing with a profusion of bright
red geraniums and yellow nasturtiums.

Otherwise the house could have used some tender
love and care. A new roof and a fresh coat of paint
would have spruced the old place up nicely.

But one glance at the area surrounding the house
and Savannah could tell instantly where the owner's
time and efforts were spent. She hadn't seen such a
wildly abundant garden since she had last set eyes on
Granny's, back home in Georgia.

Tomato plants struggled to hold their heavy, succulent
fruit. Squash and pumpkin vines vied for space, and
beans curled their way up cornstalks that were ready to
be picked.

In the midst of an herb garden that Savannah herself would have been overjoyed to have right outside her back door stood Francia Fortun. She had a basket slung over her left arm, and she was peacefully gathering what appeared to be herbs. She had a look of joy and well-being that Savannah had seen only on the faces of those who were tending a garden or holding a sleeping child.

If it hadn't been for all the tattoos and the black spaghetti-strap tank top, she would have looked like a fine Victorian lady cutting flowers for her drawing room vases.

Savannah parked the Mustang, and she and Dirk got out. When she closed the door, the sound caught Francia's attention. She turned and squinted into the morning sun, trying to see who had come calling.

Savannah could tell the moment Francia recognized them. The tranquil smile vanished from her face, and a look of annoyance, bordering on hostility, replaced it.

"It's you two," she said, not bothering to sugarcoat her tone one smidgeon.

"Yeap," Savannah said. "Just us chickens."

When she felt Dirk tense beside her, Savannah realized she had broken the cardinal Dirk rule: Don't mention chickens.

Unless they were in drumstick form, slathered in sauce and roasting on a barbecue grill, he hated chickens. He had an inexplicable phobia and couldn't bear the thought of them. Therefore, it was unacceptable to mention them in his presence. Not even in a passing joke.

She thought the number one Dirk rule was stupid as all get-out. But then, he didn't make fun of her when she did her "mousey dance," so she cut him some slack.

"I thought we were done with the interviews," Francia said.

"We're not 'done' until the handcuffs have been slapped on and somebody's getting read their rights," Dirk told her, his voice and his eyes even a bit less friendly than hers.

She tossed the basket onto the ground, far more roughly than Savannah would have predicted, considering how lovingly she had been gathering its contents only moments before.

"That's how we conduct a murder investigation," Savannah told her. "You're an expert at sauces and spices and how to cook Chateaubriand for thirty people all at once, and this guy here"—she pointed to Dirk—"he and I know how to catch killers. That's what we're good at."

"Then I guess by now you've caught the one who killed the chef, right?"

Something about the taunting tone of the young woman's voice made Savannah want to shove a big sprig or two of that freshly picked dill up her left nostril.

Instead, she glared at her and said, "We're getting very close. We've got it pretty much narrowed down . . ." She paused a moment for effect, then added, ". . . to you."

"Me? You've got to be kidding!"

Yes, no doubt about it. Francia's "cool" façade had slipped. In fact, with her eyes slightly bugged and her mouth hanging open, she reminded Savannah of a Georgia swamp frog, just waiting for a fly to pass by.

"I would never kid about murder," was Savannah's solemn answer. "Not once."

"Then you're mistaken!" Francia's face was growing

redder by the moment, and she began to breathe hard and fast, the way she had the night of the killing.

It occurred to Savannah that she might start to hyperventilate again. And this time, she just might let her.

If she had to throw up again, she could do it over there among the radishes.

Dirk stepped a bit closer to Francia, deliberately invading her space to keep her off-balance. "We've been marking our suspects off the list, one by one. Everybody's accounted for. Everybody was where they said they were. Except for one. And that's you."

Francia turned and began to walk away from them, toward the house. But Savannah and Dirk followed her. She had taken only a few steps when she must have reconsidered and realized they weren't about to be left behind.

She whirled back around and faced them. And the look of rage, raw and searing, in her eyes surprised even Savannah.

Having arrested murderers, rapists, robbers, and abusers of all kinds, she thought she had seen every variation of anger under the sun. But in a temper contest Francia Fortun could have competed with the best—or worst—of them. Savannah had seen friendlier looks on the faces of criminals who, one second later, had attempted to kill her.

She couldn't help wondering if those angry eyes were the last sight that Chef Baldwin Norwood had seen before leaving this earth.

"I can't be your only suspect," Francia shouted. "Of all the people who hated that guy, you'd try to pin his murder on me? What about Perla? She had every reason to kill him."

"Like what?" Savannah asked.

"Pick a reason. Any reason. I'm sure she had a dozen or more. She'd put up with his womanizing and his abuse for fifteen years, and then he kicked her out for another woman?"

"What woman?" Dirk asked.

"I don't know. Probably some bimbo he picked up in a bar the night before. It wouldn't matter to him."

"When did he kick her out?" Savannah wanted to know.

"Last week. He told her to pack her bags and get out . . . that he had bought his new girlfriend an expensive ring and was taking her to Santa Tesla Island. He told Perla by the time he got back, she'd better be gone. And she was. But she let the whole world know that she intended to sue him for everything he had. Palimony and all that."

Savannah turned to Dirk. "The luggage," she told him. "That mountain of suitcases in the living room."

"She said they were getting ready to take a trip," Dirk said, remembering.

"Trip? There's no trip," Francia interjected. "If there was a pile of luggage in the living room, it was because Perla was moving back into the house now that he's dead. She'll probably wind up with everything he had. And she should. She worked herself half to death and put him through the top culinary school in Paris. But do you think he appreciated it? Hell, no. She got nothing in return for all she did for him. Not even a ring on her finger. Are you going to tell me that's not a motive for murder?"

"It might be," Savannah said. "But it doesn't matter.

She has an alibi. She was with her daughter at the Pantages in Hollywood, watching a show. They proved it."

"That's true," Dirk said. "I checked it out myself. They were there. So much for your 'I'll blame it on Perla' plan."

Francia's chin started to quiver, and Savannah thought she might begin to cry. Her cockiness seemed to be turning to desperation. "Well, what about Yale? He and Chef Norwood hated each other for years."

"Why was there bad blood between them?" Savannah asked.

"Because Norwood destroyed Villa Nuevo. It was a beautiful restaurant, and it was making both of them a ton of money. Yale worked hard at putting that restaurant together and making it a success. We all did. Except for Norwood, that is."

"You're saying Norwood ruined the place they owned together?" Dirk asked. "How did that happen?"

"He drank constantly, especially when Yale went away on business trips out of the country. Then Norwood just went wild. He wouldn't show up to work, and when he did he was worthless. He invited huge groups of his so-called friends for these big parties, and he never reimbursed the restaurant. It didn't take long for it to start going under. When Yale returned from China this last time, Norwood had just about scuttled the ship. The only thing left to do was file for bankruptcy and close the doors."

Savannah thought back on what Otis Emmett had said about Yale visiting ReJuvene the night of the tasting and arguing with Norwood. No wonder they had exchanged some harsh words. If Chef Norwood had done that to her restaurant, she would've been ready to bury him in his double-breasted white jacket.

"And then," Francia continued, "as if that wasn't bad enough, Norwood abandons ship and takes his staff with him. He didn't even give Yale any notice or time to hire another team."

"Yale must've considered suing him," Savannah said. "He certainly had good reason to."

Francia glanced around, as though checking among the orange trees for eavesdroppers. She lowered her voice. "Yale threatened to sue him. Of course he did. Who wouldn't? But then Norwood played the orgy card."

Savannah wasn't sure that she had heard her correctly. "*Orgy* card?"

"Yeah, a few months ago Norwood took Yale to Las Vegas with him on some kind of a business trip. But, of course, with a sexual animal like Norwood, it turned out to be more monkey business than anything else."

"Monkey business?" Dirk asked, feigning disbelief. "Go figure."

Francia nodded. "Norwood arranged an orgy with some hookers for the two of them and sprang it on Yale. He went for it, and boy did he regret it. They hadn't been back home for five minutes before Norwood told everybody in the kitchen. Bragging about it. Later, when Yale told him that he was going to sue him for ruining Villa Nuevo, Norwood threatened to tell Yale's wife about the orgy. Needless to say, Yale dropped the lawsuit."

"Listen," Dirk said, "I know a little about Yale Ingram myself, and he's no altar boy. I don't know if I buy your story there, Francia."

Shrugging, Francia said, "Believe it or not, but it's

true. Yale used to mess around with a few of the waitresses. But his wife caught him and sent him to Sexaholics Anonymous. She told him if he ever had another slip, that was the end of the marriage."

"She probably would've considered an orgy a slip," Savannah commented. "I know I would. If any man of mine did that, he'd find himself slipping, all right. Into a hole in the ground about six feet deep."

Chapter 18

Savannah heard a distinctive pinging coming from the vicinity of her purse. As her heart pounded, she reached inside, pulled out her cell phone, and looked at it.

The message was from Dr. Dalano's office. Her appointment was in half an hour.

Shoving the phone back into her purse, she glanced over at Dirk and saw that he was watching her intently. She had to wrap up the interview with Francia and get back to San Carmelita, pronto. One look at Francia's defiant face told her that this conversation was going nowhere anyway.

Savannah knew, all too well, what a perp looked like right before confessing to their particular transgression. Usually, their spirits were broken and dejected as they resigned themselves to society's inevitable punishment.

Francia was a million miles from broken or dejected. There wasn't a chance in Hades that she was going to kneel here in the middle of her garden, confess, and beg for mercy.

Judging from the angry fire that still smoldered in her eyes, they were lucky that they hadn't been stabbed with an asparagus spear or clobbered with a corncob.

Savannah reached up and lightly brushed the tip of her nose with her forefinger. It was their secret code that the other one wanted to leave a place.

He gave her a slight nod and turned to Francia. "We're gonna get going now. But I guess I should say congratulations on your new promotion to master chef there at the restaurant. You know, the promotion you wouldn't have gotten if ol' Norwood hadn't wound up on the wrong side of a knife handle."

Francia didn't reply. She just continued to give him that nasty look that would have chilled the spines of lesser souls than Dirk Coulter.

"You take care now, hear?" Savannah said with only a moderately sarcastic tone. She looked over at the tomato plants, overly burdened with their bounty. "I reckon it'd be too much to ask for one of those vine-ripened beauties to take home with me."

Again there was no answer. Just the steely look.

"Yeah. That's what I thought," Savannah told her as she reached for Dirk's arm and propelled him toward the car.

"Boy, did you get a load of her?" Dirk said once they were out of earshot. "She's mean as a circular saw when you cross her."

"You can't really blame her," Savannah replied. "If somebody accused me of killing another human being, whether I'd done it or not, my reaction would be pretty much the same as hers. Calling somebody a cold-blooded

murderer right to their face . . . probably not the best
way to make friends and influence people."

"Maybe not. But it's a good way to shake up a suspect, so's you can find out what they're made of."

"And what do you figure she's made of?"

"Let's just say, if I had pissed her off and then wound
up hanging out with her in a dark alley, I wouldn't turn
my back to her."

"Amen."

"But then, I'd say the same about you."

"Why, thank you, darlin'." She reached down and took
his hand. "You silken-tongued, sweet-talkin' laddie."

Savannah's and Dirk's mood was considerably less
cordial when she dropped him off, fifteen minutes
later, at the police station house.

In fact, the atmosphere between them was more than
a bit chilly. It was plumb Nordic.

As he started to climb out of the Mustang, he turned
back to her, and with an angry, guarded look on his
face he said, "I can't believe this, Van. Not only are you
not going to let me go with you, but you won't even tell
me where you're headed?"

"I'm sorry," she said, fighting the urge to either yell at
him or burst into tears and hug him. She wanted badly to
do both. "It's no big deal. I just—"

"The hell it's not. It's gotta be a big deal or you
wouldn't keep it from me. Since when do you and me
have secrets?"

She reached over, grabbed his hand, and squeezed it.
He didn't squeeze back.

"Sweetie, please. This is something I need to do on
my own. And I need you to understand. Okay?"

"No. It's not okay. How am I supposed to understand something when I don't even know what it is? Maybe you should just trust me, give me a chance to understand."

She glanced at her watch. "Dirk, I need to get going. Get them to loan you a radio car to take over to Yale's office. See what you can wring out of him. I'll touch base with you later."

"When?"

"Later." She gulped. "I love you, darlin'. You know that, right?"

His eyes searched hers, and she could see his anger turning to sadness.

The lump in her throat tightened. She felt like she was swallowing a chunk of rough cement.

She could handle his anger any day, but the thought that she was causing him pain was almost more than she could stand.

She began to question her decision to do this alone. But another glance at her watch told her that this wasn't the time to change plans. As Granny Reid often said, "Don't go changin' horses midstream."

Once again, she squeezed his hand.

This time, he raised hers to his lips and pressed a kiss into her palm. "I love you, too, Van. Be safe, sweetheart."

"I will."

"Promise?"

"Promise."

He got out of the car, closed the door, and walked up to the station house entrance.

Savannah pulled out of the parking lot and onto the road.

In her rearview mirror she could see him, still standing there beside the door, watching her . . . until she turned the corner three blocks away.

Several years ago, when Savannah had first met Dr. Anna Dalano, she had thought it unusual for a physician to have five piercings on each ear.

Oh, Dr. Anna's choice and earrings were tasteful enough—diamond studs, descending in size from the earlobe upward. But it was still a bit unorthodox. As was her inch-long, spiked blond hair with its blue tips.

So was calling your family physician "Dr. Anna."

But on a day like today, when Savannah was feeling as nervous as a cow with a buck-toothed calf, the informality was welcomed. She much preferred having Dr. Anna, with her ten earrings, sitting across from her wearing a pretty blue sweater set and a necklace with a skull and crossbones pendant, than the traditional, grim-faced fellow in a white smock.

"It's been a while since we've seen you," the doctor said, flashing her an open, friendly smile. She glanced down at Savannah's chart, which was lying open on her desk. "I guess that means you've been feeling pretty good."

"Yes, I have." Savannah hesitated, then plunged ahead. "Until lately."

"And what's been going on lately?"

"I've been really tired and cranky all the time, wanting to kill Dirk." The doctor smirked, so she added, "More than usual, that is."

Dr. Anna picked up the pen and began to scribble notes on the chart. "Anything else?"

"I've had some headaches. I haven't been sleeping well. And I've had these weak, shaky spells where I feel dizzy. Yesterday, it was bad enough that I fell down."

Dr. Anna looked up from her writing and gave Savannah a quick once-over. "Did you hurt yourself?"

"Just my pride. I was at the beach. Dirk and about a million little kids were watching."

"Any nausea?"

"A little bit. You know, from the dizziness."

The doctor scribbled for, what seemed to Savannah, an eternity. Finally, she set her pen aside and gave Savannah a long, searching look that told Savannah nothing.

Like most physicians, Dr. Anna had a great poker face.

Finally, she cleared her throat and said. "Savannah . . . when was your last menses?"

Savannah sat in Dr. Dalano's waiting room, pretending to read an article in *Cosmo* about the ten most romantic places to have sex in the great outdoors without getting arrested. But she had a feeling that it was that very activity that had led her to the doctor's office.

How many times had Granny told her when she was a teenager, "It only takes once, Savannah girl. A few minutes—ten seconds, if the knucklehead's particularly bad at it—and your life changes forever."

It had only been once, about a month and a half ago, under the wisteria-draped arbor in her backyard when the light of the full moon and her husband's irresistible charms had seduced her. Throwing caution to the wind—along with a pair of her sexiest lacy panties—she had taken a chance on Mother Nature.

Caught in the throes of passion, she had forgotten that Mother Nature simply adored babies.

I could be pregnant, she thought. *Pregnant. A baby. Pregnant with a baby.*

And how do we feel about that, Savannah? asked that quieter, far more calm and collected voice deep inside.

We? We? Who's we? Are you going to carry this baby with me? Are you going to be there in the delivery room, panting and pushing? Are you going to help with the 3:00 a.m. nursing?

Quiet, sane Savannah didn't answer.

Yeah, that's what I thought. If I'm pregnant, it's me. Just me.

Well, and Dirk.

Savannah smiled, remembering how Dirk had been with the kids on the beach—laughing, throwing the ball for them, picking them up and twirling them around. She pictured him petting and caring for Diamante and Cleo, whispering sweet nothings into their fuzzy little ears. Any guy who was that good with animals would make a great father.

Dirk, a dad. The very thought warmed her heart and allayed most of her fears. If those tests that she was waiting for came back positive, she would not be alone in this. Not at all.

Sometimes life gave you a nice surprise, a gift you weren't expecting. And this just might be the biggest one she'd ever received.

While she and Dirk hadn't been officially "trying," she was sure he would welcome the news. In fact, as she imagined the joy they would have, telling each member of their family and friends, she could already see the delight on their beloved faces and—

"Savannah."

Granny would beam and shout, "Praise the Lord!" Waycross and Tammy were bound to cry. Ryan and John would—

"Savannah. Would you come with me, please?"

It was the nurse, standing in the door, beckoning her back to the office area once again.

This was it! Now it would be official. Her world was about to change forever, and for the good.

She jumped to her feet, filled with so much pure happiness she thought she might just float away. She rushed to the door and hurried through it, more than eager and willing to face the most important role she had ever played.

"Menopause?"

The word hung in the air between Savannah and her doctor like a giant, black storm cloud blotting out the sun.

And her dreams of ever becoming a mother.

Dr. Anna gave her a sweet, sad smile. "I'm so sorry, Savannah," she said. "Didn't you consider that as a possibility when you missed your last cycle?"

"No. I've always had irregular periods. I finally just stopped trying to chart them, years ago. I didn't even realize that I'd missed one until you asked me . . . I . . . oh, no, I didn't consider . . . I didn't . . ."

The tears she had been fighting for weeks started to flow hot and heavy as she covered her face with her hands and began to sob hysterically.

Dr. Anna got up from her chair, walked around the desk, and knelt beside Savannah's chair.

"There, there," she said, patting her patient on the

back. "I'm sorry this took you unaware like this. I thought you suspected you were in peri-menopause. The headaches, irritability, insomnia, even the dizziness—those can all be symptoms of menopause."

"But, but aren't . . . aren't they . . . *hiccup* . . . for pregnancy, too?"

"Yes, the symptoms of pregnancy and menopause are quite similar for some women."

"Well, I guess I'll, I'll never"—she accepted the tissue the doctor offered her—"never know about the, the pregnancy pa-a-a-art."

Her sobs commenced all over again, even worse than before.

Dr. Anna put an arm around her shoulder and rocked her gently. "I'm really, really sorry, Savannah. I didn't know becoming a mother meant so much to you."

"Me either."

"I beg your pardon?"

"I didn't know either." She stopped and blew her nose, filling the tissue. The doctor quickly gave her another. "Not until I told you I'd missed a period and you said let's do a test and I said okay and you said go wait in the waiting room."

"I see."

Dr. Anna rose from her knees and pulled an extra chair close to Savannah's. She sat down and said, "Out there in my waiting room . . . that was the first time you've ever really thought about motherhood?"

"No, of course not. I used to think about it when I was taking care of my little brothers and sisters. I had eight, you know."

"Yes, I recall you telling me that. And back then, when you fantasized about becoming a mom, what did you imagine?"

Savannah laughed, but the sound was bitter and ragged. "I thought: I'm sure as hell not going to have nine kids!"

Dr. Anna laughed with her. "I can understand that. But did you have your heart set on it?"

Savannah thought about it and couldn't come up with a ready, definitive answer. "I guess. I mean, doesn't everybody?"

"No."

"No?"

"No. *I* didn't fantasize about motherhood. I dreamed of being a doctor. That was all."

"You actually decided not to ever have children."

"I most certainly did. Motherhood is wonderful. The most important job in the world. But I believe that every little baby who comes into the world deserves to be really, really wanted. So if a woman doesn't truly want a child, I don't think she should have one. Of course, that's just my opinion."

She took a clean tissue and dabbed at the tears on Savannah's cheeks. "Did you really, really want to have children, Savannah?"

For a long time, Savannah sat there, searching her mind and her heart for the answer. The true answer. Not the one she felt she was expected to speak.

She stopped crying and folded her hands in her lap, regaining control of her emotions.

Finally, she said, "I'd never really thought much about it. I figured I'd get married someday and motherhood being the natural progression and all—"

"For most people."

"Yes, for most people. And I suppose I figured children were out there in my future somewhere." She took a deep breath. "But I don't live in the future or the past all that much. My present is pretty darn full. It's pretty much all I can handle from day to day."

"That's a good thing, Savannah. I think a lot of people would be happier if they lived in the present, too."

"I never really decided," she continued. "And I guess, if you postpone making a decision about something for long enough, sometimes the decision gets made for you."

"And sometimes our hearts knows what's best for us and 'decide' by 'not deciding.'"

Savannah wiped her eyes and blew her nose. "And that's okay?"

"I don't know. Only you can say if that's what happened."

Again, the two women sat for several long moments in silence as Savannah processed all that had been shared between them.

Eventually, Savannah stood and tossed her used tissues into a nearby trash can. Then she smoothed her hair and her blouse and donned her best "tough gal" face.

"I don't know yet," she told Dr. Anna. "I feel a lot of things right now. When it all gets sorted out, I'm not sure what's going to come out on top."

The doctor stood, put her hands on Savannah's shoulders, and gave her a kiss on the cheek. "*You*, my brave friend. *You* are *always* going to come out on top."

Savannah laughed. A little. "How do you know?"

"I'm a doctor. We know everything."

Chapter 19

When Savannah arrived home, it was to a house filled with guests, and she had to admit she was somewhat relieved.

All the way home from the doctor's office, she had rehearsed at least a dozen versions of the same speech that, sooner or later, she was going to have to present to Dirk:

"Guess what, honey. That pretty young thing you married a few months ago. . . . Well, she's turned into an old hag now and can't have babies. Hope you weren't counting on being a dad."

That was about the best version she had come up with thus far. So she knew the speech still needed some work.

She truly regretted the fact that, before the marriage, she and Dirk had never had one single "baby" talk. It was a conversation that every couple needed to have before walking down the aisle. But perhaps it was even more important, since they were marrying in their forties—a bit late for starting a family.

Driving home, she had been hoping against hope that maybe, just maybe, he would be on the same page as she. Only without the hysterical sobbing in the doctor's office part.

When she pulled into her driveway and saw not only Dirk's borrowed radio car, Tammy's pink Volkswagen, and Waycross's General Lee, but also Ryan and John's Bentley, she had breathed a sigh of relief. Although it did trouble her to know that she was avoiding alone time with her own husband.

That had never happened before. But then it wasn't every day that a woman was told she wouldn't be having any babies. Ever. Or a man either, for that matter.

As bitter pills went, that was a pretty nasty one to have to swallow.

When she entered the house and walked into the living room, she saw Tammy and Waycross huddled together at the desk in the corner. They were staring at the computer screen as Tammy's nimble fingers flew over the keyboard. She knew they were hard at work because they gave her only the briefest of nods before going back to whatever they were doing.

Ryan, John, and Granny were sitting on the sofa. On the coffee table before them was Savannah's suspect poster board. The threesome was crouched over it, intently discussing every person named there.

She didn't see Dirk, and that worried her. But she didn't want to go looking for him either. If she found him alone in another room, he would no doubt demand to know where she had been and what had happened. The last thing she wanted was to have that conversation when there was a house full of guests and no privacy.

Sitting down in her comfy chair, she scooped both of the cats onto her lap. As always, they were thrilled to see her, rubbing their faces against her cheek and the palm of her hand, demanding petting.

Considering the events of the past few hours, she found their unconditional love and affection all the more precious.

"Looks like y'all called yourselves a meeting of the Moonlight Magnolia Detective Agency," she said. "Guess I didn't get the memo."

In unison they turned from what they were doing and looked at her, a bit sheepishly.

"We're sorry, love," John said. "But Ryan and I, we were so discouraged and downcast that we could barely stand ourselves."

Ryan added, "So we decided to drop by here unannounced and inflict our disgruntled selves on you. Guess it's your lucky day."

"Not really," Savannah muttered under her breath. Then she cleared her throat and said, "Why so glum? Is there any special reason you're all down in the mouth? That's out of character for you guys."

That was when she noticed that their normally impeccable attire was actually quite grungy. John's dove gray slacks were dirty on both knees, and Ryan's white shirt had black smudges that looked like grease on the elbows and down the front. Their hair was a mess, and Ryan had a streak of oiliness on his right cheek that matched the mess on his shirt.

"You two look like you've been in a pig wrestlin' contest and the pigs took the blue ribbon," she told them.

"That's about how I feel, too," Ryan replied. "After hearing what Otis Emmett said about no one entering

or exiting the restaurant's rear door, we realized that
the rod and the knife that Dr. Liu described still have to
be somewhere in the kitchen area."

"Or down the hallway that leads into the bathroom,"
Granny added.

"Or in the bathroom itself," Dirk said as he walked
into the living room, juggling several coffee mugs in
his hands.

Waycross jumped up from his seat at the desk and
hurried over to help him. He took two mugs from Dirk,
walked back to the desk, and offered Tammy one.

She simply shook her head and gave him a sweet
smile. "I've already had my daily half-cup. But thanks
anyway."

Waycross walked over to Savannah's chair and placed
the mug in her hands. Catching sight of her tear-swollen
eyes, he said, "You all right, sis? You look like you've
been crying."

"Naw. It's just my sinuses acting. You know, the
Santa Ana winds and all that mess."

"I didn't know you have sinus problems," he per-
sisted.

"I do today. Okay?" she snapped back. "Now what
were you all saying about looking for that rod and
knife?"

Although she was trying to avoid Dirk's eyes, she
could feel him staring at her from the other side of the
room. He had been watching her since he had walked
in from the kitchen. But now that Waycross had brought
attention to her red eyes, her detective husband was giving her the piercing, see-all-know-all Sergeant Coulter
special.

For a moment, she knew what it felt like to be in the

sweat box with Dirk doing the interrogating. He had that intimidating "I know all your secrets" look down pat. No wonder criminals folded like a poorly wrapped burrito when he questioned them.

"We looked everywhere," John said. "We're positively flummoxed. Haven't a clue where the bloody things are."

"The other night," Savannah said, "when you had that meeting with the staff . . . did anybody go back in the kitchen or the bathroom?"

"Absolutely not," John told her. "The crime scene tape is still across the doorway, and we told them in no uncertain terms not to set foot in there."

Ryan added, "And they didn't. We had our eyes on them the whole time. Nobody went in there. It's been sealed since the crime occurred."

Dirk walked over to Savannah, slid her footstool over beside her chair, and sat down on it. Placing his hand on her knee, he said softly, "How did your . . . um . . . errand go?"

Suddenly, she felt as though everyone in the room was staring at her, giving her the same old hawk-eyed look as Dirk.

She took a quick glance around the room and saw that she was right. They were all staring at her with big question mark eyes.

Why did her friends and family all have to be detectives? It made it nigh to impossible to get away with anything.

She turned back to Dirk and said calmly, "Thanks for asking, but lousy. By the time I got there, they were all sold out of my size. You know how those stupid clearance sales are."

The room was silent.

If a cricket had been chirping five miles away, they could have all heard it and understood every word it was saying.

"How did your interview with Yale Ingram go?" she asked Dirk.

"Okay." His expression was still guarded and hurt, and that went straight to her heart. "I asked him why he stopped by the restaurant the day of the testing. He said he wanted to see the new place, wanted to see what Norwood had thrown him over for."

"Really straightforward stuff," Savannah said.

"Yeah. He was pretty nice and polite about it all, until I suggested that maybe the reason he stopped by that day was to tell Norwood that he had dropped the lawsuit . . . so Norwood wouldn't tell his wife about the orgy."

"The what?" A wide-eyed Tammy whirled around in her seat, suddenly all ears.

"Come on now, girl," Granny said. "I'm an old lady from the one-stoplight town of McGill, Georgia, and even I know what an orgy is. It's when more than two people get together and commit a bunch of debauchery and wickedness and call it 'fun.' And I'll have you know, it was your generation that thought up that hooey. Until y'all invented it, there weren't such things in the world. My generation wouldn't have dreamed of such a thing."

For a moment, visions flashed through Savannah's mind of the depravity of the Roman Emperors, the promiscuous ancient Greeks, and several rather lascivious accounts she had read in the Old Testament. But out of respect for her grandmother, she decided to let Granny think the flower children of the sixties had doomed mankind with their newly discovered sexual promiscuity.

"Anyway," Dirk continued, "Yale told me at the time of the murder he was addressing a group of investors in the valley. Over a hundred of them, as a matter of fact."

"And we've verified that here on the Internet," Tammy proudly announced. "They even posted a video of his speech on Facebook."

"Well, heck," Savannah said, "if it's on Facebook it has to be true."

Granny tapped her finger on Savannah's suspect board. "No matter how you slice this cake, you just keep coming back to the same thing. It must've been this Francia girl. And she must've stashed that rod and that knife someplace. Y'all just haven't found it yet. And I know why."

Everyone turned to Granny, eager to hear her words of wisdom.

"And why is that, Mrs. Reid?" John wanted to know. "Please, do tell."

"Because so far the only ones who've been looking for those things were Savannah—and she's been pretty muddleheaded lately—and menfolk. And everybody knows that when a man's looking for something and it doesn't up and fall right into his outstretched hand, he ain't got a clue."

She stood and began to collect the empty coffee mugs from around the room. "There's only one thing left to do. We all hightail it outta here, get our backsides over to that new restaurant of yours . . . which I've been dyin' to see anyway. I'll betcha with some women along—gals who ain't been discombobulated, that is—we're gonna find us some murder weapons."

* * *

"Okay, you boys were right. There ain't no weapons here," Granny said as she collapsed onto one of the restaurant's dining room chairs and propped her elbows on the table. "Leastways, not those particular weapons . . . the ones that did the deed."

As Dirk, Waycross, and Tammy followed her lead, taking seats at the large, round table, Savannah sat next to Granny and draped her arm across her grandmother's shoulders.

"I agree with you, Gran," she said. "Of all the zillions of knives in this joint, there's not one that matches that description, with the partially serrated blade. And when Dirk and I were scrounging around for that rod the other day, it was measly pickings."

Ryan walked over to their table, carrying a tray of glasses filled with ice. John followed with a large, frosty pitcher of water. They set it in the middle of the table and took seats.

Savannah reached for the pitcher and began filling the glasses for the overheated and overworked group of searchers.

"I've gotta tell you, this case is making me crazy," Dirk said, rubbing his eyes. "We've got all of these suspects, all these motives. And every one of them has an alibi."

"Except for Francia," Ryan replied.

"Francia Fortun, as in, our new replacement chef," John said, shaking his head. "I must confess, comrades, I'm sinking deeper and deeper into the well of depression by the moment."

Dirk gave a dry chuckle. "And you know what they say about those wells being colder than a—"

"Watch it, young man," Granny snapped. "I know that quaint little phrase, and a whole lot more to boot. But I don't go using them in mixed company."

Dirk blushed and ducked his head. "Sorry, Granny."

Tammy giggled. "Colder than a flat frog on a Philadelphia freeway in February?"

Dirk perked up. "Yeah, right. That's what I meant to say."

Savannah slid a glass of water across the table to John. "Try not to worry, sugar. This is all going to work out in the end. You just wait and see."

"That's for sure," Waycross agreed. "You're gonna have this fine establishment up and running like a top in no time."

Granny nodded. "These trials and tribulations will soon be a thing of the past."

"Just as soon as we nail the killer," Savannah said.

She pressed her fingertips to her aching temples, intending to give them a brief massage. But she glanced around the table and saw that Granny, Dirk, and Waycross were all watching her intently, worried looks on their faces. So she thought better of it and folded her hands on the table in front of her.

"It has to be Francia Fortun." Tammy gave Ryan and John a sympathetic look. "I'm sorry, guys. I know that would leave you in a really bad place chef-wise. But she's the only suspect without an alibi."

"That's true," Ryan agreed reluctantly. "She's the only one who had opportunity."

Dirk sniffed and leaned back in his chair, hands behind his head. "Yeah? Well, there's no way I could sell that to the prosecutor: 'She's the only one who could have done it, so she did it.' That ain't gonna fly."

Everyone at the table sat still and quiet for a long time. Savannah could tell by the depressed looks on their faces that they were as pessimistic about this case as she was.

For the first time in years, she was beginning to think that a homicide she was working on might go unsolved. Possibly forever. And while, sooner or later, that was a sad reality in every investigator's career, she had no intention of surrendering the battle just yet.

There had to be a way. There was always a way.

To Savannah's way of thinking, the cause of justice was a sacred endeavor. And she liked to think that she and her loved ones, who were seated around the table, fought on the side of the angels.

More than once she believed they had received a bit of celestial assistance when working a case that appeared to be stuck at a dead end. She couldn't help thinking that now would be a good time for a bit of divine guidance.

Glancing to her left, she saw that Granny was chewing her bottom lip, her forehead wrinkled in a deep scowl, her eyes narrowed.

Savannah knew the look.

When she had been a kid and saw "The Look," she knew that either she or one of her siblings was about to "Get It." That expression on Granny's face indicated that she had just figured something out. Like: Marietta hadn't spent the night at her girlfriend's house after all but had lied so she could sneak out with that worthless Randall Cooter kid again. Or: Macon's new bicycle that he said he found in a ditch somewhere bore an unsettling resemblance to the one reported stolen at a carnival over in Ringgold the week before.

"What is it, Granny?" she asked. "Have you got something?"

"I do believe I might."

Dirk perked up. "Then let's have it."

"Now ain't the time to be shy," Waycross added.

Granny drummed her fingertips on the table. "I don't want to get everybody's hopes up. It might be nothin'."

"Don't worry about that, love," John said. "'Nothing' is all we have at the moment anyway. That's the only good thing about floundering down here in the Well of Despair. There's nowhere to go but up."

"Okay, then. Here goes." Granny drew a deep breath. "Who says this Francia Fortun was the only person in the kitchen area when the chef was murdered?"

"Are you suggesting someone else was in there, too?" Savannah asked.

Granny shook her head. "No. I'm literally asking you—who said that she was the only person in there? Who told you that?"

"An eyewitness," Dirk said.

"Eyewitnesses can be wrong," Granny argued.

"Yes," Savannah said. "But this particular witness seems reliable, and he's unbiased. He has no reason to lie."

"Unless *he's* your killer."

Granny's simple statement hung in the air, like smoke after a fireworks explosion.

"Think about it," she continued. "We've pretty much proven that what he said happened couldn't have happened. It's not possible."

"What do you mean?" Savannah asked.

"He told you that Francia went inside to go to the bathroom. The chef got killed, according to Dr. Liu, with a rod, knife, and meat cleaver. And nobody but y'all who were officially working the case have gone in and out of that room since then. Except for those three kitchen workers, Francia, Manuel, and Carlos. And none of them carried the weapons out. Right?"

"Right," Savannah said. "We checked them. Nobody was carrying anything on their person."

"Now, see there?" Granny smiled. "According to your feller, nobody left with the weapons, and yet the weapons ain't there. That just makes no sense. And I learned a long time ago, when somethin' don't make sense, most times it's 'cause it ain't true."

Savannah began to chew on her bottom lip, just as Granny had done, as the pieces of the puzzle rearranged themselves in her head. "We based all of our assumptions on what Otis Emmett told us," she said.

"Sure we did," Dirk replied. "He was the one in the back alley with a front-row seat to everything that was going on. He was the one keeping an eye on the back door when it all went down."

"So he says," Granny answered. "But who was keeping an eye on him?"

"He's a vet," Dirk said softly.

Savannah reached over and touched his hand. "I know, darlin'. But even veterans are human beings. Precious as they are, some of them lie from time to time."

Tammy had her tablet out and was vigorously working the screen. The light of discovery glowed in her eyes. "He's more than a vet," she said. "He got a medal for taking out a bunch of enemy snipers single-handedly and saving a dozen of his fellow soldiers."

"Great," Dirk said, sinking even lower in his chair. "You're suggesting that our killer could be a decorated war hero."

"I don't like it any more than you do, Dirk," Ryan said. "But Granny's right. It doesn't make sense that—"

Tammy gasped, and everyone at the table turned to stare at her, watching as the blood drained from her face.

"Oh no," she said. "You're not going to believe this."

Waycross laid his hand on her shoulder. "What is it, sweetie?"

"It's how he killed those enemy soldiers. They were hiding individually in various places along the top of a ridge. He had to sneak up on them and take them out quietly, one by one."

Time seemed to slow for Savannah, as it did at moments like this . . . important moments, when a case turned 180 degrees.

She knew what Tammy was going to say even before she spoke the words: "He used an ASP baton and a Ka-Bar—"

"—U.S. Marine Corps fighting knife." Dirk shook his head, looking heartsick. "I used one myself. It's exactly the right length and has a combo blade, partially serrated. Why the hell didn't I think of that before?"

"Because you couldn't bear to, sugar," Granny told him sweetly. "You soldiers never stop being soldiers, ever. And you're all brothers. How could you stand to think a brother could do such a thing?"

Dirk rose from the table, ran his fingers through his hair, adjusted his jeans, and checked the Smith & Wesson in his shoulder holster. He turned to Ryan and John. "He's probably still out back in the alley. Do you two wanna come along when I talk to him?"

"The guy who closed down our restaurant?" Ryan asked.

"The bloody maggot who murdered our chef in our own kitchen?" John added. "Let me at him."

As the three men started for the door, Granny said, "Those fellas take their restaurant business mighty serious."

"You have no idea." Savannah jumped to her feet. "Let's go, too. With any luck, they'll need some assistance."

Chapter 20

Otis Emmett wasn't in the alley.

But fortunately, the Moonlight Magnolia gang found a young lady loitering in the vicinity who was a good friend of his, and she was all too eager to talk.

Wearing nothing but a low-cut tie-dyed tee-shirt and crocheted shorts that left little to the imagination, the woman introduced herself to the group as "Chicago."

At first, Savannah thought it was a ridiculous name. But on second thought, she decided she was in no position to judge, considering her own name and those of her eight siblings, also named after cities in Georgia.

The crocheted shorts, though . . . she had no problem condemning those. She could see all the way to Kalamazoo, and if Chicago moved just wrong, she was afraid she might see Kalamazoo, too.

However, Chicago was friendly enough and helpful as she rattled on about how handsome, smart, brave, and strong Otis Emmett was.

Apparently, true love could blossom in alleys as abundantly as anywhere else.

After listening to the woman prattle on about her beloved for several minutes, Dirk asked the million-dollar question. "So, tell me, Chicago . . . do you happen to know where your boyfriend is right now?"

She blushed and giggled, more like a maiden in an all-girl parochial school than a gal who was making a public spectacle of herself. "Aw-w-w. Get out. Otis isn't my boyfriend. I wish he was, but he's just not that interested. I think the war did something to him. He's a really sweet guy, but he just doesn't seem to—"

"Chicago!" Savannah's last nerve snapped. She could almost hear it twang. It had been a long day and it was only midafternoon. "Girl! Listen up. Where . . . is . . . Otis?"

"Oh, he's at his mom's."

"His mom's?" Dirk asked.

"Yeah. She comes and picks him up here in the alley every Saturday morning and takes him home with her. She fixes him his favorite meal and lets him shower and stuff. She's always offering to wash his clothes, too, but he doesn't want to put her out too much. She's old, see, and it's hard on her just to drive here and get him. Last week she had a wreck and totaled that junky old car of hers. Otis was so upset when he heard. She really needed that car, and she couldn't afford another one."

"Why doesn't Otis live with his mom?" Ryan asked.

"He just has too many problems to live with anybody, even his own mom. I asked him one time if he'd like to move in with me somewhere, if we could get the money together to rent a room or something, and he told me that he's too messed up to be with anybody.

Even his own family. It's a shame, too, because Otis has so much to offer. He's just the most—"

"When does this charming lad of yours usually return from his mother's home?" John asked.

Savannah could tell by the strained look on his usually jovial face that he, too, was feeling the stress. She was hoping Chicago wouldn't say, "Around midnight."

"Right about now," was the welcome answer. "She usually pulls up over there and . . . Oh, hey! Look at that! There they are!"

Savannah turned to the left, where Chicago was pointing, and indeed there was a car pulling in. It was an older PT Cruiser, but the electric blue paint glistened in the afternoon light. A used car dealer's sticker was affixed to the rear driver's-side window.

"Oh, good!" Chicago exclaimed as she clapped her hands and wriggled her barely covered butt. "He said she might get a Cruiser. I love those cars. Maybe she'll let me drive it sometime."

Savannah saw that the male members of her gang had donned seriously somber faces and were standing at attention, waiting for Otis Emmett to exit his mother's car and walk their way.

They were positioned back a bit, in the shadow of the building and close to its rear wall, so they wouldn't be so obvious.

Tammy and Gran looked equally grim and were partially hidden behind a stack of produce crates.

Savannah reached over and took Chicago firmly by the upper arm. "Listen, girlfriend," she said, "you're gonna wanna haul those bare buns of yours out of here."

"What do you mean?" Chicago's eyes were wide and frightfully vacant.

Savannah couldn't help but feel a surge of concern

for Chicago. The streets—any streets, even the streets in as nice a town as San Carmelita—were no place for a woman with vacant eyes, wearing crocheted shorts, and showing off her Kalamazoo.

"Just trust me," Savannah told her, giving her a gentle push in the opposite direction. "Something's going to go down here in a minute or two, and you don't want to be any part of it. Skedaddle now."

Chicago didn't need to be told twice. With a confused and frightened look on her face, she turned and ran away as fast as her flip-flops could take her.

"So much for standing by your man," Savannah muttered as she watched her scurry around the corner.

Turning back to the action at hand, Savannah saw Otis open the passenger door and lean over and kiss his mother on the cheek.

Savannah felt sorry for the woman in the car. Before the day was over, she might receive the sad news that her son had been arrested for a vicious, cold-blooded murder. What woman could hear something like that and ever be the same again?

No one.

Otis closed the car door. When he stepped away, he waved once more to his mom. She blew him a kiss and drove away.

He watched until her car was gone, before turning around and walking toward them. Savannah's pulse raced as she reached under her jacket to unsnap her holster.

She reminded herself—as was the rest of the group, she was sure—that this man coming their way might look like a street bum but he was a trained Marine who had taken out enemy sharpshooters with the most rudimentary of weapons.

He wasn't someone to trifle with.

Having escorted Chicago off the scene, she was farther away from the suspect than the rest of her gang. So
she quickly closed the gap and hurried to stand next to
Dirk.

On the other side of him, Ryan and John were ready,
too. They carried no weapons, but they had their FBI
combat training, should they need it.

Waycross brought up the rear.

"Let me," Dirk whispered, his face as serious as she
had ever seen it.

They all understood and moved back a bit, letting
him step forward to intercept Emmett.

The moment the two men's eyes met, Emmett's body
stiffened, as though he was standing to attention.

Watch the hands, Savannah thought, her academy
instructors' voices echoing in her mind. *It's the hands
that kill you, not the face. Watch the hands.*

Otis Emmett's right hand was balled into a fist. His
left held a battered backpack.

Suddenly, Savannah was afraid—very afraid—for
her husband. This man was highly dangerous, but she
knew Dirk would cut him some slack because he was a
veteran.

She only hoped his generosity didn't get him hurt.

Or worse.

Emmett stopped walking and stood perfectly still as
he looked around. He glanced from one member of
their group to another, as though sizing each one up.
Then he turned his attention to Dirk, who was now
only a few feet from him.

"I need a moment of your time," Dirk was saying.
"I've got something important to ask you, and I need
you to stay calm. If you do, then so will I. Okay?"

Emmett shot Savannah another quick look, and she

knew he was taking note of the fact that she had her hand under her jacket.

He was no fool. He would know she was armed.

Dirk had both hands open and out in front of him, but Emmett had to know he was armed, too.

Those were at least two guns he would have to contend with. Even if he was carrying his knife and billy club on him, he had to realize he was at a disadvantage, should he try to fight.

But there was no way to tell what people would do. Under stress, they often chose the most foolish of their options.

"Okay," he told Dirk. "What do you want to ask me?"

Dirk took a step closer.

Savannah did, too. Just in case.

"We're following up on a couple more leads," Dirk said in his calmest, quietest voice. "And I need to ask you for a favor."

"What favor?"

"I'd like to have your permission to take a look inside that backpack you're carrying."

Though his body didn't even flinch, the expression on Otis Emmett's face was the same as someone who had just received a swift roundhouse kick to the solar plexus.

For several long moments, he said nothing. And when he finally spoke, his voice sounded high and tight. "Why do you want to look inside my backpack?"

Dirk drew a deep breath and stepped even closer until the two men were face-to-face. "Come on, buddy," he said. "You know why. Just let me do what I gotta do. Okay?"

When Emmett didn't reply, Dirk slowly reached down and took hold of the backpack's shoulder straps.

Emmett tried to jerk it away, but Dirk held fast and said, "Don't do it, man. Don't go there. Nobody has to get hurt today. We're just going to take this nice and slow. Let it go now. Just let go. Everything's gonna be okay. I promise."

Emmett stared at Dirk, his face growing redder by the moment. Savannah could see his pulse pounding in his temples. His entire body began to shake violently, as though he were standing in a Category 2 hurricane.

But he let go of the pack.

Dirk took two steps backward, out of Emmett's reach.

"I'm going to have to look in here sooner or later," Dirk told him. "You can make me get a search warrant, or you can give me permission to look right now. But either way, it's going to happen. Understand?"

Emmett's body sagged, as though he were some sort of helium balloon that had lost half of its air. "Yeah," he said. "You might as well. Go ahead."

"Thank you." Dirk unzipped the backpack and looked inside.

Savannah held her breath as he searched the pack's interior briefly. Then he closed it and set it on the ground behind him.

"Why?" he asked Emmett. "You're a Marine, a hero. There's nothin' on earth better than that. But you throw it all away, live here in an alley like a cat that was dumped on the side of the road."

"That's what I feel like, okay?" Emmett blurted. "They dumped me. I got back stateside and they turned their backs on me like I was nothin'! Nobody shows us vets any respect anymore."

"That isn't true," Dirk told him, his voice soft and controlled. "I've shown you respect. My wife showed

you respect. Everybody standing here right now re-
spects you for your service to our nation, for your hero-
ism. And there's a lot more of us out there in the world,
so don't tell me that."

"You don't understand."

"I understand better than you think. I know what it's
like to kill enemy soldiers because your country tells
you to. I know what it's like to come back home to a lot
of people who don't have a clue what that took out of
your soul. But what I don't understand is how you could
use the training the Corps gave you to murder a soft, de-
fenseless guy like Norwood, who didn't stand a chance
against you."

"He disrespected me!" Emmett shouted. "I asked him
nice if I could have a bowl of something, anything out of
his kitchen. Something he was just going to throw away.
But he called me a 'damn bum' and pushed me away
from his door."

Tears filled Otis Emmett's eyes and spilled down his
cheeks into his beard. "I fought for him. I risked my
life for his family and everybody he knows. I watched
my buddies die for him, and I nearly did myself, but
that bastard couldn't give me a stale piece of bread?"

The alley was silent for a long time as no one spoke.
No one moved.

Then Dirk reached behind his back and brought out
a pair of cuffs. "Chef Norwood was a sorry excuse for
a human being, I'll grant you that," he told Emmett.
"And he shouldn't have treated you, or anybody else,
that way. But that didn't give you the right to kill him."

Savannah tensed and so did Ryan and John as Dirk
stepped behind Emmett and started to cuff him.

But the defeated soldier surrendered without resis-
tance.

Once Dirk had finished his task, they all began to breathe again.

Their homicide case was solved, their suspect had confessed, and Dirk had him in custody.

Savannah turned to John and said, "See, what Granny said was true. This trial and tribulation y'all have been going through . . . now it's just a thing of the past."

Chapter 21

As Savannah sat in her comfortable chair, sipping a big mug of hot chocolate—which she had secretly laced with Baileys Irish Cream when Granny wasn't looking—she felt incredibly guilty.

Usually, when Dirk made an arrest and she had assisted him, she accompanied him to the station house. Once the prisoner was booked, she helped him with the copious, monotonous paperwork.

It was one of the worst parts of being a cop.

But tonight he had offered to do it himself and encouraged her to go home and rest. She had gratefully accepted, knowing what it cost him to suggest such a thing.

Not only would he be stuck at work for several hours longer, but he would miss the chance to have her alone in the car on the way home. And she knew he was dying for some one-on-one time so that he could ask her what had happened earlier.

Of course she was going to have to tell him before the day was done. But she still hadn't decided what to say. So she was putting it off for as long as possible.

"You're sure quiet this evening, sweet pea," Granny said as she sipped from her own Baileys-free mug of hot chocolate.

"I'm okay," Savannah said. "It was just a big day, all the way around."

Granny's sharp eyes studied hers. "Hmmm. And here I thought it might've had something to do with that sale you went to this morning. Not finding what you're looking for, that can be pretty disappointing."

It was Savannah's turn to search her grandmother's face. And yes, there it was, the sarcasm, that knowing look that said, "You're lying. Your pants are on fire. And I can smell them all the way over here."

Granny cast a look across the room to the corner where Tammy and Waycross were, once again, sitting at the desk. Shoulder to shoulder, they were staring at the computer screen, researching something on the Internet.

She lowered her voice and said to Savannah, "If you wanna talk about that, you know, sale you went to— I'm all ears."

Savannah could feel the terrible knot tightening in her throat again, and she didn't trust herself to speak. She just busied herself with sipping the chocolate.

They sat quietly, until Tammy and Waycross turned in their chairs to face them.

"Okay," Tammy said, "we've got to talk."

"About what?" Granny asked.

"About this case that we just supposedly solved," Waycross said.

"What do you mean, 'supposedly'?" Savannah asked. "Dirk took him in. By now Emmett's booked and Dirk's halfway through the fives. It's a done deal."

"But we have our misgivings," Tammy told them.

"What misgivings? He confessed. We all heard it loud and clear," Savannah reminded her.

Waycross cleared his throat and shuffled uneasily on his chair. Like a good younger brother, he had always been uncomfortable when confronting his older sister. But he had been known to do so, from time to time, when he felt strongly enough about something. "We were as sure as you are that Otis killed the chef. We still are. But we were wondering why he stabbed and chopped him up so bad. I think you guys called it 'overkill.' Is that really over a missed bowl of soup or piece of bread?"

"Hey, I've seen people do worse." Savannah shook her head. "I had a case, years back, where one brother stabbed another one right through the heart with a steak knife. Turns out, he did it because the victim had nabbed the biggest porterhouse at a family barbecue. When you think about it, it's pretty stupid to kill another human being. There's hardly ever a justifiable reason for it. I guess a missed bowl of soup's as stupid a reason as any other."

Waycross wasn't convinced. "But Otis was a soldier, trained to kill, and good at it. Dr. Liu said that Norwood was probably dead as soon as he got whacked over the head. And he sure as shootin' was after he got that stab to the aorta. So what was the meat cleaver to the head all about?"

Savannah shrugged. "Again, who knows why anybody does what they do? We've got his confession. He had the knife and the baton and some blood-smeared leather gloves right there in his backpack. You can be sure that Dr. Liu is going to be able to lift DNA off all those."

Granny piped up, "I agree with Savannah. We got him dead to rights. I think you two are in a stew over nothin'."

But Tammy wasn't ready to surrender yet either. "What if somebody hired him and told him to do it that way—all gruesome and bloody like?"

Savannah smiled. "You've been watching too many movies, Tamitha, my dear."

"Yeah, I'll bet that's it! That's what it was, a murder for hire!" Waycross was suddenly so excited that he looked like he was about to burst. "Somebody paid him to do it, and they told him to mess Norwood up real bad."

Tammy started wriggling and waving her arms around. "That's right! And his mom just bought a car. And a PT Cruiser at that! Those cars keep their resell value, even the old ones."

"And that Chicago gal," Waycross continued, "she said his mom was poor, and obviously Otis is poor. . . ."

"So where did Mom Emmett get the money to buy the Cruiser?" Tammy grabbed Waycross and they hugged each other in a wild, crazy way that made Savannah feel, frankly, a bit uneasy.

The kids had lost it.

Yes, no doubt about it, they had gone over Niagara Falls on a garbage can lid.

"How much does an old PT Cruiser cost these days?" Waycross wondered out loud. "Turn around there, sugar, and check it out on the Internet."

Tammy spun around in her chair, and in no time her fingers were flying over the keyboard and websites were popping up right and left on the monitor.

Savannah looked over at Granny, who rolled her eyes and shook her head.

But something kept Savannah from rolling hers, too. She didn't know if she agreed with the kids about their "overkill" theory. But that business about Otis's mother buying a car when she was supposedly dirt poor—they might have something there.

"Five thousand dollars!" Tammy exclaimed. "That's how much she would've paid for it, more or less."

Savannah decided to play along, for a moment, just to make them happy—and because five thousand dollars was quite a bit for a poor person to pay for a car. "Okay, so if it's the way you guys say, and somebody paid for a hit . . . who's the somebody?"

"Well, it certainly wouldn't be Francia," Waycross reasoned, "or Carlos or Manuel. Maybe that Yale guy?"

"He had an airtight alibi," Savannah reminded them. "Though he could have paid for it, so we'll keep him on the back burner."

"Which takes us to the girlfriend, Perla Viola," Tammy said.

Savannah licked some of the cream off the top of her drink. "She was at the theater with her daughter in Hollywood."

"Says her, says the daughter," Waycross interjected. "But who's to say they're telling the truth?"

"They had tickets to the show and the *Playbill*. Dirk saw them, verified them."

"So what?" Tammy said. "You and I could get tickets to a play and the *Playbill*, too. That doesn't mean we stayed and watched it all the way through."

Tired as she was, Savannah's wheels started whirring. Tammy was absolutely right. Perla Viola and her daughter could have bought the tickets and then come directly home without seeing the play. That would've put them back in San Carmelita in plenty of time for the murder.

"You aren't really saying that you think Perla was there when Otis killed him, are you?" Savannah asked them.

Tammy and Waycross looked at each other, then Tammy shrugged. "No, I guess not. But that doesn't mean she didn't pay Otis to do it."

"And," Waycross added, "if I was paying somebody to commit a murder for me, I'd be sure I was in another town and had proof of it. Wouldn't you?"

Granny turned to Savannah. "They might be onto something, sugar. Did you tell me that the chef had thrown his girlfriend out and taken a new gal to Santa Tesla Island for a long, romantic weekend? That he'd given the latest girl some kind of nice ring? Most women would take a mighty dim view of that."

Suddenly, Savannah saw Umber Viola, sitting in her mother's living room, sunburned, toying nervously with her fingers.

One finger in particular.

The ring finger of her left hand.

The finger that had a white area that wasn't sunburned.

"Holy cow," she whispered.

"What is it?" Tammy asked.

She and Waycross jumped up from their desk chairs and rushed over to Savannah. Tammy sat down on Savannah's footstool and Waycross plopped himself down on the floor beside her chair.

"You thought of somethin'," Waycross said. "Spit it out, Sis."

"I'm afraid of what I'm thinking." Savannah closed her eyes, as though it would somehow erase the vision of that young woman with the sad doe eyes in so much pain, touching the white band on her finger where a large ring had recently been but was there no longer.

"You're thinking that Perla gal hired that fella to do it, ain'tcha?" Granny said.

"I'm hoping Perla did," Savannah replied. "Because I can't bear to consider the alternative."

Once a plan had been put into place, which included Tammy and Waycross visiting every one of the half-dozen pawn shops in San Carmelita first thing in the morning, the young couple said good night, leaving Savannah and Granny alone.

Still waiting for Dirk to return, and for their inevitable heart-to-heart talk, Savannah sat quietly in her chair, petting the cats.

Granny watched her from the sofa, a look of loving concern on her face. Finally, when the silence grew too long for comfort, she said, "You know, puddin' cat, there's an old saying that goes somethin' like this: 'A mother can only be as happy as her saddest child.' The same goes for grandmothers and grandchildren, too. And tonight I'm feelin' pretty poorly."

"I'm so sorry, Gran. You know the last thing I'd want to do is bring you down. Please don't worry. Everything's all right."

"Then how come your face is as long as a Kentucky fiddle?"

Savannah gulped. "I can't say, Granny. Please."

Horrified, Savannah watched as tears filled her precious grandmother's eyes. "Then it must be somethin' plumb awful, because you and me, we could always talk about 'most anything."

Savannah jumped up and ran to her grandma. She sat next to her on the sofa and gathered her into her arms. After kissing the top of her shining silver hair, she said, "No, Gran. It's not something awful. It's something that's perfectly natural. It's just . . . well . . . I figure I owe it to Dirk to tell him first—him being my husband and all. Once I've told him, you can ask me anything, and I'll tell you the straight-up truth. I promise."

Granny placed her hands on either side of Savannah's face and looked deeply into her eyes. "Ah. Okay. I understand."

"You do?"

"Yes, I reckon I do. But I'll wait for you to tell me yourself. You're right. You should tell Dirk first. I'm proud of you for honoring your husband in that way. You're a good wife, Savannah girl."

As Savannah gazed at her grandmother's face, her expression so soft and loving in the rose-colored light of a nearby lamp, Savannah thought she was the most beautiful woman she had ever seen.

Her eyes were still the deepest, richest shade of blue, like fine sapphires—exactly like Savannah's. And her hair formed such a lovely, shimmering halo around her head. No doubt that had been part of why the young, childish Savannah had thought her some sort of secret angel.

Of course, being more than eighty years old, Gran had lines galore. But although society might condemn her for having them and try to sell her all sorts of products and procedures to get rid of those wrinkles, Savannah loved every one of them. Given the opportunity to erase them all, Savannah would have considered the idea preposterous, almost blasphemous. She would have kept her grandmother exactly as she looked right at that moment for all eternity, if she could.

You didn't mess with perfection. And her blessed grandmother was as close to perfect as Savannah ever expected to encounter here on earth.

Granny twined one of Savannah's dark curls around her forefinger and said, "You know, sweet girl . . . you're not only a wonderful wife, but in your lifetime you've been an amazing mother to a whole lot of God's creatures."

Savannah wasn't sure she'd heard correctly. "What?"

"I said you're a fine mother, too."

"But . . . I've never been—"

"Don't be silly. Of course you have. You've had a mother's heart almost from the very beginning of your years. Sadly, you had to. But it's done you good in the long run. And you've done a lot of good for others because of your early trials. You've played the motherhood role for so many orphaned souls who've crossed your path."

Savannah considered her words, then said, "I guess I've always felt maternal toward my brothers and sisters, but . . ."

"And those two cats, which you rescued from the pound, and all the critters you had before them. And the thousands of people in need who you encountered when you were a police officer, and even now in the work you do. How many tears have you wiped away? How much good advice have you handed out? How much practical, everyday help did you offer to people? How many wounds have you bound and how many broken hearts have you ministered to? Thousands, Savannah. That's how many. And if that ain't bein' a mother, then I don't know what is."

Savannah's heart filled to overflowing and tears spilled out of her eyes. But they were good tears. Healing tears.

Granny knew.

Of course she did. Gran always knew.

But she was respecting Savannah's right to share her news with Dirk first by not requiring any sort of answer.

Gran kissed away her granddaughter's tears and stood. "I just heard a car pull into your driveway," she said. "Sounds like a big engine, so it's probably your husband in that borrowed policeman's car of his. I'm going to go on upstairs and go to bed now."

Savannah stood with Gran and walked her to the foot of the stairs.

"Don't you worry about a thing," Granny told her before ascending. "I'm going to say a big ol' prayer for you and your man tonight, and this is all going to work out just fine in the end. You'll see."

As Savannah watched her grandmother climb the staircase to go to bed, she was even more sure than ever of one fact: Angels did, indeed, still walk the earth.

And sometimes, they wore floral print caftans.

Chapter 22

As Savannah took Dirk's hand and led him out to the backyard and the wisteria arbor, it occurred to her that maybe this wasn't the best plan. The moonlight streaming through the beautiful lavender blossoms overhead, and the heady perfume of her rose garden, reminded her of that lovely night they had made love in this very spot.

The night when, for a little while today, she had thought that they might have conceived a child of their own.

She had thought, just in case things didn't go so well, that the backyard would provide more privacy than their bedroom—which was right down the hall from Gran's guest room.

However, now that she was here, in the moonlight, smelling the roses, remembering . . . she decided it hadn't been such a great plan.

But they were there, and judging from the anxiety

bordering on agony that Dirk was radiating, she knew she couldn't wait any longer.

"Sit down over there, sweetheart," she told him, leading him to a comfortable wicker chair.

As he did what she had asked, she pulled another chair around so that she could sit on it and face him directly.

He was terribly silent as she settled into her seat, leaned forward, and took his hands in hers.

"You know, of course, that I didn't go shopping today," she began.

"I'm a police detective, Van. I know you went to the doctor. Now tell me what you found out."

When she hesitated, he said, "Quick. Babe, I'm dyin' here."

"Dr. Dalano ran some tests and . . ."

She stared down at his hands, unable to look him in the eyes.

When she finally did venture a glance, she was shocked to see that his eyes were already wet with tears. In all the years she had known him, she had never seen him looking so forlorn.

"Just tell me, darlin'," he said. "Whatever it is, we'll get through it. I promise you. I'm here for you. I always will be, no matter what."

Okay, she told herself. *Do it. Dive right in. It has to be done, so say it now and get it—*

"I can't have babies."

"What?"

The words she had been holding back all day began to tumble over themselves, fighting to come out. "These crazy symptoms I've been having . . . I thought I might be pregnant. Then I missed a period, but I always miss periods, so no big deal, but then the doctor ran some tests, and she says I'm in peri-menopause."

"Perry Mena-who? Who's he?"

"Peri means 'before' or 'around,' or something like that. Anyway, it's not officially menopause until I've missed a whole year of periods, but she said my reproduction system has changed, and not only am I not pregnant, but I waited too long and now I can't ever have babies."

Looking at his face, so blank, so empty, tore at her heart. He was obviously in shock. Terrible shock.

She began to cry, hard, as she had in the doctor's office. "Oh, Dirk, I can never give you children, and you're so sweet and good with kids. You deserve to be a father, but I can't have your babies, and I'm so, so sorry!"

Still he sat there, motionless, just staring at her.

She ached for him to say something, anything. Even if he told her that he wanted a divorce, it would be better than this awful silence.

"Dirk, I wish that—"

"Wait." He placed his fingers over her lips. "The doctor said you're going through the change of life? That you're . . . past your childbearing years?"

His fingertips kept her from speaking, so she nodded.

"And that's why you've been so tired and dizzy and why you fell down?"

Another nod.

Suddenly, he grabbed her in a hug that was so tight, she could scarcely breathe. And he began crying, too, wracking sobs that shook them both as he crushed her to him.

Oh no, she thought, panic and grief overwhelming her.

He was taking the news far worse than she'd thought he would. He must have really, really wanted kids.

She couldn't give her husband babies, and he was devastated.

She didn't know what to do. Certainly, she had seen Dirk tear up from time to time over the years. Though he would never admit it, he was a sentimental sort of guy, and even a sad or inspiring movie would cause him to pretend he'd gotten some of Cleo's fur in his eye.

But she had never seen him sob uncontrollably like this. And it broke her heart to think she was the cause of it.

"I'm so sorry, honey," she said, holding him close and stroking his hair. "I didn't realize it meant so much to you to have children. If you want a divorce, I understand."

Abruptly, he released her. "What?" he said, his deep voice tremulous.

"I told you that if you want a—"

"I heard you. Why would you say a dumb thing like that?"

"Because you're so upset. You're crying. Obviously, you really had your heart set on being a dad."

He gave her a long, quizzical look, then he started to laugh.

At first she thought he had become hysterical, then she saw the broad smile on his face and the joy in his tear-wet eyes.

He took her face in both of his hands and kissed her forehead, each cheek, her chin, and then her lips—most tenderly.

"Oh, Van," he said, his breath warm and moist on her cheek as he pulled her close. "I wasn't crying because you can't have babies, sweetheart. I was crying because I'm so relieved. The way you were acting, I was sure you had cancer or . . . or . . . a fatal case of creeping crud-itis or whatever. I thought my wife was gonna die on me. But you're okay, and that's all I care about, Van. That's all I ever cared about. You."

A tsunami of relief, like she had never felt before, swept over her.

He was telling her the truth. He didn't care. Except about her.

"I love you," she said, looking into her mate's eyes, seeing the love and devotion reflected there.

In all of her years, having said those three words countless times, Savannah had never meant them more.

"Menopause, hmm," he said, nuzzling her neck. "Does that mean we won't have to use birth control anymore?"

"After twelve months of no-show from Aunt Flo."

"And you've got a couple of those months out of the way already?"

She gave him a sexy grin. "Yep. Down the hatch. In the bank."

"Then how's about you and I meet back here, ten months from tonight, and make wild, insane, mind-blowing love under this, this contraption. . . ."

"Arbor."

"This arbor. Whatcha say, babycakes?"

"I say, we'll raise such a ruckus that the coyotes up on the hills will be howling at the moon!"

Over breakfast the next morning, Savannah tried to keep a straight face and not make goo-goo eyes at her husband too much, considering that Granny was sharing the same table.

But it wasn't easy. After the moonlight sweetness and the intimacy that had followed in their bedroom, she had started her day fully sated. All without eating a bite.

Certainly, Gran had picked up on the fact that all was peaceful on the western front, and the three of them enjoyed quite a pleasant meal—considering.

Considering that she had broached the topic with Dirk that maybe, just maybe, the suspect who he had arrested yesterday might not be the only offender in his murder case.

"Let me get this straight," he said over a well-buttered biscuit, dripping with the peach preserves Gran had brought with her on the plane. "You want me to investigate Umber Viola for the capital crime of 'murder by hire.' And you ask me to do this because Otis Emmett's mom bought a used car. One that, for all we know, she's making payments on."

"And the sunburn," Savannah reminded him.

"Yes, and because she had a sunburn, which you think she got on a trip to Santa Tesla with her mother's boyfriend—who just happens to have raised her since she was about five."

"Which makes it all the more wicked and perverse, if it's true," Granny chimed in.

"And the band of white skin on her ring finger." Savannah nudged his leg under the table with her fuzzy house slipper.

"Yes," he said, "because no one in the history of the world has ever worn a ring to the beach, gotten burned, taken the ring off, and had a white mark like that one!"

Savannah stuck out her lip in a pout. "Well, when you say it like *that*, Mr. Smarty-Pants, it sounds stupid."

"That's because it *is* stupid, Van. Emmett confessed. We've got him. Case closed."

"Not if Tammy and Waycross have anything to do with it," Granny said with a smirk. "They're gonna be bargin' through that door any second now."

Two heartbeats later, there was a brief knock at the kitchen door, then it opened and Tammy and Waycross sailed in.

Dirk froze in midchew, then said to Savannah, "How did she do that?"

"She's got great ears and can hear cars coming a mile off. She can even tell whose car it is."

Gran blew on her nails and polished them on her chest. "Hey, you don't raise nine teenage grandkids without developing some special skills along the way."

"Good morning, everyone," chimed the sunshine girl as she danced over to the table and took a seat next to Granny.

Waycross sat beside her, an enormous grin on his adorable freckled face.

Savannah knew her baby brother, and she knew that look. They had something good.

"We've got something good," he said.

"I knew that." Savannah took a sip of her coffee. "Stop pussyfootin' around and cough it up."

"First of all, Tammy was up most of the night doing research," he began.

Savannah leaned over and whispered to Gran, "That means she hacked into somebody's account illegally, without a warrant, committing a felony. And because she's so smart, she can do that stuff and not get caught and thrown in jail. That's why she's an extremely valuable member of this team."

Gran nodded. "Gotcha."

"I found out something interesting," Tammy said.

"More solid evidence that either Perla Viola or her daughter, Umber, had something to do with Baldwin Norwood's murder?" Dirk asked, grinning.

"You're on board with this? That's fantastic!" Tammy started to bounce up and down on her chair.

"Settle down, Tams," Savannah told her. "You need to learn how to recognize sarcasm when you hear it."

"We'll see what you think once you've heard this," Waycross told Dirk. Turning to Tammy, he said, "Tell them about the phone calls, honey bun."

Savannah paused, biscuit halfway to her mouth. Tammy was "honey bun" now? Interesting.

"I accessed Umber Viola's cell phone records—"

"You mean 'hacked,'" Savannah interjected.

"Whatever. And the night she was supposedly at the Pantages, watching *Phantom* with her mom—you know, like in the seat right next to her mom—she made six phone calls during those two hours."

"That's horrible!" Dirk said. "I go crazy if somebody uses their phone in a movie theater. But in a joint like that, you pay a couple of hundred dollars per seat!"

"Make fun if you must, Pee Pee Head, but who do you think she was calling? Just guess. It's really cool."

"Otis Emmett?" Dirk asked with a smirk.

"Well, no. That would have been really super cool, but still. . . . She was calling her mom! And talking to her for four, five, even seven minutes!"

"No way!" Dirk gasped. "That's positively criminal.

I'll go pick her up right now and charge her with creating a nuisance in a fancy theater and disturbing the peace of everybody around her." He shook his head. "What are people thinking these days? Using their cell phones to talk even when they're sitting right next to somebody."

Tammy turned to Savannah. "I am not talking to him anymore."

"I understand. And I, too, think that is extremely cool. Obviously, they lied about their whereabouts that evening, and that's quite suspicious."

"Just wait'll you hear the cherry on the Dairy Queen Snickers Blizzard," Waycross crowed.

Dirk turned to Savannah. "They put a cherry on those?"

"Hush." She nodded to Waycross. "Go ahead, darlin'."

Waycross slipped his arm around Tammy's waist and gave her a sideways hug. "Listen to this! We went out to the pawn shops this morning as soon as they opened. We downloaded a picture of that Umber gal that we found on the Internet and showed it to them. The third place we went to . . . bingo!"

Savannah perked up. "Bingo?"

"Bingo!" Tammy lifted her arms over her head and did a little boob jiggle dance that caused Gran's eyebrows to rise a notch and a half.

"Please translate 'bingo,' bimbo," Dirk grumbled.

"They knew her. The owner said she came in there the morning of the murder and sold him a three-carat canary yellow diamond ring. He paid her five thousand dollars for it, and she demanded to be paid in cash. He said he always pays in cash anyway, but she was making a big point about how that was the only way she'd sell it."

Savannah looked at Dirk. He looked back, and she knew his wheels were turning right along with hers.

"Come on. We have to at least check it out," she told him.

"I can't," he replied. "Emmett's arraignment is today, and I have to be there."

"Then you won't mind if I do it, right? I'll just drop by and have a little chat with Umber. See what I can drag outta her."

Dirk picked up a piece of bacon and popped it into his mouth, then stood and gathered up the dishes. "Look at you," he told Savannah, "sitting there, asking permission. Like you're not gonna do it anyway, whether I want you to or not."

"Why, darlin'," she said, batting her eyelashes at him and turning up the Southern drawl several notches. "I don't know what you're speaking of. I wouldn't dream of undertaking such an endeavor without my dear husband's blessing."

Once he had shoved the utensils into the dishwasher, he turned toward the living room. "Go for it," he said. "Just keep me posted. And be careful."

Once he was gone, Waycross turned to Savannah and said with a grin, "You've got that down pat, sis."

"Whatever are you speaking of, brother of mine?" She downed the last swig of her coffee.

"Giving Dirk-o the illusion of control," Tammy replied.

"It's a fine art, and she's a master," Granny told Tammy. "Watch and learn, young woman. Watch and learn."

Chapter 23

Savannah had her work cut out for her, trying to track down Umber Viola. The young woman hadn't been at the Norwood mansion, but a helpful neighbor suggested that she might be found at the local library. Apparently, she read to a circle of children there on the weekends.

It didn't make Savannah feel any better to hear that Umber was a charitable soul who entertained kids on her own time. Savannah would have much preferred that she was a shallow, mean, foolish person. It would have made it much easier to accuse her of murder.

When Savannah inquired about her at the library, the head librarian told her that Umber had called in sick and canceled her reading session.

But as Savannah was leaving the library, a teenage girl, who had been sorting books on a rolling cart, hurried over to her. She glanced around, as though making sure no one was listening. Then she whispered, "I heard Umber went to the pier to think and just be alone for a while. She's taking this thing that happened in her family—you know, the murder—really hard."

"Yes," Savannah replied. "It was a terrible thing. Thank you so much for your help. And for the work you do here at the library. Libraries are so important."

By the time Savannah found Umber on the pier, it was well past lunchtime. Savannah was feeling a bit tired and more than a little cranky.

But at least I know why now, she thought. *And much to my husband's relief, I'm not gonna be kicking the bucket anytime soon.*

As she climbed the steps to one of the longest wooden wharfs in Southern California, she could see Umber Viola standing down at the end. Her back was to the shore. She appeared to be gazing out at the horizon, where Santa Tesla Island appeared to be floating on a downy pillow of fog.

Savannah walked the length of the pier, passing fishermen cutting bait, lovers strolling hand in hand, and some kids flying dragon and pirate kites.

Finally, she was standing directly behind Umber, and what she saw, now that she was closer, caused her pulse to race.

On a bench, only a foot or two away from the girl, was a pair of designer sandals, neatly placed side by side. And next to the shoes was a sweater, folded oh-so-perfectly. On top of the sweater lay a pair of earrings, a watch, and some bracelets. . . .

And a white envelope with the word "Mom" written on it.

From Savannah's vantage point, she could see that Umber wasn't gazing out at the island in the distance.

Instead, she was staring down at the waves crashing against the barnacle-encrusted pilings far below. Tears were streaming down her face.

"Umber," Savannah said softly.

It seemed to take the young woman a moment to register Savannah's gentle greeting. But finally she turned around and gave Savannah such a blank look that Savannah thought perhaps she didn't recognize her.

Finally, Umber said, "You shouldn't be here. I don't want you here. I don't want anyone here. I need to do this alone."

Savannah pointed to the nearby bench. "There's no reason for you to be alone, sweetie. I'm here now. Come sit over here and talk to me for a while. You might feel much better if you did."

"There's no point in talking. What's done is done. And it can't be undone."

"That's true," Savannah told her. "But we can still try to make the best of an awful situation. I'd like to help you. I believe I can, if you'll let me."

Umber shook her head. "There's nothing you can do for me. I did a terrible thing, and now my life is over, too."

Savannah stepped closer to her and put her hand on the girl's forearm. "Your life is not over. If you come forward, turn yourself in, and explain what happened—"

"Then maybe I won't get the needle. Is that what you're saying?" She wiped her tears away with her sleeve. "I know that they can execute somebody for what I did. Paying somebody to kill a person . . . that's like hiring a hit man, isn't it?"

"I won't lie to you. You committed a very serious

crime, and you'll have to pay for it. But still, the best thing you can do for yourself is explain what happened."

"Nobody's going to listen to me. Nobody cares. Nobody's ever cared."

"That isn't true. I care. And I'll listen."

Gently, Savannah tugged Umber's arm and slowly guided the young woman over to the bench, where she sat her down.

One by one, Savannah picked up the items that were laid there and gave them back to their distraught owner. She slid the bracelets back over her arms, wrapped the sweater around her shoulders, handed her the earrings, and put the sandals back on her feet.

Savannah discreetly slipped the envelope into her own pocket.

Then she sat down beside Umber. She reached for the woman's hand, which was damp and cold, and folded it between her own.

"Take your time, honey," Savannah told her. "We're in no hurry. Just tell me what happened and why."

"Baldwin was like my dad, you know? He and my mom got together when I was just five. I hardly even remember what it was like before him."

"If he helped raise you, he *was* like a father to you," Savannah said. "I'm sure you loved him."

"I did. And he always said that he loved me, too. But now that I'm older, I know why he said that. So that he could do things to me. He made me feel special, so that I wouldn't tell on him."

Shivers ran down Savannah's back, and they had nothing to do with the chilly ocean breeze. "I'm sorry, sweetheart," she said. "He had no right to do those things."

"He even told me that I was the only reason he was

with my mom. He said he hated her for all the mean things that she said and did to him and to me. He said he wanted to leave her. But he couldn't take me with him, because the law wouldn't allow it."

"He was certainly right about that," Savannah told her.

"He always told me that, once I was grown up, he would take me away from my mom, and he and I would live happily ever after without the wicked old witch around. It was like this special secret that we had. We had a lot of secrets."

"Tell me what happened, leading up to his . . . passing."

"It started on my birthday," Umber said. "For my present he gave me a pretty ring with a big yellow diamond. When my mom saw it, she got really jealous and threw a fit. She said it looked like an engagement ring, and it wasn't appropriate. They had a big fight, and she accused him of loving me more than he ever did her. She said he shouldn't have given me a diamond ring when he had never given her one after all their years together."

Umber stopped to take a breath, and Savannah said, "Yes, a thing like that might cause an uproar in anybody's household."

"My mom was going to throw me out of the house, send me away to live with my aunt in New York. But Baldwin got really mad and told her that she was the one who was leaving, not me. He said we were going away for a few days to Santa Tesla Island. And by the time he got back, she'd better be gone."

Savannah patted the girl's cold hand. "That must've

"That's how much I hated him," she was saying. "I didn't just want him dead, I wanted him chopped into pieces so that he couldn't come back and hurt me and my mom again."

Savannah put her arms around the girl and rocked her, just as she would have a younger sibling—or a child of her own.

"Sh-h-h," she said. "There, there. The worst is over now. From here on, things will be better for you, Umber. I promise. You'll see."

But as Savannah sat there, trying to console the broken child in her arms, she couldn't help thinking how terrible it was that her words were actually true. Compared to the hell Umber Viola had been living in for the past thirteen years, prison would probably be an improvement.

And how awful was that?

Chapter 24

Once again, it was opening night for ReJuvene, and Savannah and company sat at their table, watching the rich, famous, and beautiful assemble for the restaurant's repeat performance.

Savannah looked around the dining room, enjoying its flickering fireplace, glistening waterfall, antique brickwork, leather furniture, and romantic lighting. It was every bit as beautiful as she remembered it. Maybe even more, because of all Ryan and John had endured to bring the amazing establishment to fruition. Again.

"This place is really living up to its name tonight, isn't it?" she said to her loved ones gathered around her.

"I don't know," Dirk said as he smeared an obscene amount of butter on an onion roll. "What does ReJuvene mean?"

"It's Spanish for rejuvenate, renew, restore. Something like that," Savannah told him. "Or maybe it's Italian or French. I don't know. They speak at least five languages fluently, you know."

"Oh." He poked most of the roll into his mouth. "I thought it was a word they made up so they could use both of their initials in it."

"Yeah, me too," Waycross piped up.

"Peasants, both of you," Savannah told them, shaking her head.

Instead of being insulted, they laughed at her.

"I speak Pig Latin," Waycross said. "Oes-day at-thay ount-cay?"

Dirk picked up another roll and pretended he was going to throw it at Savannah.

"Don't you dare! If you embarrass me tonight, I swear I will—"

"Chill out, darlin'. I'm not going to embarrass you," he said, tossing the bread back into the basket. "I promise I won't scratch any of my private zones, belch, or fa . . ." He cut a quick look at Granny and saw she was giving him a threatening scowl. ". . . or do anything that might offend the lovely ladies sitting at this table."

"How about me?" Waycross asked.

Dirk leaned toward him and whispered, "Let's just say, if I feel the need to pass gas, it'll be in your direction."

"Gee, thanks. You'd better be nice to me."

"Why start now?"

Waycross grinned. "You'll find out later."

"Yeah," Tammy said, snickering. "Later."

"O-okay," Dirk said, buttering another roll.

Savannah ignored their silliness and watched as Ryan

and John moved gracefully about the room, greeting and charming wherever they went.

Tonight there was none of the tension that had marred the previous opening. Under the supervision of Chef Francia Fortun and her sous-chef, Carlos Ortez, the kitchen was working smoothly, turning out delicious, flawless dishes one after the other.

The waiters, including Maria Ortez, worked the tables with friendly efficiency, making sure every diner's needs were well satisfied.

A few moments before, servers had distributed flutes of champagne, telling the guests to ready themselves for a special toast.

And special it was, indeed, when Ryan and John delivered a sincere thank-you to everyone who had helped to resurrect ReJuvene. Savannah's heart warmed when her name and those at her table were mentioned among the honored.

When the time came to sip the bubbly, Dirk leaned across the table and said to Granny, "Well, are you going to join us, Gran? I know you object to Demon Rum, but how about a sip of some fizzy?"

Savannah tensed a bit, hearing Dirk's offer. Granny was an extraordinarily tolerant person in many ways, but she had witnessed too much suffering caused by the overconsumption of alcohol to ever be a fan. She had been a bona fide, card-carryin' teetotaler her entire life, and she wasn't likely to amend her ways at this late date.

But she did smile at Dirk when she said, "No, thank you, sonny boy. I don't mind if y'all do, it bein' a special occasion. But I'll do my toastin' with this here fine iced tea. I'm sure there's just as much good luck in a glass of this as a bottle of that bubbly stuff."

When they all lifted their glasses, Savannah couldn't help but notice that Tammy also chose to forego the champagne and celebrate with a simple club soda.

Since when did the Sunshine Girl not imbibe? She might have a lot of rules about sugar, salt, and flour, but Savannah couldn't recall any time before when Tammy had refused a glass of spirits.

"Aren't you celebrating with us tonight, Tams?" Savannah couldn't help asking her friend. "It's not like you to sit out a dance."

Tammy looked at Waycross and snickered.

He looked at her, blushed, and snickered back.

The champagne bubbles hit Savannah's bloodstream and sent a rush of effervescence throughout her system.

Or was it something far better than champagne?

Maybe what she was feeling was joyful anticipation as she watched a rush of love and the excitement flow between her beloved brother and the sweetest woman she had ever known.

"What's this?" Dirk asked, looking from the giggling twosome to Savannah and back. "Am I missing something here?"

"Sh-h-h," Savannah said. "I think Tammy and Waycross might have some sort of announcement to make. Am I right, little brother? Tamitha?"

"Well," Tammy said, jumping around in her seat. "Most people get married and then they buy a house and then they have a baby. But, thanks to you, Savannah, I already have a house."

"Yes, and . . . ?" Savannah could feel her heart getting ready to take flight.

Waycross picked up Tammy's hand and kissed it. "And this morning, I asked Miss Tammy here if she'd do me the honor of being my wife."

Tammy's effervescence overflowed, "And I said, 'Yes, yes, yes!'"

The table exploded with lots of screaming, laughter, jumping up from chairs, running around, hugging and kissing—much to the astonishment and delight of the other diners.

When all was said and done, Savannah found herself on her knees between her brother and friend's chairs, her arms around both of their necks.

"I knew it! I knew it!" she said, strangling them with hugs. "When? When are you going to have the ceremony?"

Waycross blushed and Tammy giggled. "Um, we don't know for sure," Tammy said. "But it's going to be soon."

"Yeah, real soon," Waycross said. "'Cause we do know for sure when the little one's coming, and that's gonna be in about six and a half months."

"Little one? Little one?" Savannah went from kneeling to sitting as her knees gave out beneath her. She turned and looked at her friend's tummy and saw that maybe, yes, there it was. A wee bit of a bump. Actually, she had noticed it a week or so before, but thought it was just the result of Tammy eating all those extra half-cookies. "A baby," she said. "Oh, Tammy, honey, that's wonderful!"

She kissed her friend's cheeks, then turned and did the same to her brother.

Gran had left her chair, too, and was standing behind Tammy. She bent down and gave her a hug. "Congratulations, sweetie," she said. "What a blessing this is going to be. We'll not only have you in our family, but a new youngun to love in the bargain."

Tammy ducked her head and said, "We were a little bit afraid to tell you, Granny, knowing how you feel about, well, certain things. I hope you aren't disappointed in us."

Granny's eyes shone with kindness and wisdom as she replied, "Darlin', we aren't going to worry about what's gone on in the past with so many blessings coming up in the future. For all you know, you and Waycross here are gonna have a passel of kids before you're done."

Gran cleared her throat and lifted one eyebrow. "That's the thing about babies. . . . They take nine months to hatch. All except the first one. There's some kinda rule that says: The first one can come at any time."

Everyone laughed and continued to chatter excitedly.

Savannah got up from the floor and straightened her skirt and her hair. She looked around and realized that they were, indeed, making a spectacle of themselves at the Moonlight Magnolia table.

Oh well, she thought. *What else is new?*

From the other side of the room, Ryan and John were beaming in their direction, and the rest of the diners appeared to be enjoying their not-so-private celebration, so she decided there was nothing to worry about.

Then she felt Dirk standing behind her. His big warm hand slid around her waist as he pulled her close. "How are you, babe?" he whispered. "Are you okay with, you know, all of this?"

She looked down at her precious friend, her dear brother, and her blessed grandmother, all of whom appeared to be the happiest she had ever seen them.

She leaned her head over on her husband's shoulder and said, "Of course I am, darlin'. With all these miracles of love happening all around me, I've never been better!"

If you think going home again is hard, try being a plus-sized PI with a troubled family legacy. But Savannah Reid is no shrinking violet. She's ready for her high school reunion, complete with mean girls, ex-beaus—and murder charges . . .

When Savannah Reid fled McGill, Georgia, all those years ago, everyone figured the chubby girl from the wrong side of the tracks wouldn't be back. But with the hope of seeing her beloved Granny Reid, Savannah makes a triumphant return with her handsome husband on her arm, ready to face the past at her 25th high school reunion. When her nemesis Queen of Mean Jeanette Parker shows she hasn't changed her stripes one bit, Savannah rises to the challenge—and *finally* comes out on top. Until Jeanette's dead body shows up in the swamp and just about everyone is ready to pin Savannah for murder . . .

Of course, Savannah's own Moonlight Magnolia Detective Agency comes to her rescue. But even her best buds are having trouble keeping Savannah out of jail, despite the fact that Jeanette has more than enough enemies—and quite possibly the blood of her recently deceased husband on her hands. Savannah never thought going back to school would be so hard. But she's learned a thing or two in her time away, and she's ready to finally make the grade when it comes to the ultimate high school redemption . . .

Please turn the page for an exciting sneak peek of G.A. McKevett's KILLER REUNION coming in April 2016 wherever print and e-books are sold!

Chapter 1

Staring across the table at her dearly beloved, relatively new husband, Savannah Reid wondered if any man in the history of the world had been bludgeoned to death at the kitchen breakfast table because he read his newspaper too loudly.

If not, Dirk was in danger of becoming the first.

Would they list him in *The Guinness Book of World Records*?

Would Madame Tussaud build a special display in the Chamber of Horrors at her wax museum, dedicated to the unfortunate victim and his dastardly wife?

Savannah could just envision it now: the wax version of Dirk slumped forward onto the table, his face buried in his oversized bowl of cornflakes, the *San Carmelita Star* spread in front of him, taking up far more than his reasonable half of the table. Standing slightly behind and looming over him would be the figure of Savannah herself—her flannel Minnie Mouse pajamas spattered with blood, a broken coffee mug in her hand—wearing the maniacal grin of a woman who had finally, utterly, irrevocably snapped.

"Whatcha thinkin' about?"

"What?" Jerked from her morbid and far too pleasant reverie, Savannah realized that he was speaking to her.

"I asked you what you were thinking about just now." He reached down, grabbed the right lower corner of the newspaper page, and with the amount of energy commonly expended to hurl a discus seventy meters or more, he heaved it to the left. The deafening racket, created by what should have been such a simple movement, set Savannah's teeth on edge and caused her to grip her *Beauty and the Beast* mug so tightly that the Beast grimaced. She braced herself for what would inevitably come next.

No sooner had the leaf settled into place than Stage Two of Page Turning commenced—the dreaded Smoothing of the Paper.

The love of her life and current source of great torment began to slap the recently turned sheet with his open palm. Moving from corner to corner in a clockwise motion, he pounded each area repeatedly and thoroughly. That accomplished, he attacked the center of the page, smacking, smoothing, and flattening with all the vim and vigor of an arachnophobe who feared his morning paper was infested with a horde of black widow spiders.

"So, what *were* you thinking about?" he asked again, leaving the paper for a moment and assaulting his cereal.

"Why do you ask?" She watched him raise an impossibly large spoonful of flakes to his mouth and shovel it in.

He gave her a sweet, loving smile, enhanced by the flakes dangling from his lower lip and the milk oozing from the right corner of his mouth. "I was just wondering, because you look so happy, so contented."

She shrugged and batted her eyelashes in her most demure Southern belle fashion. "Why, just a little daydream," she drawled.

"About?"

"Madame Tussaud."

He looked puzzled for a moment, then dropped his spoon into his bowl. The clang of metal hitting metal sounded like Quasimodo and the bells of Notre Dame announcing the top of the hour. But it was a necessary evil. After he had broken two of her favorite china bowls, Savannah had restricted him to using an indestructible graniteware bowl—the dark blue, white-speckled kind that cowboys used around their campfires. Or so she'd assured him. She had given the bowl to him for his birthday and had told him it was a vintage collectible that had actually been used on the set of *Bonanza*.

Yes, she was learning that successful matrimony required a certain degree of ingenuity, bolstered by an occasional whopper of a soul-blackening lie.

"Madame Tooth-So?" He quirked one eyebrow as he searched his memory banks for the reference, then nodded knowingly. "Oh, yeah. I remember her. She was that gal we busted who was running the cathouse on Lester Street. The mayor was playin' footsie with a couple of her gals when we rousted the place."

Savannah laughed, wax museum horrors momentarily forgotten, as the memory took her back to the "good

old days" when she and Dirk had both been cops, partners even. Dirk was still with the San Carmelita Police
Department, but she and they had long since parted
ways.

But that didn't stop her from wallowing in the mem-
ories.

"Yes," she said. "As I recall, he was tickling more
than their feet when we charged through the door of that
bedroom."

"And remember the look on the captain's face when
he saw you hauling his mayorship in . . . cuffed and
wearing nothing but his boxers?"

Savannah groaned. "That had to be one of the bigger
nails in my law-enforcement coffin."

Sharing a companionable laugh, they were, once again,
on common ground. Domestic tranquility had been restored.

Dirk stood, picked up his bowl and spoon, and carried them to the sink. As he rinsed them and placed
them into the dishwasher, Savannah congratulated herself on the minor improvement in his behavior. Who
said a wife couldn't change her husband if she only
nagged loudly and frequently enough?

"Wanna ride along and keep me company today?" he
asked as he pitched the abused but gloriously spider-
free newspaper into the recycle bin.

Another uptick on the Civility Meter.

She eyed him suspiciously. "Won't this be your fifth
day staking out that strip-joint dive there in Twin
Oaks?"

He shot her a guilty look. "Yeah. So?"

How typical of him to invite her along when his as-
signment was as exciting as watching a snail marathon.
"I'd best stick around here and pack for the trip." She

sighed, thinking about her upcoming journey back in time. Back home to the tiny rural town of McGill, Georgia, where she had been born and reared, not to mention teased and tormented.

A chance to reconnect with her past at a joyous event called a high school class reunion. Woo-hoo. She could hardly wait.

But then, she would also be celebrating Granny Reid's birthday. And that would make the effort all worthwhile.

Or mostly worthwhile.

Dirk donned a self-satisfied smirk and said, "Rather than leave it to the last minute, *I* packed last night."

"Big whoop-de-do. Underdrawers and your spare toothbrush. You fellas have it easy."

"And you gals take way too much junk and expect us guys to lug it for you."

She thought of all the clothes spread across her bed upstairs, next to her still empty suitcase. Yes, he had her there. In an attempt to wear something that showed off her overly generous bustline without accenting her overly abundant butt line, she would be dragging half of her closet to McGill and back.

Okay . . . *he* would be.

Bless his little pea-pickin' heart.

She stood and carried her own bowl to the sink. Once she'd rinsed it and placed it into the dishwasher, she turned and slipped her arms around his waist. Hugging him tightly against her, she closed her eyes and breathed in the delicious smell of him: freshly applied deodorant, shave lotion, and the faint unique scent of his skin. He smelled like protection, companionship, and strength. But mostly, he smelled like love.

Reluctantly, she released him, and as he walked away to gather up his essentials—cell phone, notebook, badge, and weapon—she did a quick mental tally of how long it would reasonably be until she laid eyes on him again.

If the stakeout was a bust, eight and a half hours. If he actually nailed some dude or dudette dealing meth out of the so-called "gentlemen's" club, it would be ten or twelve, at least, by the time he had them snuggly situated behind bars and had completed all the paperwork.

"Be careful, darlin'," she said as he headed for the back door.

"I always am."

She thought of what a usual shift entailed in the world of Detective Sergeant Dirk Coulter. The safest thing he did all day was merge into rush-hour traffic on the 101 freeway with an apple fritter in one hand and a mucho grande coffee in the other. "Yeah, well, be more careful than that."

He gave her a grin that warmed every part of her body, and said, "Love ya." Then he sailed out the door and slammed it, rattling the dishes in the cupboards and sending her cats running for cover.

"You better love me, boy," she replied as she turned back to the sink and the half-washed coffeepot. "After all I put up with offa you, you'd better be plumb nuts about me."

"You okay, babe?"

Dirk reached over and placed his hand on top of Savannah's. She was hanging on to the armrest of the airline seat as tightly as she usually gripped the lap bar of a triple-loop roller coaster.

True, she wasn't crazy about landings, but she usually didn't mind them this much. She seldom broke out in a cold sweat and felt the overwhelming need to shriek, "We're all going to die! We're all going to die!" as the plane banked, then straightened and descended, lining up with the runway.

Below she could see Atlanta, Georgia, spread before her, remarkably greener than the beige desert landscape she had left behind in Southern California.

She liked green. She loved the smell of the Georgia pines and the peach orchards. Hearing the soft, sweet drawls, so like her own, did her heart good.

Then there was the less health-conscious regional cuisine. It probably did her heart far less good, but it certainly nourished her spirit, and that alone was worth the trip.

She was looking forward to fewer kale chips and bean sprout wraps and more pecan pie à la mode and peach cobbler.

There was a lot she loved about Georgia and Georgians. So, ordinarily, she didn't mind a homecoming.

She had been back a few times in the past twenty years and didn't recall experiencing quite so much dread at the prospect of being returned to the bosom of her native soil.

"It ain't the soil's bosom I'm worried about," she muttered. "It's the natives."

"What?" Dirk gave her a quizzical look, the one he wore when she spoke her thoughts aloud without any explanatory preamble.

"Nothing. I'll be okay," she told him with a sigh as the wheels hit the tarmac and the plane bounced along, as though happy to be on land once more. "Everything will be fine and dandy . . . just as soon as I see Granny."

* * *

Indeed, all was right with Savannah's world the moment Dirk drove the rented car off the two-lane rural highway and down the narrow dirt road leading to her grandmother's house. The mere sight of that tiny shotgun shack lifted her mood and brought peace to her soul in a way that no luxury estate on earth could have done.

It wasn't so much the run-down structure, with its peeling paint, sagging front porch, and missing tarpaper roof tiles, that warmed Savannah's heart. It was what this humble piece of property represented. Or, more importantly, *whom*.

As children, Savannah and her eight siblings had been removed from their mother's custody and placed in the care of Granny Reid. Savannah would never forget the night when superheroes dressed in dark blue uniforms, with shining badges pinned to their chests, had scooped her and her brothers and sisters into their strong arms and had delivered them from their dark world of chaos, squalor, neglect, and abuse.

They had been driven away from their furious, shrieking mother in big, powerful black-and-white cars with magical red and blue flashing lights on their tops. And from the moment those heaven-sent warriors had transported them to this little house at the end of the dirt road, their childhoods—their lives—had changed forever.

Humble but tasty meals appeared three times a day, with the punctuality of a Marine Corps mess hall. Fresh, clean clothes were available every morning, and a bath with plenty of soap and vigorous scrubbing was required every evening.

Good manners and bedtime prayers were mandatory. Discipline was consistent and fairly administered, tempered with copious amounts of love in the form of hugs, kisses, encouragement, and sage advice.

Now, all these years later, although Savannah wasn't exactly giddy at the prospect of reuniting with her school chums, she considered it worthwhile just to see Granny in her own natural habitat.

"It'll be nice to visit with Granny here, in her own house, for a change instead of at our place," Dirk said.

Savannah was often taken aback by how frequently and how precisely his thoughts echoed hers. It had been bad enough when they were partners on the force and friends, but now that they were married, it certainly appeared that "two had become one."

A little scary, she thought, *considering it's Dirko*.

"I'll bet that's what you were thinking, too," he said. "You ever noticed how often me and you are thinking the same thing?"

"Knock it off. You're creeping me out."

"What?"

"Nothing. Pay no attention to me. I'm just out of sorts, you know, what with the reunion and all."

"What are you talking about? It'll be great! A chance to rub elbows, drink punchless punch, and eat dried-out cake with a bunch of knuckleheads you never wanted to see again for the rest of your life."

"Yeah, well, that's the least of it," she replied as, once again, she felt tiny drops of sweat appear on her forehead. Perspiration that had nothing to do with the humidity of a Georgia summer.

Dirk pulled the car up to the front of the house and killed the engine. He reached over and took her hand in his. Giving her fingers a squeeze, he said, "Okay, so that's the *least* of it. What's the *most* of it?"

She gulped. "Let's just say I wasn't exactly socialite

material back then. The clothes I wore, my hairstyle and makeup, or lack thereof, were all hot topics of lunchroom gossip. That and the fact that I never showed up for school functions."

"Not even football games?" he asked with a look of shock and horror. "Why the hell not?"

Savannah gave him a sweet smile; that was her guy, all right. Always the jock. Missing a sporting event, anytime and for any reason, was simply unthinkable.

But her expression soon turned solemn again as she recalled the long hours spent on Gran's back porch with the wringer washer. She could still hear the hypnotic rhythm of the machine's agitator as it sloshed the load back and forth in its tub of hot, soapy water. She could still smell the acrid scent of bleach and strong detergent in the humid summer air.

She would never forget the anxiety provoked by feeding washed, wet clothes through the powerful wringer as she tried to keep her hand from slipping between the hard rollers, which would have surely crushed her fingers.

Then there were the endless afternoons and weekends spent in the backyard, where baskets overflowed with cold, wet laundry, and miles of heavy-laden clotheslines sagged with clothes flapping in the breeze.

"I didn't have time to hang out with the other kids," she said, "because I was too busy hanging their clothes out to dry. And then for extra fun, on weekends we scrubbed their houses." She chuckled wryly and shrugged. "Gran and I had a lot of mouths to feed, and, Lord, how those younguns could eat."

Dirk lifted her hand and pressed a kiss to her fingers. A look of sadness and a hint of repressed anger crossed his face as he said, "I'm sorry, sweetheart, that you had to work so hard, and you were just a kid."

"Oh, I didn't mind the work," she replied. " 'Hard work never killed nobody,' as Gran frequently told us. What I minded was the other kids—a certain group of girls in particular—never letting me forget that I was beneath them."

Dirk pulled her close and nuzzled her hair. "*You* ain't beneath *nobody*, darlin'. And tomorrow night the two of us are gonna walk hand in hand into that gymnasium, with all its tacky crepe paper and balloon decorations. And my head's gonna be held high. The lady I'll be escorting will be not only my wife and the prettiest woman ever to come out of Georgia, but also the best person I've known in my life."

Savannah looked into her husband's eyes and knew with every cell of her being that he meant it. He told her that often, and she usually delivered a smart-aleck response, like "If I'm the best person you've ever known, boy, you need to get out more."

But at that moment, sarcasm was the farthest thing from her mind. "And I love you, too. Plumb to pieces."

"I know you do. But we better get in that house right now, 'cause your granny's at the window, watching us make out. And from the scowl on her face, I'd say she disapproves."

Savannah sighed and laughed. "Reckon some things never change."

Chapter 2

"It's not that I minded the two of you swappin' slobber in front of my house," Granny told Savannah and Dirk once she had hugged them hard enough to make their ribs ache. "Seein's how y'all are married now, it's allowed and even encouraged. But not when I'm in here, itchin' to get my hands on you."

Savannah gave her grandmother an extra hug and marveled at the essence of pure feistiness that radiated from this eighty-plus Southern belle, wrapped in a pink and purple floral caftan. Her thick silver hair was neatly arranged, every curl in place, and from her ears dangled fuchsia chandelier earrings.

Every birthday since Gran had turned eighty, she had challenged herself to do something "new and daring." Wearing shoulder-sweeping chandelier earrings was last year's bold fashion foray. Savannah couldn't wait to see what this upcoming birthday would bring. Granny had already warned everybody to beware; it was going to be a doozy.

"So, where is everyone?" Savannah asked, looking around the strangely empty house. She had expected to be mobbed by a gaggle of Reids and Reid younguns. Even half of her siblings, along with their rambunctious offspring, could fill the average living room.

"I told 'em not to descend on you like a pack of hyenas the minute you got here this evenin'," Gran replied. "They'll all be swoopin' in like a flock o' pigeons first thing tomorrow mornin', bright-eyed and bushy-tailed, lookin' for breakfast."

Savannah grinned at the imagery of bushy-tailed pigeons, but mixing her metaphors was just part of Gran's charm, so Savannah wouldn't dream of correcting her.

"They'll be lookin' for you to cook for 'em, you mean," Savannah said.

Gran chuckled. "I don't mind. Vidalia's biscuits are heavy enough to sink a battleship, and Marietta fries her eggs so hot, they have them tough ruffle things around the edges. I don't mind cookin', especially for you, sugar."

With eyes the same striking sapphire blue as Savannah's, Gran gazed lovingly up at her granddaughter. But the affection quickly turned to concern. "What's the matter with you, girl?" she snapped.

"What? Oh, nothing, Gran."

"Yes there is. Somethin's amiss for sure."

She grabbed Savannah's hand and pushed her across the tiny living room to an ancient plaid sofa covered with a large afghan—just one of Granny's many creations that decorated the otherwise plain but cozy house.

"Sit yourself down right there," she said, "and tell me all about what's ailin' you."

Gran gave Dirk a shove toward the overstuffed armchair in the corner, its threadbare areas covered with snowy crocheted doilies . . . also products of Gran's skilled fingers. "And since you're my grandson-in-law now, I'll let you sit in my comfy chair."

"Why, thank you, Granny. I'm deeply honored," Dirk said. He settled into the chair, but after placing his hands briefly on the doily-covered armrests, he seemed to think better of it and folded them demurely on his lap. He looked anything *but* comfy.

Savannah grinned, watching her husband squirm. Dirk had never been at ease among "girlie" stuff. Discarded beer cans, empty pizza boxes, and rusty TV trays were what he considered to be perfectly acceptable items of home décor. But ruffles and floral prints sent him into a dither. So an overtly feminine home like Granny's was the stuff of nightmares for a manly man like him. He lived in mortal terror that he would break a delicate ceramic angel or snag a lacy something or spill iced tea on an heirloom quilt.

Savannah had tried in vain to convince him that a woman who had raised nine children in a tiny house was quite adept at gluing broken items and removing even the most stubborn stains.

Savannah couldn't count the times over the years when she had heard Gran say to her or one of her siblings, "Accidents happen, sugar dumplin'. Don't fret. There ain't nothin' in this house that means half as much to me as *you* do."

Whatever Gran did or said, it came from a heart filled with love. Even interrogations like the one that was about to begin.

But no sooner had Gran settled herself next to Savannah on the couch than they heard the back door open, then slam closed. No doubt, it was one of the

Reid offspring. Neighbors and friends would have been polite enough to knock.

Savannah was grateful for a possible reprieve from the pending "What's wrong with you?" Gran cross-examination.

"Yoo-hoo! Granny? You here?" yelled a less than melodious female voice from the kitchen.

"In the front room, Marietta," Gran called back.

"I brought your casserole dish back, like you told me to. I didn't get a chance to wash it. I'm pokin' it here in the sink."

Savannah braced herself as the approaching *click-click* of high heels announced the arrival of Marietta. She was sister number two, right behind Savannah in the long line of siblings. Miss Mari was Savannah's least favorite of the batch.

She actually qualified as one of the other reasons why Savannah wasn't thrilled to be "home."

"I thought I'd fetch it over here before that ornery, nasty, mule-headed sister of mine and her old man come sailin' in," Marietta babbled as she made her way from the kitchen, through the bedrooms, and toward the living room. "I'm gonna try my best to avoid cross-in' paths with—" Marietta stopped so abruptly in the living room doorway that she nearly fell off her four-inch zebra-striped mules. "Oh. You done got here."

Savannah flashed her sister her best fake smile, which looked more like a grimace worn by wolves fighting over the carcass of a dead elk. "Sorry for the inconvenience," she said. "If I'd known, I would've asked the captain to circle over Atlanta a few times before landing."

Propping her hands on her ample hips, Marietta lifted her chin and stuck out her chest, which, in typical Reid gal fashion, was more than voluptuous. So voluptuous, in fact, that if she took one deep breath too many, she might "volupt" right out the front of her low-cut leopard-print blouse.

As Savannah took in the tiger-striped purse, it occurred to her that Miss Marietta wanted to make sure every male in the county knew that she would be a virtual tear-cat between the sheets, if only they were fortunate enough to get the chance to bed her.

A shockingly large percentage of them had lucked out at one time or the other. Much to Granny's consternation.

But Savannah just thought her sister looked like a billboard advertisement for a zoo. Also, she had seen enough of Marietta's heavy-duty body-shaping foundation garments hanging on the shower curtain rod to know that it was mostly false advertisement.

Granny cleared her throat and said, "I'll thank you girls to be civil to one another when you're under my roof. And if you reckon you can muster it, a smidgen of sisterly love would be a fine thing, too."

Marietta tossed her head, wriggled her hips, and delicately patted her oversized bouffant as she flashed a sideways look at Dirk that could definitely be classified as come-hither.

Dirk looked down, suddenly fascinated by the design of the doily on the armrest.

"It's a lot to ask there, Granny, expecting the two of us to pretend we even *like* each other, let alone *love* one another," Marietta said. "This here precious sister of mine pert near took my head clean off the last time I saw her. Whopped the holy tar outta me right there in the middle of her living room. And me, a guest in her house. It was plumb shameful."

Savannah opened her mouth to retort, but Granny placed a warning hand on her knee and gave it a squeeze.

"I remember that squabble all too well," Gran said. "If you'll recollect, I was in the house when it happened and heard you squawkin', Marietta, all the way upstairs to the guest bedroom, where I was tryin' to get a nap. I also remember 'tweren't nothin' but a pillow fight and your big sister didn't give you one lick amiss that day. What you got, you had comin'.'"

Savannah could be quiet no longer. "That's for sure, missy. You go flaunting your womanly wiles—which may or may not be all that wily—in front of another woman's husband, you're going to get trounced. Especially when that woman's your big sister."

Marietta gave Savannah a catty smirk. "Well, now, you always was a sight bigger than me, 'specially in the hip area, but I figure I better watch what I say on that topic, or I might get beat to death for that, too."

Savannah smiled, recalling the Catfight of the Century with the sort of delicious satisfaction reserved for those whose portion of well-deserved revenge had been a long time coming.

So what if the battle had done more damage to her sofa accent pillow than it had to her overly flirtatious, highly immodest sister? Having to restuff a cushion was a small price to pay for getting to knock the stuffing out of a sister who so thoroughly deserved it.

Secretly, Savannah half hoped that Marietta would flash Dirk another unsolicited view of her scant knickers. Probably also leopard print. Savannah had no doubt that given the chance, she would score a knockout in round two, as well. But, of course, that sort of sporting event could never occur on such hallowed ground as Granny Reid's living room.

Maybe before the visit was over, she'd have the opportunity to lure Miss Hussy Pants into a dark alley or a peach orchard and rearrange her hairdo once again.

One could always dream.

But as Savannah was fantasizing about the gory details such a rematch might offer, the front door opened, and Alma Reid entered the house. Like a sudden and unexpected parting of the clouds, Alma's sunny presence immediately dispelled the darkness.

At least for Savannah.

If Marietta was her least favorite sibling, Alma was dearest to her heart. Shy and sweet, ever thinking of others, Alma seemed the exact opposite in every way to Marietta—to the point where Savannah couldn't help wondering if they were truly from the same gene pool.

Savannah jumped up from the sofa, ran to Alma, and folded her into a hearty Reid embrace. When Savannah finally released her, Alma gazed up at her older sister with adoring eyes and said, "Shoot f'ar. I wanted to be here when y'all got in. I've been dyin' to see you. It's been so long."

Casting a quick glance at Marietta, Savannah saw her roll her eyes. Yes, Marietta and Alma were as different as a soft pink rosebud and an out-of-bloom prickly pear cactus.

As Alma hurried over to Dirk and he rose to greet her, Savannah felt the gentle nudge of Granny's elbow in her ribs. "You doin' all right, dumplin'?"

Savannah managed a chuckle and said, "Right as rain after a long dry summer."

"Bull pucky."

Okay. So much for fooling Gran, Savannah thought. When would she learn that it was nearly impossible to hide your inner being from someone who knew you better than you knew yourself?

"It's just that . . . well . . . coming home . . . It's a mite hard," Savannah confessed.

She was surprised and annoyed to hear the shakiness in her own voice. Savannah liked to think of herself as a pretty darned tough cookie. Getting choked up about a simple thing like coming home to your birthplace and the loving arms of your family didn't exactly fit Savannah's carefully constructed self-image.

She preferred to think of herself as a gal who ate nasty criminals over easy for breakfast, along with a side order of sharp nails—all spiced with a drizzle of rattlesnake venom.

And while she didn't fully believe her own illusion, she certainly didn't see herself as a weepy female, prone to getting the vapors over nothing.

"It ain't easy, Savannah girl, comin' home. You got a lot of history here, and not all of it's good."

"That's for sure," Marietta piped up. "I wouldn't want to be in your shoes, coming back to town, seeing people you haven't seen in ages, looking twenty-five years older and a heap wider through the backside. And speaking of shoes, I hope you brought some good ones, not those old lady loafers you usually wear."

Granny shot Marietta a reproving look. "Miss Mari, I will thank you to keep your words soft and kind while you're under my roof. Your sister here is facing what you might call 'the dark night of the soul,' and we should strive to be supportive in her time o' need and sorrow."

Savannah stifled a chuckle; Granny had a tendency to wax dramatic and poetic at times like this. "I wouldn't say it's a particularly 'dark night,' " she said. "I'm just a bit nervous about runnin' into people I was glad to be rid of when I left here."

Breaking his uncharacteristically long silence, Dirk added, "Don't worry about Savannah, Granny. She's fine. Since she started goin' through this change of life business, she'll start bawlin' over an inspiring margarine commercial."

Silence reigned in the room.

The level of estrogen-charged indignation rose by the moment.

Finally, it was Marietta who came to Dirk's rescue. "I don't know what all the fuss is about. Tell me the truth, Savannah. These people you're so in a tizzy about seeing . . . Do you like 'em?"

"Do I *like* them?" Savannah didn't even have to think about it. "No, I can't stand them. They're a bunch of conceited, snotty bit—" She gave Granny a quick look. "Um, disagreeable females who made my life miserable. I wouldn't give you two cents for the whole batch of 'em, not if they were dunked in chocolate and rolled in pecans."

A sly grin crossed Marietta's face as she reached up and fingered her rhinestone earring thoughtfully.

As Savannah locked eyes with her sister, she seemed to sense that she was about to hear something important. Something life changing. Something profound.

From *Marietta*.

Go figure.

"Well, now, dear sister of mine," Marietta said, her Georgia drawl as thick as sorghum syrup. "Here I figured you were a whole lot smarter than that. If you don't give a hoot about them, got no use for 'em, and

think they're just a pack of disagreeable, worthless females . . . why the heck would you care what *they* think
of *you*?"

Later that night, as Savannah snuggled close to Dirk
in Granny's bed, beneath Gran's handmade tulip quilt,
she whispered, "I feel guilty, taking the best bed in the
house. But Granny wouldn't accept no for an answer.
That's Southern hospitality for you."

"Yeah. Thank goodness for Southern hospitality.
After being scrunched up in that airline seat for hours,
it feels good to stretch out. I'm dead tired. Good night,
darlin'."

"Thanks for coming with me," she whispered. "I know
traveling long distances—you know, like out of town—is
not really your thing."

He chuckled and pulled her closer. "No problem.
But I'll let you make it up to me. Sometime when I'm
not too tired to breathe."

Laying her head on his shoulder, she ran her hand
lightly over his chest and felt the warmth of his skin,
the masculine bristling of hair against her palm.

"That was something else, what Marietta said, huh?"
she whispered. "Imagine Miss Prissy Leopard Pants
coming up with something all enlightened like that."

Dirk replied with a snore.

It was another hour or so before Savannah drifted
off to sleep, still pondering the simple logic of her sister's statement.

Why *would* she care what these people thought of
her? As long as she had the affection and respect of
those she loved, wasn't that all that truly mattered?

Yes, ole Marietta had nailed it.

Finally, as sleep overtook her, Savannah's last thought was, *True wisdom has come . . . out of the mouths of babes. Or, in this case, a nitwit, dingbat floozy. Wonders never cease!*

Breakfast at Gran's house was an event. A *major* event.

Not exactly Christmas Eve or Thanksgiving dinner, but close.

In the Reid household every meal was an extravaganza. If not for the sophistication of the cuisine, then for the sheer volume of it.

Savannah had always been astonished at the amount of food it took to feed her clan and the space required to seat even her next of kin.

The cheap aluminum dining table with its gray, pearlescent surface, which had borne the burden of thousands of such feasts, had been stretched with extra leaves made of plywood until it practically filled the old country kitchen.

Less fortunate city folks who seldom consumed more than a bagel, donut, or fiber bar with their morning coffee might have been astonished at the glorious, if somewhat gluttonous repast spread upon that humble table. But the Reid family considered it perfectly normal to begin the day with a hearty, calorie-dense, and cholesterol-laden breakfast.

Granny Reid appeared to live in mortal terror that some member of her family might faint dead away in the street late some morning from lack of nourishment. And the townsfolk would gossip about it for the next fifty years. Long after Gran was resting peacefully in the cemetery on the hill, McGillians would be shaking their heads, tsk-tsking oh, so sadly, and whispering about how "Granny Reid always was a mite stingy with her sausages and overly tight with her buttered biscuits, and a body had to practically pry the jam jar out of her hand."

Rather than have her legacy tarnished, her character disparaged in such a brutal fashion, Gran made sure that everyone who pushed away from her table had to readjust their belt, loosening it at least two notches just to be able to breathe.

Savannah had never once questioned where she might have inherited the tendency to overfeed her guests. And she would bet dollars to donuts that not one person around Gran's table that morning would suffer a hunger pang again. At least not until lunchtime.

Gran presided at the head of the table, as was her honor as the octogenarian matriarch. Though she did little sitting. She was constantly jumping up to add a bit more cream gravy to the bowl, a few more biscuits to the basket, and peach preserves to the crystal candy dish that had been pressed into service for Savannah's sake.

On either side of her sat Savannah and Dirk. The chair next to Gran's had always been Savannah's by firstborn birthright. And although her siblings had complained about it from time to time, Gran had always defended Savannah's position by pointing out the added responsibilities shouldered by the oldest child in a family of nine kids.

"Them who works the hardest gets the seats of honor," she had proclaimed time and again to quell a row.

That also explained why the grandchildren were

lined up, sans chairs or any other form of creature comfort, at the kitchen counter, their plates in front of them and dour expressions on their faces. In Granny's home it was still the 1950s, and although she was fine with them being seen and heard, they were definitely *not* in charge.

"How come when Aunt Savannah comes to call, us kids have to eat standin' up instead of sittin' at the table?" whined one of sister Vidalia's adorable eight-year-old twins.

"Oh, hush your bellyachin'," Vidalia snapped, turning around and swatting Jack's backside. "It ain't because Aunt Savannah's here. Not this time, anyways. It's 'cause you and your sister were jumpin' like a pair of wild jackrabbits on the table last Sunday a week ago and broke the other leaf. So you're standin' at the counter, and it's your own blamed fault."

She turned her wrath on her daughter. "Jillian, stop playing with that bowl of oatmeal, or I swear, I'm gonna make you wear it for a hat, oats and all."

She crumbled some biscuits onto the high chair trays of her second set of twins, who were seated behind her and next to Savannah.

A moment later, Savannah felt a half-chewed, soggy bit of something hit the side of her neck. *Apparently, the kid doesn't like Gran's biscuits*, Savannah thought as she wiped away the slimy blob with a paper napkin. Thankfully, it hadn't been buttered.

She thought of Tammy, her health-conscious assistant and best friend back in San Carmelita, who was five months pregnant. Savannah made a mental note never to sit downwind of that child, either, in the coming months. The kid would probably smack her with a half-gnawed-upon celery stick.

Farther down the table sat the rest of Savannah's family. At least the ones who were still living in town.

Next to Vidalia was Butch, Vi's long-suffering husband. Between his hard work as an auto mechanic in McGill's only garage, Vidalia's frequent hissy fits, and two sets of twins, poor old Butch did well to retain his sanity. More than once he had threatened to "cut my strings and go straight up." And while Savannah wasn't sure quite what that meant, she wouldn't have blamed him if he had.

Next to him, wearing her usual baggy black pencil skirt and equally saggy plain white shirt, sister Cordele looked like a twenty-seven-year-old going on seventy-seven.

Her dark hair was slicked back, held with an extreme amount of gel, and fastened with a black barrette. Though, in typical Reid fashion, the tiny ringlets at her neckline were managing to escape and curl down onto her tightly buttoned collar. As always, the look on her pretty but unadorned face was as severe as her fashion choices.

Beside Cordele sat Jesup, Cordele's exact opposite. Jesup had allowed her thick, dark hair to go on its own flights of fantasy, and it pointed in every direction, in a wild array. Except for where she had shaved off a wide strip just above her right ear and had had her initials tattooed on her scalp. She had gotten the name of a boyfriend, now five guys ago, over the left.

Granny had not been thrilled.

Though Gran had been slightly less irate than when Jesup had come home sporting a Celtic ink chain around her neck. And far less unhappy than when she had gleefully displayed a new skull and crossbones on her left buttock.

More than once, Savannah had heard Gran praying under her breath for strength while dealing with Jesup. The phrases "cross to bear" and "thorn in the flesh" had been uttered, along with the words "beat the tar outta."

The rest of the gang was absent from the breakfast table for a variety of reasons.

Much to Savannah's delight, Waycross had moved to San Carmelita and would soon be marrying Tammy.

Atlanta had relocated to Nashville, where she was fulfilling her life dream, singing backup at a recording studio.

Macon, the family rare-do-well, was serving the last two weeks of a three-month hitch in the county jail for yet another DWI. Like their mother, he had yet to learn that cheap whiskey and curvy country roads weren't a complimentary mix.

"Marietta told me to send you her regrets," Vidalia said, nabbing another biscuit for herself. "She had something important she had to do, or else she'd have joined us this morning."

"Like watch her toenail polish dry?" Dirk muttered into his coffee mug.

Savannah noted his scowl with a minor sense of alarm. Her husband wasn't particularly jovial this morning. Far from it, in fact.

If nothing else, Dirk was a creature of habit. But he was trying desperately to eat his breakfast—while having to share a table occupied with Reids galore—without a newspaper to smack and abuse, and without his *Bonanza* bowl.

Not for the first time, she realized this solitary, routine-enslaved curmudgeon had sacrificed a great deal to become her mate.

No wonder she loved him.

Snatching the biscuit basket from Vidalia, she said, "As far as Marietta, I'll just bet she was plumb overcome with contrition at missing the chance to see me again."

Vidalia looked slightly puzzled. "If that means she was all broke up about it, I'd have to say she looked like she'd survive. Maybe even thrive. I wouldn't feel too sorry for her, if I was you."

Savannah grabbed the platter with the bacon and sausages as it made a second round about the table, and helped herself. "I saw her last night. That was enough to hold me for a while."

"She said you were frettin' about having to see the old gang at the reunion tonight," Butch offered, making a rare contribution to the conversation. "But if it's that uppity snit Jeanette Parker you're worried about seeing, you can rest easy. She's got a lot more on her mind right now than tormenting you."

"That's for sure," Alma said, jumping up from the table and hurrying to the refrigerator to fetch more butter. "She's a widow, fresh made."

"And your ole beau, Tommy Stafford," Cordele added, "he's the sheriff now. And he's been doing his best to prove that her bereavement was intentional. On her part, that is."

Savannah perked up and nearly choked on her bacon. "Really? Jeanette Parker married Mr. Barnsworth, and now he's dead?"

"Dead as a roadkill skunk," Butch supplied.

Granny nodded. "And the whole sorry affair smells even worse. Jacob Barnsworth has gone on to his eternal reward, and that Jeanette gal has her sticky fingers on all his money. "

"And on a lot of other women's husbands," Vidalia

added with a giggle. "You know she's always been a slut."

Gran cleared her throat. "Now, Vidalia, you know we don't use language like that in this household. I much prefer 'maiden of ill repute.' "

"Or two-bit hussy," Savannah suggested.

Nodding thoughtfully, Gran said, "Considering the female in question, that would work, too."

Dirk gave Savannah a mischievous grin over the rim of his coffee mug. "I wasn't impressed with that old boyfriend of yours the last time we were here," he said. "Maybe I can offer Sheriff Tom Stafford the benefit of my extensive expertise. Maybe you and me could nail this Jeanette gal for murder, Van. Now, wouldn't that be fun?"

A thrill coursed through Savannah's body and soul, and it had little to do with the caffeine content of Granny's potent coffee or the sugar in her preserves. It had a lot to do with the fantasy of settling old scores and maybe even reaping a long-delayed harvest of pure ole vengeance.

Of course, such reveries weren't noble, virtuous, or particularly worthy of a fine Southern lady. But the more Savannah thought about it, mulling over the possibilities, the more she imagined how delicious such a scenario might be.

Sweet, indeed. Maybe even sweeter than Granny Reid's best apple butter.